# A LOVE TO
# LAST FOREVER

# A LOVE TO LAST FOREVER

*Brides of Gallatin County*

BOOK TWO

# TRACIE PETERSON

BETHANY HOUSE PUBLISHERS

*Minneapolis, Minnesota*

To my grandchildren
Rainy, Fox, and Max

You have given me great
joy and love. You are a blessing
beyond compare.

Love,
Nanna

# Books by Tracie Peterson

*www.traciepeterson.com*

*A Slender Thread* • *I Can't Do It All!*\*\*
*What She Left For Me* • *Where My Heart Belongs*

### ALASKAN QUEST
*Summer of the Midnight Sun*
*Under the Northern Lights* • *Whispers of Winter*

### BRIDES OF GALLATIN COUNTY
*A Promise to Believe In* • *A Love to Last Forever*
*A Dream to Call My Own*

### THE BROADMOOR LEGACY\*
*A Daughter's Inheritance* • *An Unexpected Love*
*A Surrendered Heart*

### BELLS OF LOWELL\*
*Daughter of the Loom* • *A Fragile Design* • *These Tangled Threads*
*Bells of Lowell* (3 in 1)

### LIGHTS OF LOWELL\*
*A Tapestry of Hope* • *A Love Woven True*
*The Pattern of Her Heart*

### DESERT ROSES
*Shadows of the Canyon* • *Across the Years*
*Beneath a Harvest Sky*

### HEIRS OF MONTANA
*Land of My Heart* • *The Coming Storm*
*To Dream Anew* • *The Hope Within*

### LADIES OF LIBERTY
*A Lady of High Regard* • *A Lady of Hidden Intent*
*A Lady of Secret Devotion*

### WESTWARD CHRONICLES
*A Shelter of Hope* • *Hidden in a Whisper* • *A Veiled Reflection*

### YUKON QUEST
*Treasures of the North* • *Ashes and Ice* • *Rivers of Gold*

\*with Judith Miller      \*\*with Allison Bottke and Dianne O'Brian

TRACIE PETERSON is the author of over seventy novels, both historical and contemporary. Her avid research resonates in her stories, as seen in her bestselling HEIRS OF MONTANA and ALASKAN QUEST series. Tracie and her family make their home in Montana.

Visit Tracie's Web site at *www.traciepeterson.com.*

# CHAPTER ONE

## November 1879

*Lady Effingham offered Lord Wodehouse a coy smile,* Beth Gallatin read in the privacy of her room. *She beckoned him forward with a simple nod and batted her eyelashes at him as he approached. "You are possibly the most beautiful woman in the room," he told her. "Only possibly?" she asked, frowning. She then gave him a seductive look that had never failed to entice the heart of any suitor.*

*How is that done?* Beth wondered. She put the book aside and went to pick up her mirror. For a moment she studied her features. She wasn't a bad-looking woman; in fact, many had told her she was quite lovely. Touching a hand to her cheek, Beth thought herself a bit too pale, perhaps, but otherwise her skin was smooth and youthful.

"And why not? I'm only twenty-two." She stared hard

at the reflection again, but this time she tried her best to give what she thought might be a seductive expression. It didn't work, however—she looked as though she might be sick instead. She tried again but was equally frustrated with the result. "Now I look angry or at least unhappy."

She put the mirror down. "What makes a woman seductive?"

She'd often observed the soiled doves at Rafe's Saloon as they crooned and called to the passing cowboys. They would pose against the porch supports with hints of smiles upon red, pouting lips. Was that seductive?

Beth glanced at the clock and realized she'd lost track of the time. Reading had a way of doing that to her, and *The Courtship of Lady Effingham* was most mesmerizing. Beth could easily put herself in the place of this opulent character—this daughter of a duke. How romantic it all was. Lady Effingham lived on an ancient estate, the child of English nobility. She was the most beautiful of women, with golden yellow hair and blue eyes, and every man who saw her was dying of love for her.

A heavy sigh escaped Beth's lips once more. "My hair is reddish brown, and my eyes are more green than blue. And as far as I can tell, there isn't a single man in the world dying of love for me."

Well, there was Nick Lassiter. Beth knew she'd caught Nick's eye since she'd come to the area with her father and sisters several years ago. Nick was definitely handsome—a dark, brooding sort, rather like Lord Wodehouse. Beth couldn't suppress a giggle as she imagined Nick dressed in fine English attire, bowing low before her.

She gave a curtsy as if the event were truly happening.

"Oh, Lord Wodehouse, how very dashing you look today." She laughed once again.

Beth knew she was acting like a silly child, but she was a hopeless romantic. Proof could be found in the stacks of books and dime novels that were hidden at the back of her closet and out in the shed. Anytime she was in Bozeman, Beth would secretly buy one or two books and hide them away for quiet moments when she could dream.

But what about Nick?

He was handsome enough, and he made her laugh. Kind and polite, he always managed to stir something inside her. Of course, sometimes that something was anger, but he could definitely bring about a response.

"And he *is* attending church now," Beth reminded herself. She'd always tried to keep her heart free of entanglements where Nick was involved because he wasn't a God-fearing man. She had known him to take a drink at Rafe's Saloon. And once when he had burned his leg quite badly, Beth recalled he had said a curse word. But at the time, that seemed completely understandable. Surely God made provision for such things.

"But is he the man of my dreams? Is Nicholas Lassiter my Lord Wodehouse?" How could she know? How was a person supposed to figure out whether or not someone was their true love? Did love always sweep you off your feet and make itself known? Or could it creep in and surprise you?

Knowing that her sister Gwen was bound to come looking for her, Beth tucked the book away and headed downstairs. She paused for a moment at the sight of Gwen kissing her husband good-bye. This was their routine most every morning as Hank headed off next door to open his store.

*They're so in love,* Beth thought. A twinge of jealousy

11

wrapped itself around her heart. How was it that Gwen had found love twice in her life and Beth hadn't found it at all? Gwen had been married to Hank's younger brother, Harvey, but then he'd died and now Gwen was married to Hank.

Beth blamed her singleness on their father. He had dragged them from one place to another after the death of their mother many years ago. George Gallatin was too restless to stay in one place, and his daughters were victims of his wanderlust. Beth had hated him for that, yet she knew it wasn't really her father she hated so much as the disruptive way of living he imposed upon them.

She frowned. Thoughts of their father always brought guilty feelings. Prior to his death the previous May, Beth had overheard him talking about moving again. She'd been livid but, because she was eavesdropping, had said nothing. But she had prayed. She had asked God to stop them from moving, no matter what it took. What she hadn't counted on was that it would take the death of her father.

Beth also hadn't counted on the sense of relief she'd felt when, at his funeral, she'd realized he could no longer force them to move. She was ashamed, but she couldn't deny the truth of her feelings.

"Oh, there you are," Gwen commented as she turned in the doorway. "I thought perhaps you were sick."

"No, just lazy," Beth said with a smile. She came down the few remaining steps and glanced out the still-open door. "Looks like another nice day."

"Yes, it's been so mild, I thought I might open everything up and air the place out again today."

"I suppose it will snow soon enough, so we might as well take advantage of the nice weather," Beth admitted. "I'll do some more laundry. There's additional bedding that I can hang out to air, as well."

"That would be good. Mr. Murphy and his men are due back today, and I'm sure they'd appreciate everything crisp and clean." Gwen fussed with an errant strand of hair before smiling at Beth. "I do believe Mr. Murphy is rather sweet on you."

"Adrian . . . ah, Mr. Murphy is very nice." In her thoughts about Nick, Beth had nearly forgotten Adrian. "But he seems to enjoy traveling too much."

Gwen looked at Beth with a puzzled expression. "What's wrong with that? His job with the railroad survey team requires that he travel."

Beth swept past Gwen. "I like it here."

"That doesn't mean you can't travel."

Beth frowned. "I think I'm traveled out. Do you realize we've lived here longer than any other town or city?"

"I suppose so. I guess it's never been that much of a concern to me."

"Well, it is to me. I like having things in their place, and I like knowing where that place is. It gives me a sense of belonging, and that comforts me. I think the only thing that could entice me to leave would be to have a home of my own, but even then, I'd want it nearby."

"But surely you wouldn't pass up true love for such a reason."

Beth thought about this for a moment. Adrian was quite attentive, and like Lord Wodehouse, he seemed charming and interesting. "I suppose I don't know," Beth finally admitted. "I've never been in love before. I would have to weigh the matter with great care. It seems to me that if a man loved me, he would be willing to adapt and make changes for me."

"But you wouldn't have to change for him?" Gwen asked with a smile.

Beth realized she'd probably said too much. "Oh, it isn't important. I don't know why I went on so about it." She glanced around the room. "What would you like me to start on first? Is there still baking?"

"Yes." Gwen started for the kitchen. "I have five loaves of bread rising. We need to make dinner rolls, as well."

"I can certainly help with that," Beth said, hoping her sister would just forget about their conversation. She hurried past Gwen and immediately went for her apron. The last thing Beth wanted was to have to explain why she felt so fiercely about staying put. She'd never told her sisters about her secret shame—her relief at their father's passing—and she never intended to.

"I know you want to avoid my question, but I do wish you would consider it carefully," Gwen said.

"What question?" Beth asked innocently.

Gwen rolled her eyes. "You know perfectly well what question. Do you truly believe you shouldn't have to change?"

Beth finished securing her apron before looking up at Gwen. "I would hope that God, knowing my heart, would send me someone who'd be happy with me as I am."

"And if He doesn't?"

"Well, I haven't really given it much thought." But that was a lie, because it was all that Beth thought about. "I suppose I could just stay single all of my life." She offered a forced smile. "I'll be the spinster Gallatin. I'll bake cookies for children and grow very plump eating fruitcake."

Gwen laughed. "Oh, there is no chance of you being a

spinster. You are much too pretty and too kindhearted. Besides, if not Mr. Murphy, there's always Nick."

"But he isn't a Christian."

"Well, I don't know about that. He's been attending church with Simon, and Hank tells me they've discussed the services on more than one occasion. Perhaps he is closer to God than you're giving him credit for."

Beth nodded. "Perhaps." She thought again of Lord Wodehouse and Nick in English attire. It was an amusing thought and immediately put her in a better frame of mind. "At least Nick seems content to live right here."

Hours later Nick was pushed to the edge of Beth's thoughts as she strolled along the banks of the Gallatin River with Adrian Murphy.

"I'm glad you had some time to walk with me. I wanted to talk to you about . . . well . . . my leaving."

Beth tried not to sound surprised. "Leaving?"

He smiled and pushed back his light brown hair. "Well, my team will be heading back East to rally with the men who sent us. We're going to discuss the various routes and surveys and probably won't be back to the area before spring—maybe summer."

"That's too bad. I know we'll miss you all." Beth toyed with a stalk of dried grass. As she straightened, Beth grew aware of Adrian's nearness. She smiled. "It's been very good for our business to have you here."

"I was hoping you'd say something more personal."

Beth looked at him and shook her head. "More personal? What do you mean by that?"

"I thought we were starting to get to know each other pretty well. Perhaps there might be something more permanent for our future."

"Our future?" Beth asked, knowing she probably sounded ridiculous repeatedly echoing the things he said.

He grinned and took hold of her hands. "You must know that I esteem you greatly. I enjoy our time together."

Beth thought of Lady Effingham and her various courtships. What would she say at a time like this? Adrian hadn't declared his love for her—he'd said he esteemed her. Beth wasn't even entirely sure what he meant by that, but it didn't stir her heart as she had supposed such words might.

"I hardly know you," Beth finally murmured. Her response was nothing like the daring and confident Lady Effingham, but it would suffice.

"I feel like I know you very well," he said, rubbing the back of her hands with his thumbs. "But I'd like to know you even better. I was hoping you might wait for me."

"Wait for you?"

He nodded. "Until spring, when I return."

Beth tried to lose herself in Adrian's gaze, but something held her back. "I can't make you promises, Mr. Murphy. It wouldn't be right for either of us. Especially since we have no real understanding."

He frowned and traced a pattern with his fingers as his caress moved up her arms. "Maybe this will change your mind." He leaned forward and closed his eyes, and Beth realized he meant to kiss her.

"There's a bear," Nick's voice boomed out, causing Beth to

jump back. "Or I should say a bear's been seen in these parts. Since it's warm, he's not gone to hibernate just yet."

Beth's body trembled from head to toe. Like a naughty child who'd been caught pulling the cat's tail, she felt her face flush and looked away. Adrian appeared to feel no such embarrassment.

"What kind of bear?" Adrian asked.

"Black bear. He was bothering folks earlier in the year and now seems to be back at it again. He's no doubt looking for extra food."

"No doubt."

Beth looked up and tried to steady her wobbly knees. "Thanks for letting us know."

"Well, you can't be too careful," Nick said, fixing Beth with a stern gaze. "A lot of animals will take advantage of the weak."

Beth realized he meant to imply Adrian, and for a moment she found it rather thrilling. Nick was jealous! It was just like chapter six, when Lord Wodehouse found Lady Effingham dancing in the arms of the American sea captain.

"Well, I suppose it would be best to get back to the house," Adrian said, glancing downriver. "I wouldn't want anything to happen to you."

Beth pulled her thoughts back to the moment. "Yes, I'm sure Gwen is wondering where I've gotten off to. There's always a lot of work to do, and I must do my share." She looked at Nick and smiled. "Thank you so much for the warning."

Nick watched the couple walk off together and fought the urge to follow them—to come between them. Adrian held on to Beth possessively, and she certainly didn't fight him to release her.

*Is Murphy what she wants?*

The thought was annoying and discouraging all at once. *I'm just a simple man. I'll probably never have exciting stories or romantic words to give her.* He knew from their conversations that Beth seemed caught up in a world of which he could never be a part. She read books that took her far away from Gallatin House.

*Does she want to leave this area? Does she want riches and wealth?* He shook his head as Murphy escorted her out of sight. Nick had wanted to court Beth ever since her father had brought them to the area. He'd enjoyed her enthusiasm for life and her playful nature. Even after enduring her pranks, he still found her captivating and charming.

So what should he do about it? She always put God between them. Her reply when he'd asked to court her in the past had been that she couldn't because he wasn't a Christian.

And lately Nick could see why. To be a true believer, as he understood it, meant to give a real commitment to change your life and live it in a way pleasing to God. It wasn't about just saying the words; it was far more important to live the truth of what you believed. As his brother had once commented, "Anyone can say they're saved by God from their sins, but their life ought to show that to be true. It ought to look different from the person who isn't a man of God."

That made sense to Nick, but he still wasn't completely convinced that he could be an honest-to-goodness Christian. His life had been marred by bad choices. Could God forgive that? Would God even want him?

❦

On Sunday Gallatin House was packed with people as they gathered to hold church services. Curt Flikkema, the circuit rider, was preaching, and Beth was pleased to see that Nick and Simon Lassiter were in attendance. It was the third time she'd noticed them in the services, and Beth could only hope that the preaching was affecting them both. After all, Gwen had mentioned their talking about spiritual matters with Hank. Surely that was a good sign.

She felt funny coming face-to-face with Nick again after nearly being kissed by Adrian. Amazingly enough, he had said nothing about the encounter and treated her as though it had never happened. Beth had thought to try to explain the matter, but then she couldn't figure out why it seemed so important that he should know.

"Guilt is the result of knowing that we had a choice to make and did not make it well," Pastor Flikkema began. "We did not choose the path we knew to be the right one."

Beth slid down her seat a bit and nervously smoothed out the dark green material of her wool skirt.

"Folks are often overcome by guilt. One simple and seemingly innocent choice or attitude takes them down the road to destruction and before they know it, they've made a mess of things."

This was far from the topic Beth had hoped to focus on. She knew she'd made poor choices during her life. Everyone had. She'd watched her mother die and felt terrible grief and guilt from not being able to stop it. Of course, Beth had been able to reason that away. She was a child. There was nothing she could have done at the age of seven. She'd blamed their father, however, for not being there.

Beth frowned and lowered her head as the pastor continued. It had been a long time since she'd thought about blaming her father for their mother's death. She had approached him about it when she'd been a girl of thirteen. It seemed important to take him to task after he had rather casually commented that God had taken their mother and unborn sibling to heaven because He had need of them.

"We had need of her, too," Beth had told him. "If you'd been here, she wouldn't have died."

Her father had studied her for a moment. "Bethy, the Lord gives and takes away. Your mother could have lived, only if the Lord so chose."

"But if you had been here," Beth countered, "you could have gotten her help. You could have saved them."

"Do you suppose the good Lord didn't know she was by herself? Do you suppose my working the far acreage was just an oversight on His part?"

His casual manner of passing the blame to God had angered her. Beth didn't want to blame God. God was, after all, her only solace these days. No, it was her father's fault. He hadn't protected them as he should have, or her mother might be alive even now.

"Sometimes," Curt's voice boomed out, "there is a liberty and freedom in facing the truth and accepting that no one else is to blame—no one but ourselves."

Beth straightened and folded her hands. The words pierced her heart. *No one to blame but ourselves?* Didn't she already blame herself for so much? There wasn't liberty in that. The only thing she found there was more guilt to heap upon that which she already bore.

Staring at her interlaced fingers, Beth tried her best to appear unmoved by the pastor's words. She had so long wrestled with her guilt that she was certain no one could help her. After all, while she hated feeling the way she did, Beth couldn't honestly say her father's death didn't relieve her. With Pa dead, they were free to stay in Gallatin House and run the business without fear of needing to move on in a week or a month.

*It's not that I don't miss him,* she admitted to herself, *because I do. I loved Pa as much as Lacy or Gwen. If he could have been like a normal father and settled down in one place, I would have wanted him to live forever.* She re-laced her fingers. Did that make her a terrible person?

How many times had she asked herself that question?

"Jesus offers to free us from our burden of guilt. He offers it through His forgiveness. See, we're all guilty of something— some of us bear more of a burden than others, but we've all sinned and fallen short of the glory of God, just like Romans 3:23 says in the Bible. Sin surrounds us with guilt, but it would be even worse for us if we made the wrong choice about what to do with that sin and guilt."

Beth shifted uncomfortably. It was as if God were speaking directly to her through Pastor Flikkema. *But I've tried to be free of the guilt. I've tried not to think about my horrible feelings.*

She glanced to where Gwen sat smiling and nodding. No doubt her sister had learned the secret of dealing with such things. She had been obsessed with the shame of having gone to a fortune-teller just before their mother died. Gwen had blamed herself for their parents' deaths, believing herself to be cursed. Now she sat there smiling. How was it she could so easily put aside the past, but Beth couldn't?

*Maybe because her fears weren't real, and mine are. Gwen wasn't really cursed, but I really am glad that there won't be any more moves to come.* She sighed and caught sight of Nick watching her. She looked away quickly and tried not to think of anything. It was just too dangerous to let her mind wander.

# CHAPTER TWO

Nick straightened and let the November breeze cool his face. He'd been working for some time between the forge and anvil, pounding out an order of iron brackets for Jerry Shepard. His forearms ached from the task, and he figured it was just about time for the noon stage. With over half of the bracket order complete, Nick wiped his brow before taking off his leather apron.

"Stage is coming," Simon announced.

Nick nodded. "I figured it was just about time."

"You suppose Uncle Forrest will be on this one?"

"I sure hope so. Snow could cut loose any day now. I'd hate for him to get stuck elsewhere." Nick moved toward the corral as the stage rounded the bend and the driver slowed the horses.

"He's the best wheelwright there is, so I doubt he'd suffer much for something to do. Hey, looks like one of the lead horses is limping." Simon moved forward to help the stage passengers alight.

"Welcome, all," Simon said, opening the stage door as the driver climbed down.

Nick had decided to follow Simon and see about their uncle before unhitching the horses. A petite woman allowed Simon to help her from the stage.

Shielding her eyes from the sun, she said, "Thank you."

"You're welcome, ma'am." Simon smiled.

It took only a moment to recognize the massive man who came next. Forrest Cromwell stood six feet six in his bare feet. The giant positively dwarfed the young woman, who'd dismounted only seconds ahead of him.

"Well, you boys are sure a sight for these old eyes," Uncle Forrest announced. He pulled Simon into a big bear hug. "Goodness, but you're the spittin' image of your mama."

"Good to see you, Uncle Forrest."

Nick grinned when the air whooshed out of his brother's lungs as their uncle tightened his grip. Simon gave his brother a just-you-wait-your-turn kind of look and drew a deep breath as Uncle Forrest released his grip.

"And Nicholas, just look at you. Why, the last time I saw you . . . well . . . you were hardly more than a boy." He gave Nick a hug that nearly broke his ribs.

"Good to see you again, sir," Nick said, using the last of his wind.

Uncle Forrest let him go rather abruptly. "I'm sure you remember your cousin Evan, and this little gal is his wife, Millie."

Nick and Simon smiled at the woman who'd preceded Forrest out of the stage before they turned to see their cousin bounding down the steps. This was a pleasant surprise. They'd known about Forrest joining them to set up business as a wheelwright, but nothing was ever said about Evan.

"We talked it over back in Kansas. Evan thought he might do well to come west with me and continue his wagon business. Millie was willing to risk it, too, so here we all are. I hope you have room for us."

"We'll make room," Simon assured him. "Evan, it's good to have you here. Millie, it's nice to make your acquaintance."

"Yes, this territory needs more lovely ladies," Nick offered.

The young woman beamed him a smile. She had seemed rather plain in appearance until doing this; now, however, Nick found her quite pretty.

Evan squeezed her shoulder. "Millie's an adventurous sort. I wasn't sure how she'd do on the long trip out here, but she matched us stride for stride and mile for mile. She's something else."

"Well, she'll need to be to endure out here," Simon replied. "I'm afraid you won't find the same level of comfort you probably had in Kansas."

"I grew up on the prairie," Millie told him. "There wasn't anything around us for miles. I think I'll like it here just fine."

Nick laughed. He noticed the driver motioning the other passengers over to Gallatin House. "I think you probably will, at that. There's lunch for all the stage folks just across the way. It's two bits, but the food is exceptional. You might as well go on over there and have some lunch; we'll get the horses changed out and join you."

Uncle Forrest gave Nick a pat on the back. "I could go for something to eat about now. Breakfast seems like days ago."

"What about all the cookies Millie's been feeding you on the way up here?" Evan asked.

Millie giggled. "Pa Cromwell has a bit of a sweet tooth."

"Well, you be sure to ask the Gallatin girls for some of their pie," Simon threw out. "They make about the best I've ever had."

"Sounds good to me. We'll look forward to you boys joining us. We want to hear all about this area."

Nick nodded and went to work unfastening the harness buckles. With Simon's help, they had the team changed out and the limping horse dealt with in plenty of time to join the others at lunch. The stage driver and those moving on, however, were heading out the door, even as Simon and Nick came up the steps.

"See you boys in a couple of days. Hope old Leroy's gonna be better by then."

"His shoe was loose and he packed a sharp stone underneath, but I think he'll be fine. I cleaned it out. He ought to be ready for you."

"He and Barney are the best lead team I've got," the driver replied. "I'd hate to see them put to pasture, but I don't think either one would ever work with any other horse, male or female. They've been together too long."

Nick smiled. "Not to worry. I think you'll get a few more years out of them."

The rest of the passengers—all men—scurried past to follow the driver. Some still held food in their hands, mostly sandwiches or pieces of pie. They weren't given a lot of time to eat, as a schedule had to be maintained.

"We waited for you," Millie said as Simon and Nick came into the dining room. "It wasn't easy to keep Pa Cromwell from sneaking into the kitchen, but we managed."

"You sure didn't need to," Simon said, taking a seat.

"Oh, it didn't take all that long," Evan added. "After all, Millie was rather insistent that we all clean up first."

Nick smiled. "Sounds like you keep these two walking a straight line."

The petite brunette laughed. "Somebody has to. When I met Evan, he was ornerier than any other man in town. He could drink everyone under the table, and then he just got plain mean."

"That was before I got religion," Evan said rather apologetically.

"And before Millie got ahold of you," Forrest said, laughing. "Millie was the local schoolmarm, and she had a way of getting overgrown boys to sit straight and toe the line. Evan might not have been one of her students, but he learned from her, just the same."

Evan gave Millie a wink. "She made a new man of me."

Just then Beth entered the room with a platter of venison steaks. "I think you're going to be pleasantly surprised," she told them all. "Gwen has a way with venison that leaves your mouth watering for more."

"It's true," Nick declared. He took the platter from Beth and winked. "But I happen to know that Miss Beth here also does a mighty fine job with venison stew."

Beth blushed ever so slightly. Lacy came in before Beth could reply, however. "Hope you like squash."

"Smells wonderful," Forrest said, reaching for the bowl.

Gwen arrived with a plate in one hand and a bowl in the

other. The plate was stacked with freshly sliced bread, and the bowl appeared to hold her baked molasses beans.

"It won't be hard to thank God for this bounty." Nick took a deep breath to enjoy the aroma.

"I agree," Hank said, coming in from the kitchen.

"Good to see you, Hank. I want you to meet our uncle, Forrest Cromwell. He is our mother's brother," Simon announced. "Uncle Forrest, this is Hank Bishop. He's married to Gwen."

Forrest got to his feet and extended Hank his hand. "I'm pleased to meet you. I hear you run the local store."

Hank nodded and smiled. "That's right. Glad to meet you, as well. Simon and Nick tell me you plan to set up business here."

"I do. This here is my youngest boy, Evan, and his wife, Millie. Evan is a master wagon builder. Millie will have her hands full just taking care of us."

Hank laughed. "Evan and Millie, I'm pleased to make your acquaintance."

Grace was offered, and everyone dug in before picking up the conversation again. Nick couldn't help but cast a long glance at Beth. He wondered if her thoughts were about Adrian Murphy or something else. He frowned. Why did she have to have an interest in that scallywag? Anyone could see he was just toying with her affections. He was what Nick's pa would have called an opportunist. Guys like that had a special gal in every town.

"Nick?"

He looked up, startled. "What? I'm sorry, I didn't hear what you said."

Gwen laughed. "You were scowling so, I thought maybe the venison wasn't to your liking."

He shook his head. "No, I was just caught up in thoughts on another matter. The meal is delicious, as always."

She smiled at this and turned to Forrest. "So will you need rooms here at Gallatin House, or will you be staying with your nephews?"

"They're staying with us," Simon interjected. "Just until we can get their house built."

"It'll be a tight squeeze," Forrest said, "but they have generously offered it and plan to help us build our own cabin. We're much obliged."

"Well, if Nick and Simon snore too loud, Millie," Beth said playfully, "you can always come join us here."

The young woman laughed. "They could never outsnore Pa and Evan."

Everyone chuckled at this, and the conversation drifted into comments about the community and plans for the future. Nick heard Hank comment on several new families moving into the area, but all he could really think about was Beth. Then all at once, she was speaking and asking his opinion.

"Don't you think it would be a lot of fun, Nick?"

Nick looked at her blankly. "What?"

"Your mind is definitely not here," Simon commented. He popped a huge piece of steak into his mouth, giving Nick time to reply.

Beth took the conversation in hand, however. "I said I thought it would be fun to have a community Thanksgiving meal. We could have it here at Gallatin House and invite everyone in the area. Folks could bring what they wanted, and we could just enjoy each other's company and the day. One of you men could go out and get us a nice elk or deer, or maybe we could get a pig and roast it over an open fire."

Nick nodded. "Yes. I think that would be a nice thing to do."

"Would we also invite Rafe and his bunch?" Gwen asked hesitantly.

Beth thought for a moment. "Well, despite my opinion of Rafe, I suppose it would be the Christian thing to do. It'd be nice for the girls and Cubby to join us." She perked up. "I'll ask him tomorrow after we get the breakfast dishes done."

"Better wait until after the lunch dishes are done," Hank said snidely. "Rafe's not usually up until afternoon."

⚬⚬

"So you see," Beth told Rafe while his son, Cubby, hovered near her on the porch, "we'd like all of you to come to dinner. You can bring any foods that you like, but it's not necessary."

Rafe scratched his stubbly chin. "I thought I wasn't welcome anymore at Gallatin House."

Beth stared at him hard. "We hope to forget our grievances with each other for the day and come together to celebrate our blessings."

"That's mighty good of you, Miss Beth," he said with a chuckle.

"What are you going to have to eat?" Cubby asked, practically licking his lips.

Beth smiled at the young man. "Well, we're going to have more food than you can imagine. Meats and vegetables, breads and custards. Oh, and pies—pumpkin, pecan, and apple. We're also planning to have applesauce cake."

"Can we go, Pa?"

Cubby sounded so hopeful. Beth couldn't help but feel sorry for him. "Everyone is invited, Rafe. You, Wyman, all of the girls, and, of course, Cubby. We really want to put aside our differences and just be thankful for what the Lord has provided."

Rafe looked as if he might make some snide comment, but he held his tongue. Beth thought perhaps memories of the Gallatin House cooking was too much for him to risk with flippant remarks.

"I suppose we can go, if it means that much to you, boy."

"Thanks, Pa!" Cubby looked at Beth and winked. "We'll be there!"

"Good. How many should I count on?"

Rafe considered this for a moment. "I guess put us down for nine. I have three extra girls now, you know."

Beth nodded sadly. "Yes, I was aware of that sad news." She turned to step off the saloon's low porch. "Oh, and, Rafe, leave your knife at home. Hank will take care of anything that needs to be carved."

She didn't give him a chance to reply but quickly made her way back toward Gallatin House. She glanced up just before running headlong into Nick.

"Oh, I am sorry. I wasn't looking at all where I was going."

"No problem." He smiled at her, and Beth felt a strange sort of quiver in her stomach. It was just like when Lady Effingham met Lord Wodehouse for the first time at the Duke of Winchester's masquerade ball. Lady Effingham had found herself thrown into Lord Wodehouse's arms when the duke's evil brother had tried to steal a kiss.

"I was hoping I'd see you," Nick told her. "I was just coming back from the store, and Gwen told me you were over at Rafe's."

Beth settled her nerves and squared her shoulders. She had to remember that a lady appeared refined and calm under any circumstances.

"Yes, I was extending the Thanksgiving invitation. I'm heading home now." It seemed ridiculous to say such a thing. Where else would she be going?

"Millie was at the store, hoping to find some things, but Hank told her she might have to go into Bozeman for them. I wondered if maybe you'd like to ride along?"

Beth considered the possibility of a long day in Nick Lassiter's company. She knew he was very interested in her; he'd even proposed courtship several times. She'd avoided his affections because he seemed to be fond of frequenting Rafe's Saloon. Of course, of late, he had put that aside. At least that's what Cubby had told her.

She thought of Lady Effingham again. What would she do? How would she respond to Lord Wodehouse or any other suitor? Beth remembered a passage she'd read earlier that morning. Lady Effingham had pretended to faint in order that one of the would-be suitors might catch her. She had been convinced that this would allow her to know her true feelings for the man.

Perhaps that would work. . . .

*But I can't be fainting. I have no reason to faint. Maybe if I just trip.*

She stumbled awkwardly, and sure enough, Nick reached out and took hold of her and pulled her toward him. The very action caused her to tremble. Beth suddenly remembered that Lady Effingham batted her eyelashes on many occasions to entice the men around her. She lifted her face and did her best imitation of Lady Effingham in the arms of Lord Wodehouse. Her heart seemed to race with excitement. Was this love?

"What's the matter? Did you get something in your eyes?"

Beth stopped batting her eyelashes and straightened. Pulling away, she sighed. The romance of the moment was gone. "I'm fine now. I'm sorry. Thanks for keeping me from falling."

Nick nodded but seemed confused by the matter.

*Men! They are such a mystery.*

"So do you want to go to Bozeman with us?"

Beth thought of the money she'd been putting aside to buy new books. "Yes, I believe I'd like that very much. Let me make sure Gwen doesn't mind. I know we're not expecting a stage in this evening, so it shouldn't cause too much difficulty."

Nick watched Beth walk away and smiled at the prospect of spending the entire day in her company. There had to be a way to convince her that he was good enough for her. He knew she had her Christian beliefs and all, and he wasn't opposed to such things. He believed in God and had always figured that made him a Christian . . . until lately. Some of the things Pastor Flikkema preached on had Nick wondering what was really involved with being a Christian.

He pushed aside his concern about the matter. Right now he just wanted to think about sharing the day with Beth Gallatin. It had felt so right to hold her, even briefly, in his arms. Why couldn't she see that he was the one man who would love her forever?

# CHAPTER THREE

The day before Thanksgiving, Nick was still consumed with thoughts of his day in Bozeman with Beth. It had been, to be perfectly honest, uneventful. Beth had spent almost every moment with Millie. The two women were like young girls as they giggled and shopped. Nick had finally taken himself off to check on some things Evan and Forrest had asked him to pick up.

Coupled with this, when Pastor Flikkema had led Sunday's service, Nick found his words convicting and impacting. The pastor had talked about how nothing was too big for God to forgive—that He hated all sin but wanted to offer redemption through Jesus to anyone who accepted His Son as Savior.

That confused Nick. He couldn't help but wonder what it all meant.

"You look like you've lost your last friend," Hank said as Nick stood waiting his turn at the store counter. Nick glanced around and saw the place was now empty.

"I was just thinking about some things the pastor said on Sunday."

Hank nodded. "He makes a good teacher, don't you think?"

"I do. I just don't understand."

"About what?"

Nick cleared his throat as if the words had somehow gotten caught there. "I guess it was that stuff about no sin being too big for God to forgive." He looked around again and then fixed his gaze on Hank. "Can I ask you something—just between us?"

Hank nodded. "Of course. Speak your mind."

"Well, it's just that I'm not proud of the way I lived my life when I was younger. I made a lot of mistakes. Big mistakes. I hurt people, and . . . well, I can't really talk about the details, but I don't know that God can forgive me for the things I've done."

"Why?" Hank asked, genuinely interested.

"I suppose because it seems too simple—too easy. How can it be that by merely asking for forgiveness, the past suddenly ceases to be held against me?"

"Ah," Hank said, nodding. *"Alienum est omne, quicquid optando evenit."*

"Is that the Latin Beth says you're always speaking?"

Hank laughed. "Yes, I spent a lot of time learning it in college. It means, 'What we obtain merely by asking is not really our own.' It's an old saying that I used to believe, but I don't any longer."

"Why not? Seems sensible to me. If we don't have to fight for something, it just doesn't seem to have as much meaning," Nick replied. "I remember when I was a kid and I wanted a rifle of my own, my pa made me earn it. Working hard for that rifle made it all the more precious to me."

"I know what you're saying. After my father's death, we had it pretty bad for a while. My mother was always working herself sick to provide for us. When she remarried, I learned my stepfather was fairly well off, and I was glad to hear it. I figured we could all relax a bit and take things easy. But that man had no intention of letting me take it easy. He made me work hard to learn as much as I could about business and hired me to help him when I wasn't at school. He paid me a pittance, but his actions made me all the more determined to be successful. I was driven to start my own business and make it work."

"So why don't you believe that saying anymore?"

"Because while I know there are many things that are all the sweeter for having to work for them—fight for them— God's love is not one of those things. He gives it freely. He wants to be reconciled with us. Jesus sacrifices everything in order to see us made right with His Father. We can't be saved because we deserve it or earn it—we're saved by grace. God's grace. His forgiveness comes at a high price, but Jesus paid that price so we wouldn't have to. Therefore, being forgiven is just as simple as repenting and asking."

"Even for really bad things, Hank?"

"I don't know what you've done, but I know God can and

will forgive the truly repentant. I know it, because the Bible says it's so, and I believe it."

"Just seems too good to be true."

Hank smiled and reached across the counter to touch Nick's shoulder. "But it is. You can count on it."

Nick left the store and made his way back to the stable. He thought about Hank's comment for most of the day. He couldn't see how God could look at the ugliness of his past and just let it go—just forgive him.

*I don't deserve to be forgiven. I did wrong, and then I ran away like a coward*. But even as Nick went about his chores, Hank's words continued to pierce his heart.

"Just smell that pig roasting," Simon declared, interrupting Nick's thoughts as he curried one of the stage horses. "I can hardly wait for tomorrow."

"Yeah," Nick agreed. "The girls have been out there taking turns tending that thing, and I have to say my mouth is watering."

"I'm glad we're having pork instead of elk or deer," Simon said, putting away some newly mended harnesses. "Millie's been inside, cooking up a storm, as well. That little gal is amazing."

Nick nodded and put aside the currycomb. "Simon, do you ever think about the past? About coming here?"

"Every so often. Why?"

Shrugging, Nick tried not to sound all that interested in continuing the conversation. In truth, however, he had a million questions running through his mind. "Do you regret coming here?"

"No," Simon answered without a pause.

This surprised Nick. "Not even a little? I mean, you had to leave everything on my account."

"I don't regret it; I think it was the best thing for us. I do feel bad for not being there when the folks passed on, but even then, I know they wouldn't want me to dwell on it. Besides, I didn't come here just on your account, so stop blaming yourself."

"You mean you would have picked up and left Kansas even if I hadn't needed to get out of town?"

"Probably. There wasn't a whole lot of future for me there. We already had six blacksmiths in the area, and I sure wasn't a farmer like Pa." Simon paused and looked quizzically at Nick. "So what's this really all about?"

Nick leaned against the stall and frowned. "I was thinking about last Sunday's sermon and how Pastor Flikkema said that nothing is too big for God to forgive—well, except blaspheming the Holy Spirit. I'm still not sure I really understand all there is to know, but when I asked Hank about it, he seemed to think that God would forgive murderers and thieves as easily as liars and such."

"That's what I understood the pastor to say, as well. You thinkin' your sins are too big for God to forgive, little brother?"

Nick rubbed his forehead. "You know what I did."

"Yeah, I know."

"Can God forgive me?"

Simon shifted uncomfortably. "I don't want to be the one to second-guess that. I think He can, given what was preached on Sunday. But you might want to talk to Pastor Flikkema yourself."

"Just seems too good to be true. All these years, I figured I was probably condemned—that nobody, God included, could forgive me."

"Ma and Pa did, and I sure never held anything against you. If we can put things aside, don't you think God can?"

"I guess I know that, being God, He can do anything. But the question is—will He? Will He forgive me?"

Simon smiled. "Guess you'll just have to ask Him."

Beth put small chunks of wood on the already-glowing embers. The key to successfully roasting a pig, Patience Shepard had told them, was to keep the fire consistent and not too hot. It had been a labor to tend the animal for hours on end, but Beth knew that by the time they sat down to dinner tomorrow, everyone would appreciate the effort.

Gwen was in the kitchen busy baking all sorts of goodies, while Lacy was making repairs to the chicken coop. When the winter snows finally hit and the temperatures dropped, they'd move the chickens to the back porch. But for now, they were just fine in their coop. Unfortunately, the last heavy gusts of wind had wreaked havoc with the thin wooden shingles, and Lacy had volunteered to don her trousers and tend to business.

Gazing off across the valley, Beth noted the snow-capped mountains and sighed. Sometimes she felt hemmed in by the majestic range; and other times, like now, she felt protected and secure. The mountains were like a barrier to keep out the bad things. Pa had once said they were like sentinels, watching over the valley.

"You lose something up there?"

Beth startled at the sound of Nick's voice. "I was just

admiring the mountains." She felt embarrassed by his intent gaze. "What brings you here?"

"Millie. She sent me to see if you could send her over any pork fat." He held up a jar as if for proof.

"Sure. I'll get it for you right now." Beth took the jar and went to the grease pan, where the drippings had been collecting. She took a dish towel and wrapped it around the jar before spooning in the hot juices. "I guess Millie must be a pretty good cook. You boys haven't been over to share our table much at all."

"She *is* a good cook," Nick agreed. "And I have to say, it's pretty nice having a woman in the house to cook on a regular basis."

Beth shook her head and handed him the jar. "Sounds like you're thinking with your stomach."

Nick frowned. "Well, when I think with my heart, it doesn't seem to get me anywhere."

Beth headed back to the fire. "Maybe you just don't know your heart as well as your stomach."

She looked up to find Nick giving her a rather smoldering look. Was that anger? Passion? Maybe he was just thinking of the pork again.

"I know my heart very well," he said, turning on his heel. "For all the good it does me." He stormed off, leaving Beth to wonder what in the world had gotten into Nick Lassiter. She was certain she would never understand men, no matter how much she tried.

∞

Lacy Gallatin had similar thoughts as she worked to secure

the last few shingles on the chicken coop. She had tried hard to honor her sister's wishes that she give up on searching for their father's killer. After all, the man had been shot during the hoopla of drunken cowboys shooting off their guns. No one intended for George Gallatin to be shot—at least, that's what everyone said. But he was dead, just the same, and Lacy wanted someone to be punished.

"Of course, Dave Shepard and Sheriff Cummings won't lift a finger to do anything about it," she muttered, pounding a nail. It wasn't her fault that she kept hearing rumors and leads. It wasn't her fault that Sheriff Cummings and Deputy Shepard had given up worrying about such things.

"I see you're wearing britches again."

*Speak of the devil,* she thought and resisted the urge to suddenly drop her hammer on Dave Shepard's head.

"You looked a whole sight better when you were gussied up for your sister's wedding," he added. "Why can't you just be happy to dress like a woman?"

"I think wearing lace and ruffles would be a bit awkward on the roof of a chicken coop, don't you?" Lacy retorted. She finished her job and scooted off the roof to the ladder. "Besides, you seem to spend an awful lot of time worrying about what I wear or don't wear. Maybe if you put that energy into finding who shot my father, we'd both be a lot happier."

"Maybe if I didn't have to worry about you stirring up trouble, I'd have more time and energy for a lot of things."

Lacy looked over her shoulder and down at the man. He positively vexed her with his insults and admonitions. "Dave Shepard, I am convinced that no matter what I wear, you would find reason to condemn me. If I were up here in a ball gown, you'd still be standing there growling about it for one reason or another."

"You shouldn't be on top of the roof anyway," he countered, "so I suppose you're right. You should leave something like that to Hank, or else get another man to help you out."

"Why? I'm perfectly capable of doing the job." She reached the next-to-the-last rung of the ladder and stopped. It made her a bit taller than Dave's six-foot-three-inch frame, and she rather liked having that advantage. "You simply worry too much, Mr. Shepard. You will worry yourself right into a grave if you don't stop concerning yourself with me, my wardrobe, and my job responsibilities. Now, why are you really here?"

He scowled. "I was making my way home and wondered if there was anything I could do to help you ladies prepare for tomorrow's celebration, but I see you have it all under control."

"And that really bothers you, doesn't it?" Lacy saw him grit his teeth and knew she'd hit a nerve. Why should it irritate him so much that she was self-sufficient? If he only understood about her life—her childhood—he would know why she had to be like this. There had never been anyone to depend on. Most of the time, the girls had been alone.

"I'll leave you to your chores and caustic remarks," Dave said, moving away.

Lacy started to step after him, forgetting that she was two rungs above the ground. She hit the ground hard, nearly knocking the wind out of her. She looked up to find Dave staring down at her. He was fighting hard, or so it seemed, to keep an unemotional look on his face.

Rather than wait for him to offer assistance, Lacy quickly

got to her feet and dusted off her backside. She wanted to cry out in pain at the sore spot on her hip, but she said nothing.

"I hope the britches cushioned your fall," Dave said with a hint of a smile.

Lacy thought about it for a moment, then, against her will, found the whole thing rather amusing. "I suppose your choice in this situation would have actually served me better. A ball gown and multiple petticoats would have given me a much softer landing."

He nodded. "Sometimes I can be right, you know."

"Pa always said even a broken clock was right twice a day." Lacy took a step and winced.

"Here, let me help you." Dave reached out for her, but Lacy wanted no part of it. She wasn't that desperate or that brave. She could remember how she'd felt the other times Dave had touched her. Who knew what might happen if she let him hold her now?

"I'll be all right. I just need to walk on my own and work the muscles."

"Have it your way." He shrugged and walked away, not even bothering to look back.

She supposed he was mad again but pushed aside the thought to focus on making her way to the house. The pain had lessened by the time she reached the back porch, and Lacy was convinced nothing was permanently damaged.

"Coop is repaired," she announced, entering the kitchen.

Gwen was just pulling a pie from the oven. "I wondered where you'd taken yourself off to." She turned after putting the pie on the counter. "You weren't out there dressed like that, were you?"

Lacy looked down at her clothes. "No, actually, I just

changed. A ball gown seemed far more appropriate for strad-dling a roof and repairing shingles."

Gwen looked at her oddly. "A ball gown? What are you talking about?"

"Never mind. I patched the walls and shingled the parts of the roof that needed it. The hens ought to be happy until it gets colder. Now what can I help you with in here?"

"Well, you might as well go down to the cellar and bring up the potatoes. Oh, and get me several onions, too."

The last thing Lacy wanted to do was climb down another ladder, but she also didn't want Gwen to worry about her injury. She did her best to cross the room without betraying her condition. Gingerly stepping down the rungs to the cellar floor, Lacy nearly let out a sob as she stooped to accommodate the short space. Frustrated, she wanted nothing more than to sit down and cry. But Lacy knew there was no point. Tears wouldn't solve anything. They never had. Strength was the only thing people respected.

# CHAPTER FOUR

Beth plopped a pail of water down on the counter and shook her head. "I can't believe the number of . . . *customers* . . . at Rafe's tonight. They're kicking up a real storm, and it's barely past suppertime." The thought of what surely must be happening very nearly under their noses caused her to shudder. "I don't know why God allows such things. And on the night before Thanksgiving!"

Gwen took the hot water and poured it into the sink. "It is despicable, but I hardly think it has anything to do with God and much to do with man. We are sinful in nature—some more than others, it appears."

"And such things are perfectly legal, so the law does

nothing," Lacy added rather bitterly. "Just as it usually does nothing."

Beth made an attempt to busy herself by drying dishes, but she couldn't let the matter drop. Her cheeks grew hot. "Oh, I do wish I were a man sometimes."

This startled not only Gwen, but Lacy. Her younger sister smiled. "That's the first sensible thing you've said in some time."

"Not that it does me any good to say it," Beth replied. "Talking about a thing doesn't resolve it or make it better. I could talk all night—sing it out at the top of my lungs—and nothing would change."

Gwen stopped washing the dishes and looked at Beth. "Maybe you have an idea there."

Lacy moved forward. "What do you mean?"

"Remember when we lived in that tiny town in Colorado— oh, I can't remember the name—where the ladies from the church used to gather outside the saloons and sing hymns to annoy the bar owner and discourage the customers?"

"I do remember that," Lacy answered excitedly. "They also posted the drinkers' names at the church on Sunday morning, just to embarrass them further."

"It seemed to work. I mean, it didn't get rid of drinking altogether, but they moved the bar to the far end of town," Gwen said.

Beth looked at her sisters, a smile beginning to spread. "I know a lot of hymns."

Lacy laughed. "If we bring Major, he's sure to help. Remember how he howls when we sing on Sunday morning?"

At his name, the dog's ears perked, and he got to his feet.

He seemed to understand the plan and headed toward the back door as if to encourage the group.

"I'd say the Major is all for it," Beth replied. "What about Hank?"

Gwen shrugged. "Why would Hank care if I sang hymns? He's gone back to the store to finish his inventory so he can close tomorrow for Thanksgiving."

"Well, he might not like that his wife was a part of such a scheme," Beth continued. "I wouldn't blame you if you felt you needed to stay out of it."

Lacy nodded. "Yes, men can be rather silly about things. I don't even pretend to understand how they think, but this might be one of those simple things that somehow destroys the perfect order of Hank's world."

Gwen grinned and untied her apron. "I can reorder his world easily enough. I'm coming, and you cannot keep me from it."

After quickly tidying the kitchen, the trio slipped out the back door and crept over to where Rafe's girls did their entertaining.

The skies overhead were starlit, and the moon was nearly full. Added to that, Rafe had made a path with lanterns along the back of the saloon so that there would be light enough for visitors to make their way to and from their rooms of entertainment.

Two of the newer prostitutes stood cooing and sweet-talking two cowboys. Beth thought again of Lady Effingham's seduction of Lord Wodehouse and wondered if this type of enticement truly interested men.

Gwen elbowed her in the ribs. "Did you hear me?"

"What?" Beth shook her head, rather startled.

"I asked if you thought this was close enough."

"I can sing pretty loud if I have to," Lacy replied before Beth could speak. "What shall we sing first?" Lacy asked, moving even closer to the rooms.

"How about that one hymn Pa always said was so convicting?" Beth tried to remember the name. "You know the one. He said it always made him feel like getting saved all over again every time we sang it."

"Oh, I remember," Gwen said, then started singing in a clear soprano. " 'Stand up, my soul, shake off thy fears, and gird the gospel armor on.' "

Beth and Lacy joined in, remembering with no difficulty the song they'd sung a hundred times before. They made quite the choir, and their voices easily carried on the night air. The prostitutes stopped and turned away from the cowboys to stare at the girls.

" 'Hell and thy sins resist thy course, but hell and sins are vanquished foes,' " Beth sang, wishing fervently that Rafe and his business would also be vanquished.

A door opened from the entertainment rooms, and a man peered out rather sheepishly. "Say, what's going on out here?"

The girls sang louder in reply. Beth thought it purely the hand of God that they should have come to the place in the song that mentioned, " 'What though thine inward lusts rebel.' " After all, Rafe's business was all about lusts—lusts of the flesh and man's natural desire to rebel against God's authority. These men didn't care that the women whose beds they shared were not here because they wanted to be. Beth knew for a fact that several had been forced to enter this sorry business as a means to pay someone else's debt. Poor Ellie had no desire to be here, but hopelessness had overtaken her. She'd given in to this seedy side of life in order to have a roof over her head and food to eat. How could Beth condemn her for such a choice? Had the circumstances been different, Beth might have found herself having to make such an undesirable choice, as well.

Two men stepped out from the saloon to head back to the rooms, but the ladies standing right there along the path, singing of God's salvation, turned them back inside rather hastily. Beth thought it all great fun, especially as the occupied rooms soon emptied out with disgruntled cowboys muttering about meddling women.

They were just starting the sixth verse when Rafe came barreling out of the saloon. "What in tarnation are you Gallatin girls up to now? Stop that singing and get off my property."

He glared at Gwen as if awaiting her explanation. She smiled while Lacy and Beth continued the song. "Mr. Reynolds, do you not care for hymns?"

"I don't care to have do-gooders trespassing and ruining my business. You've driven off several of my customers, and now I'm doing the same with you. Get off my land."

Gwen nodded. "Come, girls."

They walked to the property line and stepped onto their own land. Rafe bellowed out after them, "And don't come back."

The girls exchanged a look, and Gwen murmured, " 'Come Thou Fount'?"

Lacy nodded and Beth began to sing, " 'Come, thou fount of every blessing, tune my heart to sing thy grace.' "

Rafe looked at them as if they'd lost their minds. He stomped over to where they stood and began to rant again. "I told you ladies to get out of here."

"Mr. Reynolds," Gwen began while Lacy and Beth hummed softly, "as you can see, we are now on Gallatin property. You have no say over what we do here. Singing is something we love to do, and we love to sing about God's goodness and mercy."

Beth wanted to giggle as Rafe's face darkened. His eyes narrowed and his nostrils flared. He let out a stream of obscenities, which only caused Lacy to hum louder. Beth followed suit.

Gwen continued. "Mr. Reynolds, you needn't curse at us. You don't like our singing, and we don't like the business you run. It would seem we're at an impasse."

"Hardly." Rafe seemed to get control of his rage once more. "I'll send Cubby for the sheriff, and then we'll see about your impasse. You're interfering with my commerce. There's bound to be a law that will see you ladies thrown behind bars."

"And then who will feed you Thanksgiving dinner?" Gwen questioned sweetly.

Rafe balled his fists. "Why can't you mind your own business and leave me to mine?"

"Because running a stage stop is not immoral and sinful," Gwen answered.

Beth nodded and couldn't resist joining in. "We never hold people against their will. If they don't want to stay at Gallatin House, they can simply move on. Your girls are prisoners."

"They owe me money. Nothin' wrong with expecting a person to pay their debts. They'd be dead if not for me."

"That would, no doubt, be in their best interest," Lacy said. "Better dead than forced to do the things you require."

"I wonder if they'd feel the same way," Rafe replied rather sarcastically. "It's so easy for you to sit over here in your privilege and safety and say things like that, but it ain't so simple when you're the one having to live in poverty. I took those girls out of bad situations and gave them shelter and board. You Gallatin girls don't have any idea what they were up against before I helped them."

"You're right," Beth said. "We don't know what they were up against, but we sure know what they face now. You took advantage of their need to satisfy your own desires. Knives to their throats, beatings when they manage to make you mad . . . yes, I can see they have a real good life." She looked to her sisters. "I think we should go back to singing."

Rafe turned and headed back to the saloon. He opened the back door and bellowed, "Cubby! Cubby, get out here! We'll see what the sheriff has to say about this."

The girls exchanged a look and smiled. It would take time for the sheriff to come from Bozeman—if he would even make the journey. They would never be arrested for singing hymns, and they knew it very well. So did Rafe. If he didn't like what they were doing, he could move his business elsewhere.

"Cubby!"

The boy was nowhere to be found, and by now the girls and their customers had emptied out of the rooms to see what the commotion was all about. Rafe slammed the door and put his fist into the wall of the saloon. He was cursing again, but then turned and walked back toward Gwen. He shook his fist at her. "Where's your husband?"

"At the store doing inventory."

"Good. I'll go get him, and we'll see what he has to say about this."

"Oh, please do," Gwen said, nodding. "He's a great baritone."

Rafe made two steps forward and raised his hand as if to

strike her. Beth stepped between them, however, and Lacy soon followed. "You're a big bully, Rafe Reynolds. You seem to make a habit of hurting those who are helpless and unable to defend themselves. You would do well to get off of our property now and go back to your business."

"Yes," Lacy said, stepping toward Rafe as if she would take him on single-handedly. "The sheriff and his deputies are rather useless at times, but even they know there's no law against singing. Now go away and leave us be, or we'll rescind our invitation for Thanksgiving dinner."

"No need to rescind anything. We ain't coming to your Thanksgiving dinner," Rafe declared, then immediately looked as if he wished he could take back the words. He quickly followed by insulting their faith and gender before storming off to the saloon.

He was cutting off his nose to spite his face, and Beth knew he would be the angriest of them all come tomorrow. "Well, I think that went rather well," she said, turning to face Gwen.

The cowboys slinked off to follow Rafe, while Marie, the elder of the prostitutes, beat a path for the Gallatins. "What gives you the right to ruin our business? We need to make money, same as you."

"I'm sorry, but you know it's wrong. Rafe should let you all go," Gwen replied.

"Go where?" Marie asked. "I don't want to lay down and die like you suggest. I don't think I would be better off dead." She pointed her finger at the trio and shook it as if admonishing wayward children. "You have no right to judge me. I'm just doing what I have to in order to survive. Someday I plan for things to be different, but right now I'm getting by the only way I know how."

"But there have to be other ways to survive," Gwen said softly. "Marie, I never meant to be condemning, but this kind of life is wrong."

Ellie made her way over but said nothing. Marie seemed to have enough to say for all of them. "You sit over here all pious and holy, but you ain't nothin' but troublemakers. Nobody asked you to come and save us. Now we're all gonna pay the price because of your meddling. Rafe will see to it we have to work twice as hard tomorrow. I hope you're happy." She pulled her shawl close and marched back to her room.

Several of the women followed after Marie, talking in hushed voices amongst themselves. Only Ellie remained.

"We weren't trying to make things worse for you," Beth said, meeting Ellie's sad face.

"I know you weren't, but Marie is right. Rafe won't stand for this, and we'll be the ones who suffer." Her shoulders slumped in defeat.

"I told Rafe to feel free to come get you," Gwen said, explaining what had happened to Hank later that night as they retired for the evening. "I told him you had a great baritone voice."

Hank put his white shirt neatly across the back of a nearby chair. "I'm not sure it was such a good idea to rile him, but I would very much have loved to have witnessed the scene." He grinned at her.

Gwen combed her long, golden blond hair and smiled in return. "I'm afraid poor Rafe got the worst of it when he announced that he and his bunch would not be joining us for Thanksgiving. I'm sure he'll regret that for some time to come."

Laughing, Hank took hold of Gwen and pulled her into his arms. "Rafe needs to learn about keeping his mouth shut."

Gwen nodded, then sobered. "I do wish there were some way to get him to leave. The saloon business seems only to grow stronger as more people move into the area. Those girls are suffering, and apparently, we just made it worse. I thought we might actually do something good by our actions, but Marie says things will only be harder. I know it's not very Christian of me to say, but I wish Rafe would . . . well . . . fail. I wish his business would collapse, and he would move on."

"I know. I am trying to buy Rafe out. I've offered him far more money than his land and place are worth, but he isn't budging. He's certain the railroad is going to come through this area and that his land will be worth far more than it is now."

"And will it?"

Hank smoothed back her hair and kissed her lightly on the lips. "I'm not certain. I know Mr. Murphy planned to report favorably about this area, but I heard some of the other men commenting on how much easier it would be to take the route farther to the north by about eight miles."

"So far as that?" Gwen frowned. "That would certainly bode ill for us."

"I'm not convinced it would be bad," Hank said, kissing her again. This time his lips lingered for a moment longer.

Gwen sighed. "But railroads guarantee a town of its

existence. Supplies are easier to get, and people feel more confident of settling in an area that offers good transportation."

"We have the stage route here, and I doubt that would change. The drivers know the lay of the land too well. You know yourself that this route has become quite important over the years."

Gwen surprised him by pulling away. "But nothing stays the same. You said as much. It might be bad either way. If the railroad comes, then there will surely come more saloons and the kind of folks who frequent them. I always liked our little stage stop, but even now, with the store and the Lassiters expanding their business to include their family members, it's changing. It's growing so rapidly. There's a sawmill, and before you know it, we'll all be discussing schools and churches. We're already discussing a town council and mayor."

"You make it sound as if all of that is bad," Hank said, looking at her oddly.

"It's not bad, but it is different." She went to the bed and sat. "I suppose I prefer the solitude of a small community like we had. I've lived in big cities—you have, too. I just can't imagine going back to that."

"We're not exactly the size of Boston just yet," he said, sitting beside her. "And if we're wise, we'll make provisions for situations and circumstances before things get out of hand. It's all about planning. I don't intend to sit back and just let things run amok."

She smiled, meeting his blue-eyed gaze. "You sound as though you are intrigued and excited about the very prospect."

He laughed and pulled her close once more. "I'm very intrigued and excited because you are a part of it."

Beth pored over the pages of her book until her candle was a tiny stub, then finally blew out the flickering flame. With a sigh, she imagined herself dressed in regal court apparel, dancing in the arms of the handsome Lord Wodehouse. But when she closed her eyes, it was Nick's face she saw.

"Do I care for him?" she whispered.

She had to admit there was something about him that always caused her heart to beat a little faster. Beth could easily see herself at his side—as his wife. What kind of life might they have together? She tried to picture the home they might share—the children they might raise.

Ellie's sad expression came back to haunt her, however. Ellie had lost her husband, only to find herself without family or friend. Prostitution had been her only recourse. Beth shuddered. What if she married Nick and something happened to him?

"But I have family," she told herself. "Family and friends. Ellie had neither."

Beth couldn't help but wonder where God was in all of Ellie's affairs. She hadn't wanted to become a prostitute. She had very nearly died from starvation and had so few choices left to her when Rafe came into her life. Where had God been? Why hadn't He heard Ellie's cries for help? Did God only listen to certain people while ignoring others? Where were the townsfolk—the church folk? Was no one else willing to help the downtrodden?

Someone had once told Beth that difficult trials were God's ways of growing a person's faith, but the very idea that God would put Ellie through such horrors made God seem rather cruel and trite. And Beth didn't believe for one moment that God was either.

"I wish I could do more to help them," she whispered against her pillow. *If only Rafe would simply close down the saloon and set them all free.* But even as she thought it, Marie's words came back to haunt Ellie. Where would they go, even if they were free?

# CHAPTER FIVE

The mingled aromas of roasted pork, venison, freshly baked bread, and coffee filled Gallatin House and left its guests longing for the Thanksgiving meal to begin. The table was filled to overflowing with such a wide variety of dishes that Beth couldn't help but wonder if they'd made too much. Especially now that Rafe and his bunch weren't coming.

She was glad to see that the weather had continued to be unseasonably warm. This had allowed Patience and Jerry Shepard to make the celebration, as well as Dave. Lacy appeared to avoid the sheriff's deputy at every turn, but otherwise, everyone seemed delighted to share the food and festivities together.

Millie and Evan sat at the end of one large trestle table

with Forrest. Nick and Simon sat on either side of their uncle and regaled the entire table with stories of their life in Montana. Beth couldn't help but smile. This was how she'd always imagined her life: a houseful of family and friends, everyone happy and joyful. It was really all she'd ever wanted—a sense of family and community. Lady Effingham believed family to be the most important thing for a woman—family and the love of a faithful man.

Beth had always had the family, of course. Her sisters were as dear to her as anyone could be. So, too, had been her grandparents, aunt, father, and mother. But life back when they were still alive was in constant upheaval. Beth had craved stability and consistency all of her life, and now she finally had a chance for that. She and her sisters were committed to running Gallatin House, and it was the thing she was truly most grateful for this Thanksgiving. Of course, the love of a faithful man wouldn't have hurt, either. She grinned. That would have been something to be most thankful for. If only God would send Beth her very own Lord Wodehouse.

"I thought I should share the Word of God before we begin to enjoy this feast," Hank declared. He stood and opened his Bible and read from Psalm 147. " 'Praise ye the Lord: for it is good to sing praises unto our God; for it is pleasant; and praise is comely. . . . He healeth the broken in heart, and bindeth up their wounds. He telleth the number of the stars; he calleth them all by their names. Great is our Lord, and of great power: his understanding is infinite. The Lord lifteth up the meek: he casteth the wicked down to the ground. Sing unto the Lord with thanksgiving; sing praise upon the harp unto our God.' " He closed the Bible and sat down. "Jerry, would you ask the blessing?"

Jerry Shepard nodded and began to pray. Beth barely heard the words, however. She was still thinking on the verses Hank had read. God was in the business of healing the brokenhearted and binding up the wounded. He was a gatherer of outcasts— and yet He also cast down the wicked. Her father came to mind, and Beth couldn't help but wonder if God would cast down the wicked who were responsible for his death.

"Amen," Jerry said, and everyone around Beth murmured the same.

Beth glanced up as everyone seemed to begin talking at once. She tamped down her guilt once more and tried not to think of how life might've been had their father survived his wounds. It would have been awful to pack up once again and move away. Beth would have cried herself to sleep every night if that had happened. It seemed silly, she knew. Here she was a grown woman, and yet such things had the power to make her miserable.

"Would you like some green beans?"

Beth looked up to see Patience smiling and holding out a bowl. "Yes, please," Beth said, taking the bowl. "I'm afraid I was daydreaming a bit."

"Your sister was just saying that you were up quite late last night making pies."

"Ah, yes," Beth said, taking a portion of the beans and passing them to Lacy. "We were very busy. I suppose I didn't sleep all that well, either. Too excited about today." She smiled and gave Patience's arm a pat. "I'm just so glad to have you all here."

"Beth, could you bring in more bread?" Gwen asked.

"Of course." Beth got to her feet and hurried to the kitchen, where she nearly jumped a foot at the sight of Cubby. "I didn't think you were coming today."

"Pa said we weren't, but with him still sleepin', I didn't figure he'd know the difference. Do you mind if I join you? It sure smells good."

Beth smiled. "You most certainly can join us. Let me fetch you a plate." She hurried to the cupboard. "I'm sure we'll all keep your secret. No one should be punished for eating dinner when they're hungry."

"My pa wouldn't agree with you, but I don't much care," Cubby admitted.

Beth ushered Cubby into the dining room with a platter of bread and a dinner plate. "Look who's come to join us," she announced.

"Cubby! We're so glad you came. Did your father change his mind?" Gwen asked. "Are the others coming, as well?"

"No," the boy replied and took the seat offered him beside Hank. "I snuck out. Pa's still sleeping." The boy piled food onto his plate and began to attack it as if he hadn't seen sustenance in months. Beth was amazed at how much he could eat.

"How goes setting up the wheelwright and wagon business?" Hank asked Forrest.

"Rather slow at this point," Forrest admitted. "We're still trying to decide how to work things. Simon and Nick think that once we're established, the stage company will keep us plenty busy."

"I don't doubt that a bit," Hank replied. "The road from Salt Lake to here is quite difficult. I'm surprised they don't have to replace the wheels more often than they do."

"I managed to talk with some folks in Bozeman," Evan added. "There's already some wagon workers over there, but we all figured with the way the community is growing, there will be business enough for everyone."

"That brings up another topic," Hank said as everyone continued to eat. "We have expanded considerably since my arrival earlier this year. At this rate, we'll need to consider naming this area and maybe even incorporating."

"I've been thinking much the same," Jerry Shepard joined in. "The area will need law and order, to be sure."

"That's true," Lacy added. "Especially since we have so little of it now." Lacy didn't so much as look at Dave, but Beth noted his discomfort.

"Not only that," Hank said, "but as Gwen and I were discussing recently, the influx of new families will create a need for schools and churches. Not to mention physicians and additional businesses. Most of you know that I've set up an informal bank, but to be quite honest, it appears that it will quickly become a full-time job, and I'll have to add on to the store to create a place just for financial transactions."

"It can't hurt to make plans for the future," Nick said thoughtfully. "It's a good place for a town. Good source of water and transportation. Even if the train goes in to the north, we're still on the main road. With all the ranches around here, we're certain to have work."

"That's exactly what I was telling Gwen," Hank continued. "It seems to me that we should at least think about giving a name to this place."

"Well, everyone knows about Gallatin House. And since the stage has to cross the Gallatin River to arrive here, what if we called it Gallatin Crossing?" Patience suggested.

Dave nodded. "I like that idea. Most folks refer to it as the

Gallatin Place anyway. Seems like calling it Gallatin Crossing would be appropriate."

"I wouldn't want folks thinking we were putting on airs and using our last name as some sort of desire for recognition," Gwen threw out. "I mean, the county is already called Gallatin; maybe we should consider something else."

"No one is going to think anything of it," Patience assured. "Besides, like Dave said, most folks already reference this area in relationship to the stage stop. It seems a wise choice to avoid confusion."

"You don't suppose people would confuse it for Gallatin City, do you?" Beth questioned.

"No, I would hardly think so. Since Bozeman took over as county seat, that poor town has little left to it," Jerry answered. "I think Gallatin Crossing would be a fine name."

"So how does one go about making that official?" Nick asked. "How do we become a town?"

Hank grew thoughtful. "We'll need to check out the territorial law and see what's required. I doubt that it's all that difficult. I do know there is a difference between simply calling yourself an unincorporated town and incorporating. We'll take it one step at a time. The only thing that might influence our timing would be the railroad."

"And that could take years," Jerry said. "They've stopped and started that line several times before. There's no telling if it will actually get completed this time around."

"I think that's a good point," Hank replied. "Of course, once the line is determined, even if it hasn't been built, it's going to cause a stir, and land prices will go up. I'll do what I can to check out the particulars. But until then, there's no reason we can't refer to ourselves as Gallatin Crossing."

Cubby jumped up, noting the time. "It's late. Pa will surely be waking up by now. I'd best be on my way. Thanks for dinner." He didn't wait to discuss the matter but quickly headed to the back door. "Bye, Lacy," he said over his shoulder.

"Wait," Beth called out. She followed him into the kitchen. "Would you like a piece of pie? We have several just waiting."

He looked at her rather wistfully. "Sure sounds good, but I can't very well take it with me."

"If I cut the piece small," Beth suggested, "you could eat it on your way home. Then no one has to be the wiser."

Cubby nodded. "That might work. I figured to go the long way around the store and come down the road so that no one suspected. That would give me plenty of time to eat it." He grinned. "You wouldn't need to cut it too small."

$\infty$

Rafe pushed around the beans on his plate and silently cursed the Gallatin women and their stupidity. If they would have just minded their own business, he might have had the chance to eat roasted pig and some of their delicious pie. His mouth watered just thinking about it, and the beans did nothing to ease his misery.

"Biscuits are done," Wyman said, tossing a pan on the table.

Rafe took one of the hot biscuits and slathered it with butter. Wyman did likewise, and the two ate in silence. For all of his life, Rafe felt he'd gotten nothing but the short end of the stick. It seemed he always managed to sidestep the easy route and head right to a rougher path. It wasn't out of desire; it just seemed to be his lot in life.

He thought of the gathering at the Gallatin House. His girls had been upset to hear they were no longer allowed to attend the festivities. A couple of them had actually gotten quite sassy about it, and Rafe had slapped them hard to put across to the rest that grumbling and complaining wouldn't be allowed. He could grumble and complain plenty for everyone. He didn't need their help.

"So you figure we'll have any business tonight?" Wyman asked.

"Who can tell after last night?" Rafe replied, pushing his empty plate back. "I've had about all the interference I'm gonna stand for from those Gallatin women."

"What can you do about it? I know you said Bishop would like to buy you out, but I didn't think that was an option."

"It's not." Rafe got up and went to the bar. He poured himself a beer, then took a long drink. "There's no reason I should have to leave. Folks know where I'm at. Moving would just confuse them."

"Well, you wouldn't have to move all that far," Wyman said, stuffing the last of the biscuit into his mouth. He picked up his empty mug and followed Rafe's example.

"I don't have to move at all. Those uppity Gallatins ain't gonna make me leave. I have it on good authority that the railroad plans to come through here. One of the men told me it was all but a signed deal. This land is gonna be worth a fortune."

"I thought they hadn't decided. Seems to me someone said that they were looking to put the railroad through to the north of us."

Rafe shook his head. "That's just to keep people from buying up the land and chargin' the railroad an exorbitant fee. I'm guessin' if folks were to know the exact plan for the route before the railroad could secure the land, then there would be a run on the area and the prices would go way up." He grinned. "But if I start buying up land now, before the route is announced, I figure I can still get it cheap, and no one need be the wiser."

"So how are you going to do this?"

"That's where you come in. I figure with a few incentives, people will be inclined to sell."

Wyman laughed. "I can think of all sorts of incentives. People tend not to want to stay in a place that isn't safe. And since the only real law is over in Bozeman, stands to reason a whole lot of bad things could happen to folks out here."

Rafe nodded. "I figured you could come up with something. You just go on ahead and get to that. See what folks are thinkin' and what kind of misery would cause them to leave. Once they're gone and the railroad comes in, things will repopulate fast enough."

"With our kind of people," Wyman added.

"Exactly. People who aren't teetotalers—folks who don't hold to religious nonsense."

<br>

Beth readied herself for bed, all the while casting glances at her Bible and *The Courtship of Lady Effingham*. She knew she should focus on her Bible reading. She'd been sorely neglecting it for days now, but Lord Wodehouse was just about to tell Lady Effingham his dark secret.

"There just aren't enough hours in the day," Beth muttered.

She quickly combed out her long hair, then tucked it in a cap and took the candle to her bedside table. The Bible beckoned her, but Lady Effingham demanded her utmost attention.

*Maybe if I just read a little and see what Lord Wodehouse has to say, then I can put it aside and concentrate on my Scripture reading.* But even as Beth reached for the novel, she knew she would get caught up in the story as before.

She settled into bed and pulled the quilts high before opening the book. With a sigh, she began to read about Lady Effingham's opulent existence. Beth couldn't imagine what it would be like to have so many servants bustling around and seeing to your every need. Why, Lady Effingham even had a maid to do nothing but arrange her clothes!

Without warning her cat jumped on the bed, nearly frightening Beth out of her wits. She snapped the book closed so fast, she actually smashed her finger between the pages.

"Oh, Calvin, what in the world has gotten into you? I didn't even know you were in here." She reached to stroke the amber fur. "You scared me half to death."

The cat only purred and pawed at the bedding to make himself comfortable. Once he settled in, Beth drew a deep breath and went back to reading. Just as Lord Wodehouse was about to make his declaration, Major began barking.

"Goodness, but is everyone against my discovering Lord Wodehouse's secrets?" Beth got up, careful not to disturb Calvin, and went to the window. She pulled back the drapes and stared into the darkness below.

Major's bark became more intense, and she could see him

pacing back and forth in front of the house. Something moved in the shadows across the roadway, but she couldn't see what it was. Apparently, this was what had Major all worked up. Rather than see him wake the entire community, Beth quickly pulled on her robe and went to tend to the dog.

She opened the front door and stepped out onto the porch. "Major, you stop that barking right now."

The dog whined and came to her side. He didn't look up at her but instead kept his attention on the area across the street.

"What is it, boy?" Beth strained to see what might have disturbed the dog. Clearly something was out there, but whether man or beast, Beth couldn't tell. A jolt of apprehension washed over her.

"Maybe it would be just as well if we went inside," she said to the dog. "After all, we're hardly prepared to do battle, no matter who the opponent might be."

Just then, a figure seemed to separate from the darkness and move toward them. Beth froze in place. She could tell by the lumbering movement that it was a bear. Perhaps this was the animal Nick had warned her about!

Major began to bark again. He charged forward a few feet, then stood his ground and raised such a ruckus that Beth was certain others would come to investigate.

"Major, come back here," she called. She didn't know what might happen if the dog decided to take on the bear, but she knew it wouldn't be good. "Major!"

"What's all the commotion?" Lacy questioned, coming up from behind Beth.

Beth jumped in fright. "There's a bear. I'm trying to get Major, but he's trying to protect me."

"I'll get the rifle," Lacy said, leaving before Beth could speak.

With her lowest, most authoritative voice, Beth commanded, "Major, come!"

The dog barked but nevertheless turned and came back to the porch. Unfortunately, the bear seemed intent on following. Beth didn't realize Lacy had returned until a blast sounded from the rifle.

The bear immediately lit out for the trees and disappeared into the night. Of course, the shot of the rifle was already causing lamps to be lit at the saloon, as well as at the Lassiters'.

"What's going on out here?" Rafe bellowed. He staggered out the front door, pulling on his gun belt over long underwear.

By now, Nick and Simon had exited their house and were heading toward Gallatin House.

"It was a bear," Beth explained. "Major was trying to ward him off, but he didn't seem inclined to leave. Lacy had to fire a shot at him."

"Did you hit him?" Nick asked.

"I didn't even try to," Lacy told him. "I just fired into the air and hoped it would scare him off."

"Which it did," Beth said.

The soft glow of lamplight filled the door behind her as Hank and Gwen appeared. "What's wrong?" Hank asked.

"A bear," Lacy said, shouldering the rifle. "He's gone now, but no doubt he'll be back. He was probably nosing around the pit where we roasted the pig."

"Maybe we should put some traps out tomorrow," Rafe declared. "Sure would save a body from havin' to wake up to all that commotion."

"I don't like traps," Beth said angrily. "They're cruel and inhumane."

"So are bears," Rafe countered.

"We can worry about this tomorrow," Nick suggested. "I'm with Beth, however. A trap would be a danger to other animals."

Beth smiled in appreciation of Nick's declaration. Gazing at him, she noted that he was very much like Lord Wodehouse. Even in the middle of the night, with the sleep still in his eyes, he was heroic and noble. She sighed.

"Lord Lassiter," she murmured.

"What was that?" Lacy asked.

Beth shook her head. "Nothing." But she couldn't keep the smile from spreading over her face. "Nothing at all."

# CHAPTER SIX

"How did you know you were in love with Hank?" Beth asked Gwen. They were on their hands and knees, busy scrubbing the pine floor of the front room, when she posed this question.

Gwen looked at her oddly. "I don't know. We spent time together and . . . well, I just knew."

"But what about how he made you *feel*?" Beth asked, reflecting on the wonderful romances she'd read. "Did he make your chest feel tight? Did your stomach get all queasy and do flips? Did your heart burn?"

"That sounds more like a bad case of dyspepsia than love," Gwen said, laughing. She got to her feet and surveyed their work. "I feel much better now that this is all washed down. It was looking so dull before."

Beth studied the floor around them, but her thoughts were on Nick.

"I just don't want to miss it when it comes to me," she finally said. Beth glanced upward to see Gwen's expression change from smiling to confused.

"What are you talking about?"

"Love," Beth said. She stood, smoothing out the skirt of her gown.

"Goodness, what makes you think you'd miss love if it came to you? How silly. It isn't like it sneaks around and hides until you find it. Love *wants* to be found."

"And I want to find it," Beth confided. She looked around the room rather uncomfortably. "I might even have found it, but I don't know for sure."

Gwen smiled. "Is this about Adrian or Nick?"

Beth felt her face grow hot. Was it that obvious to everyone around her? She put her hands to her cheeks. "I suppose it could be about either one, but . . . well . . . I was thinking actually of Nick. Before he started showing an interest in the Bible and churchgoing, I knew I shouldn't even think of such things and I tried hard not to, even when he was always badgering to court me. Grandma Gallatin used to scare me half to death with all the terrible stories of young ladies she knew who'd been unequally yoked with men who hated God."

"Yes, but I don't think Nick ever hated God. He might not have known much about Him, but I never heard him speak negatively."

"Still, you know that Jesus said if a person wasn't for Him, he was against Him. I never could quite tell with Nick. But now he's taken an interest in the things of God and . . . well, he might have even gotten himself right with God. I don't know for sure." Beth supposed the whole conversation sounded completely ridiculous to Gwen. It was starting to sound that way to her own ears, as well.

"Are you in love with Nick?" Gwen surprised her by asking.

Beth shrugged. "I don't know. Sometimes I think I am, but other times, I just can't figure it out. He makes me feel funny—like when I see him for the first time in the day and he smiles at me." She paused and shook her head. "I know that probably sounds silly."

"No. Not at all," Gwen promised. "I feel the same way about Hank." She closed the distance between them and put her hands on Beth's shoulders. "You just need to give this time, Beth. Don't feel that you have to decide overnight what your heart is telling you. It will come through loud and clear in time. You aren't going to miss seeing the truth of it, believe me."

"Is the cake done yet?" Lacy called as she came in from the back porch.

Beth suddenly felt uncomfortable. "We can talk more about this later," she whispered. It wasn't that she didn't trust Lacy, but of late, it seemed her little sister hated most of the men in the county. No sense asking for her advice about love.

"It's cool enough to frost," Gwen said, moving into the dining room.

"Cubby's so excited that we would go to the trouble to bake him a birthday cake. I didn't bother to tell him that we had presents for him, too," Lacy said with a smile.

"Well, this will be a very special occasion. I'm hoping Rafe's cooled off enough to not protest when Hank asks if he and Cubby would like to join us for a supper celebration.

I would have extended the invitation only to Cubby, but it's hard, given he's still a boy and Rafe is his father."

"Well, he doesn't consider himself much of a boy anymore," Lacy countered. "He's got a bit of a swagger in his steps nowadays. He's fifteen, and he thinks that pretty well qualifies him to be a man."

"In much of the country," Gwen replied, "I'm sure it does. Still, I don't want to cause enmity between us and Rafe—at least, no more than already exists."

Lacy picked up the bowl of frosting that Gwen had prepared. "I suppose we'll know soon enough if they're coming. I'll get the cake frosted, anyway. Cubby's a sweet boy. I intend to see that he has a nice birthday cake, even if his pa doesn't want him to have a celebration."

∞

Nearly a week later, Lacy encountered Cubby as she led her saddled horse from the Lassiters' to Gallatin House.

"Miss Lacy? I'm wonderin' if we could talk, private-like, for a minute."

Cubby seemed nervous and almost embarrassed. Lacy couldn't imagine what might have happened to cause this, so she immediately halted the horse. "Of course. What's wrong?"

Cubby looked at his feet and shook his head. "Nothing's wrong. I just wanted to . . . to . . . talk to you." He glanced up ever so slightly. "I like talkin' with you."

Lacy smiled. "I like talking with you, too. Did you enjoy your birthday party?"

He puffed his chest at this and seemed to lose some of his

shyness. "I sure did. It was the first birthday party I'd ever had. Pa said it was a waste of time, but I thought it was a lot of fun. Made me feel real special."

It figured Rafe would try to ruin the boy's good time. The man wasn't happy in his own life, so it seemed he wanted no one else happy, either.

"I don't think birthdays are ever a waste of time. They are a person's one special day. I'm glad we could celebrate with you."

"It was really nice of you and your sisters." He acted as though he were noticing the horse for the first time. "You going riding?"

"I'm heading out to the Shepard place."

"Wish I had a horse. I'd ride along and keep you safe. You can't be too careful around here. I heard Pa and Wyman talkin' just the other day about some highwaymen."

"I doubt they'd bother with me. I don't carry any valuables, and I seldom keep to the road. I'm usually cutting across country for a faster trip." She smiled at his concern. "But thanks all the same for caring."

"I do care, Miss Lacy. I'm fifteen now, and I figure it's time I tell you . . . well . . . that I care. I care about you." He held her gaze for just a moment, then looked at his feet once again.

Lacy didn't know what to say. Here this scrap of a boy, all gangly-legged and baby-faced, was speaking of having feelings for her. "I'm flattered, Cubby—"

"Quennell," he interjected. "My real name is Quennell."

Lacy looked at him for a moment, flustered by the unexpected confession of his feelings. "I'm considerably older than you. You might have turned fifteen, Cubby, but I'm twenty now. An old maid, by most folks' standards. At least around these parts."

"You aren't an old maid, and you aren't that much older than me," Cubby protested.

"Five years can be a very big divide. Besides, I don't think much of men right now. Certainly not enough to want to keep time with them. They all seem full of boasting and false promises, or they're mean-spirited. I don't want to be bothered, and I sure don't want to hurt someone like you."

Cubby grew bold and stepped forward to within inches of Lacy. "You wouldn't hurt me, and I wouldn't hurt you. I care for you. I want to court you."

Lacy could see just how serious the boy was. She felt helpless to say anything that could dissuade his affections and ambitions.

"I think you're very sweet, but I am not going to court you." Lacy took that moment to move away from him and mount her horse. She looked down at him with a sympathetic expression. "I'm not going to court anyone."

"It's because you think I'm not worthy, but I am," Cubby said, coming alongside the horse. "I'll prove it to you, and then you'll see for yourself. I know you like me, or you wouldn't have bothered to give me a present or have a party for me."

"Please, Cubby," Lacy said, nearly distraught. "I don't want you to think I feel something for you that I don't. I don't feel that way toward anyone, and I doubt I ever will." She urged the horse forward, not daring to look back. She felt horribly heartless for her words, but she knew in time it would all be for the best. There was no sense in letting him get his hopes up for something that would never happen.

She rode across the empty field and found the path she

often took to make her way to the Shepard ranch. Lacy was glad for the time alone.

"Poor Cubby," she murmured. "I never wanted that to happen. I just wanted to be nice to him."

*Why do men have to be like that? On one hand, they are always looking for meaning where there is none, and on the other, they're oblivious to details when it matters.*

Dave Shepard came to mind. He didn't seem to realize that the death of her father had left Lacy with a driving need to make sense of it all. Dave knew that Lacy believed her father had been murdered rather than accidentally killed. But still he refused to pursue the case further.

Lacy straightened in the saddle and pushed her wide-brimmed hat back just a bit. She couldn't explain in any reasonable manner why she believed her father had been purposefully shot, but she did. It was just a gut feeling, and it continued to nag at her. Despite her promise to Gwen to try and stay out of it, Lacy knew it was no good. She couldn't leave well enough alone. Sure, her father would still be dead no matter who was to blame, but at least if Lacy could find his killer, justice would be served. Didn't she owe Pa at least that much?

$\infty$

"Do you really suppose you'll stay in Montana?" Beth asked Millie as they sat together, sewing in the front room of Gallatin House. Gwen had suggested the gathering as a way to chat and get to know Millie better, while also accomplishing some of their household tasks. Nearly an hour had passed, with Millie asking Beth and Gwen all sorts of questions about her new homeland.

"I do love it here," Millie admitted. "I loved Kansas, too, but I must say it's completely different here. It seems so far removed from everything else. I feel as if I've driven right off to the end of the world."

Beth laughed and knotted her thread. "Sometimes it feels exactly like that. Especially during the winter."

Gwen nodded. "It does seem a little bleak at times. At least many more of the stages and freighters are making it through. Used to be that winter signaled the stop of just about everything. Now the roads are being developed in such a way that so long as the drivers take a shovel or two along, they can pretty well dig their way out if needed."

"Remember the stage that got stuck about two miles from here?" Beth commented. "That was about three years ago, wasn't it?"

"It was," Gwen replied. "They were on their way up from Virginia City, heading to Helena. The snows were so bad, they had to walk the last two miles because they couldn't get the stage through. We had those folks with us for a week while the stage company dug out a path. Of course, it didn't help that it just kept snowing."

"Goodness, but it all sounds so exciting," Millie declared. "I love a good adventure."

Beth thought immediately of Lady Effingham. She, too, loved adventure and often commented about it. "I love adventure, as well," Beth added with a smile. "And believe me, we get plenty right here."

Millie laughed. "I'll say. What with bears on the prowl and Indian attacks, it seems like this is the Wild West so many easterners talk about. But I wouldn't trade it. I'm glad we came. Evan was always telling me about the letters Nick and Simon sent home after they first came here. He said the place sounded so raw and unspoiled. He's wanted to see it for nearly as long as the Lassiter brothers have lived here."

Beth saw this as a good opportunity to better know Nick, and posed a question. "I never have heard the story of why Nick and Simon settled in this area. Why did they leave Kansas, Millie?"

The younger woman shrugged and gave the slightest hesitation. "I can't really say. I know there's something of a mystery about it, but the family keeps it quiet. There was some sort of trouble—that's all I know."

"Trouble?" Beth prodded. "What kind of trouble?"

"Like I said, I don't really know. I came from Missouri to teach school long after they'd gone. I do know it involved Nick more than Simon, but because Simon was older, he took on the responsibility for his brother and brought him out here."

Beth was utterly intrigued. Nick had a mysterious past, just like Lord Wodehouse—who she'd just learned was actually a royal prince who had killed his best friend in a duel and was now on the run, hiding from his past. Could Nick's life be similar in circumstance and situation? Oh, but the thought of it delighted Beth in a way she couldn't explain. It thrilled her to imagine that Nick was someone or something other than he appeared to be. Perhaps he was hiding from an evil foe who planned to do him harm.

Beth's imagination ran rampant as she considered all sorts of problems Nick might have encountered. It made him mysterious . . . alluring.

"Of course, Forrest said it will come in time."

Beth suddenly realized she'd not been paying attention and had no idea what Uncle Forrest Cromwell was advising would come in time. The clock on the mantel chimed four, and Gwen quickly put away her sewing.

"I must get supper started. We have a stage due in at six if the roads in the mountains aren't too bad."

Millie nodded. "I should get home, too. I need to get supper started for my menfolk." She carefully folded the dish towel she'd been hemming. "It was sure nice to get to sit and talk with you gals. I hope we'll be good friends."

Gwen smiled. "I think we already are."

Beth, too, folded her sewing and put it back in her bag. Gwen would need her help in the kitchen, as Lacy still hadn't returned from the Shepards' ranch. She stretched and headed for the kitchen while Gwen saw Millie to the door. Pictures of Nick battling with a sword came to mind. Beth giggled at the thought until the dashing image turned to stare at her. The dream seemed almost real enough to touch.

"You certainly are given to daydreaming these days," Gwen said as she bumped against Beth's now-stopped form.

Beth looked at her sister oddly, then nodded. "I suppose I am."

"Well, why don't you dream a little while you climb down into the cellar and bring up some of that venison stew I made the other day? I'll warm that up and make biscuits, and you can open some apple preserves and make pies. We'll have a nice hearty meal."

With both of them working, tantalizing aromas soon filled the air. Beth had just finished laying a fire in the front room when a knock sounded at the door. Since most of the freighters and stage drivers tended to just walk in, Beth couldn't help but wonder who it might be. She went to open it just as the knock began again.

The sight of the handsome face caused Beth to stammer. "Adrian . . . I mean, Mr. Murphy."

He smiled at her and shook his head. "I much prefer you call me Adrian. You know that." He took off his hat. "Could you walk with me for just a moment? I know it's getting dark. I can't stay so we won't go far."

Beth nodded. "Let me get my shawl." She hurried to the peg where her shawl hung. What was Adrian doing here? Hadn't he returned to the railroad headquarters to discuss the survey plans?

*Well, obviously he hasn't,* she chided herself. *He's here, after all.*

She smiled as she made her way out onto the porch. "I can't be long. We're expecting a stage, and Gwen needs my help."

"I understand. I just wanted to see you one more time before I left."

"I thought you had already gone."

He smiled and took hold of her hands. "We left behind some important instruments. I rode out here to retrieve them, but I knew I couldn't pick them up without seeing you, as well."

Beth thought of Lord Wodehouse, riding over thirty miles in the rain just to see Lady Effingham. She smiled. How romantic that Adrian should have done something similar for her. Of course, it wasn't raining. And it was only fifteen or so miles.

"I couldn't leave without trying once again to secure your promise to wait for my return in the spring."

His comment took Beth by surprise, and she stopped in midstep to face him. "I don't understand."

"But you must. I asked you to wait for me . . . to wait for my return so that we might court properly."

"But you might not even return to this part of the country," Beth protested. Her senses were returning in a rather obtrusive manner. "You said so yourself. You said once the survey was complete, you would have to move on to take on the next stretch."

"That's true enough, but there's no reason we couldn't at least see each other on occasion."

Beth shook her head. "Adrian, I don't think I can make you any kind of promise. I'm sorry." She knew it wasn't what he wanted to hear. Still, it seemed the right thing to say, although she was certain Lady Effingham would have managed it with much more flourish and pomp.

To her surprise, Adrian pulled her awkwardly into his arms and kissed her. Beth had never known a man's kiss before, and the strange feel of Adrian's damp—well, almost wet—lips against her own seemed more annoying than romantic. His hand stroked at her neck all the while, as if he were calming a mare in a stall.

When she could no longer stand it, Beth pulled away. She wanted to say something impressionable, but nothing came to mind. Adrian just grinned at her like a schoolboy who'd just won the spelling bee.

"I'm sorry if I took undue advantage of you," he finally said.

"You don't really sound sorry."

He laughed. "I suppose I'm not *that* sorry, but I didn't mean to offend you. I just hoped that by kissing you, it might prove to you the depth of my feelings."

"How?" Beth asked, not actually meaning to vocalize the thought.

Adrian seemed taken aback. "Well . . . I just thought . . . I had hoped . . ." He went silent. "Just think about what I've said."

"I'm sorry," Beth said, shaking her head. "I can't make promises to you about the future." In fact, she realized she didn't want to make him promises about anything. Adrian Murphy did not hold her interest the way she had hoped. Why couldn't she just be in love with a man who obviously had feelings for her? Why did she have to go on being confused by her own heart?

He hung his head. "I'm sorry. I suppose in being so forward, I've ruined my chances with you."

Beth merely shrugged and nodded. It seemed appropriate enough and resulted in Adrian turning to walk away. He glanced back at her once, and Beth got the distinct feeling that she was supposed to call out to him, but for the life of her, she couldn't figure out what she would say. Goodness, but why didn't life come with a book of sayings, ready for any circumstance?

Walking quickly in the opposite direction, Beth nearly ran right over Nick. He took her by the arm to steady her but quickly dragged her off toward the back of the house.

"What in the world do you think you were doing?"

He was angry, that much was evident. But why?

"Do you not care for your reputation? How can you just stand out in the street and act so shamelessly?"

Confusion was quickly replaced by her own anger. Beth

tried to push away Nick's hold, but he had an iron grasp on her arm and refused to yield.

"What are you yelling at me about? I've done nothing wrong."

"You were kissing that Murphy man in the street."

Beth considered his comment. "Actually, he kissed me. I did very little."

This only served to irritate Nick more. "You are living dangerously, Miss Gallatin. That man had no right to touch you, much less kiss you."

Beth giggled. "You sound jealous."

"I *am* jealous."

His gaze burned into her with such intensity that Beth couldn't look away. His words, his stance, and especially his touch had a sobering effect on her that she couldn't understand. Her stomach seemed to tighten and then release. There were the flip-flops, but why now? He wasn't kissing her. He was yelling at her. There was nothing romantic about that.

"Why are you jealous?" Beth asked, trying to make sense of her emotions and Nick's words.

To her surprise, he released her and shook his head. "If you can't figure that out by now, you really don't know me at all." He walked away and, unlike Adrian, did not look back.

Beth fought the urge to go after him. She wanted to know more. Needed to hear his explanation, but she was frozen in place. He was jealous of Adrian kissing her. Did that mean he truly cared about her?

Nick was long gone when Beth finally headed for the house. She felt as though she were in a cloud of confusion. Her thoughts were more muddled than ever before. If this was how love made a person feel, then perhaps she would be better off without it.

⌒⧜⌒

Nick stared at the ceiling for a long time after he'd blown out the lamp. All he could think about was Beth in the arms of that Adrian Murphy. When he closed his eyes, he could see the two of them kissing. It was killing him inside.

He rolled over and pounded the pillow with his fist, making a decision about love and Beth Gallatin. He was going to stay as far away from both as he could. Experience had been a demanding teacher—a harsh and unrelenting master. He would do better to leave such fancy to his brother and forget about it for himself. After all, he knew only too well the trouble it could cause.

⌒⧜⌒

The first winter snow was gentle, with a dry, wispy snow that seemed almost ethereal. The landscape took on a glittery sheen that made everything seem fresh. The temperature remained tolerable, and everyone was in a celebratory mood. The next snow, however, brought with it frosty arctic air that chilled them with an ever-plummeting temperature. When the storm let up, at least twenty inches of snow covered the ground, and a bone-numbing cold left no one in doubt the mercury was well below zero.

January was no better than December, but with the long hours of darkness and snow, Nick concluded that he would be better off to forget about women and focus instead on the work at hand, both physical and spiritual. He decided to put Beth from his mind and vowed to himself and God that he would instead seek the Scriptures.

With the wind howling and rattling the cabin windows,

Nick pored over the book of Matthew, listening to the words Christ shared with the people. He told them they were blessed if they hungered and thirsted after righteousness—told them they'd be filled.

"You ever feel hungry for righteousness?" Nick asked his brother one night as they settled into bed. Ever since Uncle Forrest and Evan and Millie had come to stay with them, they'd been sharing a room. It hearkened back to days when they'd been boys. But now, instead of laughing and telling scary stories to get the best of each other, they often talked about far more serious matters.

"I suppose lately I have," Simon admitted. "I see things that are just plain wrong, and I'd like to know why God allows them. I try reading the Bible, but I find it confusing at times."

"I know. I feel the same way. I never was much into book learning. Still, I find myself thinking about it . . . wanting to read the Bible and know more. I guess God's kind of hooked me by the collar and won't let go."

Simon smiled. "I figured it was Beth Gallatin who had done that to you."

Nick shook his head. "I have a goal for the winter. I want to know more about God and stay as far away from Beth as possible."

Laughing, Simon climbed into bed. "I don't know how you expect to do that when she's one of the only single women in the area, and she lives just across the road."

"I didn't say I know exactly *how* to do it. I just said it's my goal. I'm hoping that by knowing more about God, the other matter will resolve itself."

# CHAPTER SEVEN

∽

## April 15, 1880

Beth waited for her sisters to tell her happy birthday, but when neither of them offered such a declaration, it seemed to sour the day. Surely they remembered.

Frowning, Beth put away the last of the breakfast dishes and sulked. She was twenty-three today. Life had seemingly passed her by and she was feeling rather desperate. Just like the gunslinger Justice Halbrook in her latest dime novel. He had no family, no friends, no home. He just drifted from place to place, trying hard to fill the emptiness inside. Well, maybe she wasn't just like him, but she knew what it was to feel empty.

All winter long Nick had avoided her like she had the pox. *And just when I started to think he might be The One.* She sighed.

Even though she'd seen him at church and other gatherings, Nick had hardly spoken two words to her. Millie said he had been hard to live with, grumbling and complaining about most everything. It just didn't seem like Nick, and Beth couldn't help but wonder why he was acting this way.

"Beth, I need you to take the wagon out to the Shepard place," Gwen told her. "Patience has milk, eggs, and butter for us."

"Say, I heard the Bradleys plan to have their cheese business up and running by next month. I can hardly wait," Lacy declared.

"It will be nice to have a ready supply and not have to make it ourselves," Gwen admitted.

Beth had to agree. Making cheese was just too much work. It was hard enough to take time out to can fruits and vegetables when they came into season. "I suppose I can go to the Shepards' for you, but—"

"Good. I want you to leave right away. It will take all day to get out there and back, and I don't want you late for supper. We have a family meeting planned to discuss the store and Gallatin House."

Things were going from bad to worse for Beth. A meeting to discuss business? Did no one remember that it was her birthday?

"Lacy, why don't you go fetch the wagon for Beth," Gwen suggested. "That way she can go freshen up and get her hat and gloves."

"Sure. I'll be right back." Lacy threw Beth a smile before heading out the door. "It's pretty warm out today, but don't let it fool you."

"Yes, we wouldn't want you to catch cold," Gwen said.

"It's one of those deceptive days that makes you think spring is really here, but just as soon as we trust it, we'll wake up to a foot of snow."

Beth sighed. "I'll be careful. I'll go and get back as quickly as I can."

"Well, don't put yourself in danger," Gwen said, frowning. "And take time to have lunch with Patience. I know she'd like that. Her daughters have been gone so long from this place that she misses the feminine company."

"But you just said you wanted me not to be late for supper."

"But there's always time for you to have lunch with Patience."

It sounded to Beth as though no one wanted to be bothered with her at home. They'd all forgotten her special day.

Nick sat at the table, nursing a cup of coffee and trying hard to get up the gumption to do something other than sit around and feel sorry for himself. All winter he'd tried to push aside his feelings for Beth, but it wasn't any use. Even with all of the extra work he'd taken on helping Evan build his house and reading the New Testament from start to finish, Nick always seemed to have plenty of time for thinking about Beth.

"You ever gonna get tired of moping around?"

Nick looked up to find Simon watching him rather intently. "I'm not moping. I'm just thinking."

"Well, it looks like moping to me. Honestly, why don't

you just go over to the Gallatin House and tell Beth how you feel?"

This surprised Nick. "I don't know what you mean." He got to his feet and took his cup to the dishpan.

"I'm thinkin' you do," Simon answered, following him. "You've been pining over her all winter. Even Ellie commented on it to me the other day. You hardly even speak two words to each other at church."

"Can't a fellow just put his mind to God when he's at church?"

Simon bellowed a laugh. The sound filled the house and instantly caused Nick to regret even talking to his brother. "A fellow sure *could* put his mind to God when he's at church, but your mind is a little crowded with other folks, and there's no sense in you denying it."

Nick shrugged. "You go on thinking what you will. Just leave me alone." He went to get his coat from where it hung behind the door.

Simon reached out his hand to hold the door in place. "Look, I'm not meanin' to pry. You know that."

Meeting his brother's sympathetic expression, Nick calmed. "I know. I'm sorry. I figured the best way to put Beth from my mind was to have nothing to do with her."

"And did it work?"

"What do you think?"

Simon chuckled. "I think you're in a sorry state. Just go talk to her."

"But she has feelings for that railroad man."

"So help her to have more feelings for you," Simon suggested. "Besides, I don't know how you can be so certain she cares for that Murphy fellow. Just because he kissed her doesn't mean she liked it. It's not like she went with him when he left."

"I know, but she couldn't very well just up and leave. He probably asked her to marry him. That's probably why he kissed her in the first place."

Simon shook his head. "Don't you think we would have heard about that by now? You know women can't keep quiet about such things. Millie would have told us."

"I would have told you what?"

Millie swept into the room, and Simon quickly diverted the conversation. "You don't suppose they've canceled Beth's party, do you?"

The young woman stepped forward with a stack of bedding. "Not at all. Last I heard, the surprise was still on. Nick, would you mind helping me carry these quilts over to Gallatin House? Gwen suggested a couple of us might even wish Beth a happy birthday and put aside any suspicions she might be havin'."

"I think that would be good." Simon pushed Nick toward Millie. "You could wish her happy birthday, then have a long overdue talk."

Nick didn't want to nurse false hope about the matter, but helping Millie did seem like the perfect excuse to get close to Beth. He took the bedding, leaving Millie free to collect her shawl.

"You'd best hurry if you want to talk to Beth," Millie said, pulling her shawl around her shoulders. "Gwen planned to have her drive the wagon out to the Shepard ranch in order to keep her busy and out of the house all day."

"Yeah, and Lacy came for the wagon nearly fifteen minutes ago," Simon added.

Nick shifted the quilts and pulled open the door. "Then let's go."

Beth had already headed out for the Shepards' by the time he arrived at Gallatin House. Just when he had in mind what he might say to her, she wasn't there. Frustrated, he left Millie and her quilts and headed over to Hank's store.

Beth's smiling face quickly filled his thoughts, and no matter how hard he tried to think of anything else, Bethany Gallatin consumed him. Why did this have to be so difficult?

Over the winter, Nick had come to understand the importance of being right with God. He'd even gotten baptized last month in the hot springs. For some reason, he'd thought this might make everything suddenly fall into place, but it didn't. Beth didn't come running to him for affection. Peace didn't rush over Nick, dispelling the demons of the past. Frankly, life didn't seem all that different, even though Hank and Pastor Flikkema assured him he had really and truly been forgiven of his past sins.

Nick stepped up on the walkway in front of Bishop's Emporium and paused at the door with a sigh. *I figured getting saved would make everything else right in a fellow's life. Seems to me it's just going on as it always has.*

"Hello, Hank." Nick spied him up on a ladder. He was wrestling with a box and grunted a greeting. "Can I help?"

Hank lost control of the crate and watched helplessly as it crashed to the floor, spilling out a variety of metal pieces. He muttered something Nick couldn't hear and climbed back down. "No. I can't even seem to help myself all that well."

"What seems to be the problem?"

"I seem to be the problem," Hank said, scooping up the fallen merchandise. "I was just doing a bit of rearranging.

Storekeeping is pretty new to me, even now. I'm learning to never put heavier items up high."

Nick laughed heartily. "I can see the wisdom in that. Still, I think you've done a great job. Your store rivals any of those in Bozeman."

"Maybe, but I'm betting their owners know more about what they're doing." He shook his head and put the broken crate and pieces aside. "So what brings you here today?"

"I guess a little cabin fever. The weather's turned nice, but I know it's probably just foolin' us."

"I'd like to think winter's over and done with," Hank replied. "I thought Boston winters were bad, but Montana beats those by a mile."

"It can be taxing, to be sure. For all the time I've been here, I find this time of year the worst. You get excited about a warm day and think you're finally headed into summer, and then without warning you wake up to six inches of snow."

"I'm not sure I'm very well suited for this life, to tell you the truth."

Hank's confession only added to what he'd said earlier. Nick could hear the frustration in his voice. "I suppose it's pretty different from back East. It's different enough just from Kansas."

"It's the isolation that sometimes gets to me. I'm used to places with plenty of noise and commotion, and then I come here, and the change is both welcoming and unnerving."

"You don't figure to leave, do you?"

Hank shook his head. "No, but I do feel a little displaced." He frowned. "Sometimes I'm not sure I'm cut out for anything here."

Nick smiled. "Well, this store has sure been good for us. You seem pretty good at running it."

"To be honest, making money is something I've always had a knack for, but when it comes to knowing how to be a husband and man of God—and even a Montanan—I feel far less equipped."

"I know what you mean when it comes to being a man of God. I've been reading the Bible all winter, and I feel like I've only just begun to see what it's all about."

"Some folks spend a lifetime trying to understand God," Hank replied. "My problem comes in the discomfort I feel when my wife knows more than I do about spiritual matters."

Nick nodded, thinking of Beth and how much it meant to her to marry a Christian. Even if he could find a way to woo her—convince her that he was worthy of courting—could he ever hope to be a spiritual leader in her life? It was an issue he'd never really considered.

<hr />

Gwen smiled a greeting when her husband came home for lunch with a guest. Someone was always dropping by Gallatin House for a meal or to soak in the hot springs. The place was rapidly becoming more than a mere stage stop.

"Mr. Vanhouten, we haven't seen you in quite a while. I heard that your wife was back East visiting relatives."

"That she is, and it's where I intend to go. The Montana winters have been too much for her, and I'm too old and cantankerous to live without a wife." He smiled and gave Gwen a wink. "Besides, it gets too cold at night to sleep alone."

"That it does," Hank said, grinning at Gwen.

She felt her cheeks flush and turned away. "Well, I'm sorry you'll be leaving us. Are you planning to sell out?" She motioned to the table and didn't wait for his response. "Please sit, and I'll bring you both some lunch."

"I'd like that."

Gwen wasn't sure where Lacy had gotten off to, but given that they weren't expecting guests for lunch, she really couldn't fault her sister. "I'm not sure if Lacy will be joining us, so we can go ahead and eat."

She ladled bowls of thick beef stew and brought them to the table. Within a few moments, she had added fresh baked bread and butter, applesauce, and hot coffee.

Mr. Vanhouten ate rather noisily for several minutes, then paused to declare, "You Gallatin gals sure can cook."

Hank patted his stomach. "A fellow could grow fat and lazy in this house."

"Hardly," Gwen countered. "We Gallatins don't keep company with idleness."

"Hank tells me business is good," the older man said, reaching for another slice of bread. "I'm glad to hear it, too. With new folks coming to settle these parts, I don't feel so bad in leaving. The last thing I'd want to do is go off and have you sitting on a bunch of land you couldn't use."

"What do you mean?" Gwen looked to her husband and back to Vanhouten.

"He means that I've just agreed to buy him out," Hank answered before Vanhouten could say anything more.

"What?" While she knew Hank could more than afford to purchase the land, it seemed strange to her that he'd said nothing at all.

"I really didn't have a chance to discuss it. I hope you'll

forgive me," Hank said apologetically. "He only asked me about it a few minutes before we showed up here."

Mr. Vanhouten nodded. "It's true. I figured Hank here was the only one with enough ready cash to buy me out quickly. Other folks would have to go seeking a loan or want to take it on credit. I need to be able to complete everything by May so I can head out to Indiana and join my wife."

"But we're not ranchers, Hank." She thought of the vast acreage the Vanhoutens held, as well as their livestock.

"I know that. Mr. Vanhouten is selling his stock to the Shepards. I'm just buying up the land around here."

"Deputy Shepard wanted to know if he could have dinner," Lacy announced as she entered the dining room. Dave followed a few steps behind, hat in hand.

"If it's not too much trouble."

"Of course it's not," Gwen replied, getting to her feet. "There's plenty. As you can see, we have another guest for the meal, as well."

"We were just talking a short time ago," Vanhouten told them.

Dave took a seat at the table and nodded. "That we were."

Lacy helped Gwen serve Dave and then took a seat beside her sister as the conversation picked up again.

"So you were saying you only bought the land," Gwen began.

Hank slathered butter on a piece of bread and nodded. "That's right. I thought it was a good purchase. I hope you agree."

"What land did you buy?" Lacy asked.

"Mine," Vanhouten answered for Hank. "I sold it all to him."

"Mr. Vanhouten has decided to move back East. Mrs. Vanhouten has difficulty with our winters here," Gwen added.

"I had no idea you were thinking about moving from Gallatin House," Lacy said in an accusing tone. She looked at Gwen as if for answers.

"I don't plan to move," Gwen replied, suddenly realizing that perhaps Hank had thoughts on the matter he'd not yet shared. She turned toward her husband. "Do I?"

He laughed, as did Mr. Vanhouten. "No. I have no plans to move," Hank assured Gwen. "I didn't even buy the house. Just the land. The house and ten acres are going to someone else."

"What fool would buy a house and so little land? Why, it's a good six miles away and surrounded by ranch and farmland," Lacy said, shaking her head. "That makes no sense."

Dave cleared his throat uncomfortably. "I guess that fool would be me."

Everyone but Vanhouten turned in surprise. It was Gwen who questioned him first. "You bought the house?"

"Yeah, I did. I thought it might be a good investment. With the town growing and all, the sheriff and I were talking about how it wouldn't be long before regular authorities would be needed over this way. I was just trying to think ahead." He frowned. "It didn't seem foolish at the time."

"It wasn't foolish at all," Hank replied. "I think it's a good idea. With the thoughts I have to plot out a real town, it will be perfect. We'll head in that direction, and you'll be perfectly situated to be our town marshal."

Dave finished eating in a rather abrupt manner and got to his feet without comment. "I guess I'd better get back to work."

Gwen could see that he was upset. Clearly, Lacy's comments had hurt his feelings.

"Lacy, come help me," Gwen commanded. She smiled at Hank. "I'll leave you two to further discuss your business dealings."

Waiting until they were nearly at the back door, Gwen turned and met Lacy's curious gaze.

"What did you need help with?" Lacy asked.

"I didn't really need any help at all, but I wanted a word with you. Don't you think you were rather harsh with Dave?"

Lacy looked completely surprised. "I didn't do anything wrong. I simply thought it was silly for someone to buy a ranch house without buying the ranch."

"I think you hurt his feelings," Gwen countered. "He looked upset."

"Let him be upset, then." Lacy shook her head. "I don't see where it's my fault. He explained why he wanted the house and land, and that much made sense. Of course, he neglected to say he needed to actually get elected to the position of marshal, but his plan made about as much sense as anything Dave does nowadays."

"Lacy, I can't believe you're being so critical. I know you two have had your differences, but why are you so angry now?"

Squaring her shoulders, Lacy met her sister's eyes with an intensity that Gwen had not expected. "It's been almost a year, Gwen. A year since Pa was killed, and still no one knows who did it. No one has been punished for it—except for us. I tried to talk to Dave about it again, and he just shrugged and told me to stay out of it."

"Oh, Lacy." Gwen reached out to touch her sister's cheek. "I'm sorry. I wasn't thinking."

"Well, I have been." Lacy pulled away. "I feel like I've let Pa down, and I don't intend to go on this way. I can't keep that promise I made to you anymore, Gwen. I have to find out who killed Pa, even if Dave Shepard and the sheriff have given up."

# CHAPTER EIGHT

⁓

The sun headed slowly west as Beth made her way back to Gallatin House. She'd enjoyed her visit with Patience, talking much as a mother and daughter might, each needing to fill that role in the life of the other. Patience's daughters were living back East, and she missed them sorely. Beth had been so long without her mother that she often longed for the comfort of speaking with an older woman.

That morning Beth had been bitter about no one remembering her birthday, but Patience had not only remembered it—she had a little celebration just for the two of them. Patience gave her a beautiful blouse, as well as several embroidered handkerchiefs. Then she surprised Beth with a special lunch that included little frosted cakes that Patience called Snow Cakes.

"I bake them in the muffin pan," Patience had explained, "and then put a little cream filling in each one, then frost them."

"But why call them Snow Cakes?" Beth asked.

Patience laughed. "Usually I only make them in the winter, because I cool the pans in the snow to make it easier to get the cakes out of the tins. I suppose I should call this batch something else."

But Beth had assured her they were delicious, no matter how they'd been cooled or what they'd been called. The fact that this dear woman had gone to so much trouble on her behalf moved Beth deeply.

"I'm so glad you girls made it through the winter in good order. It seemed a godsend that you had Hank come into your lives," Patience had told her as they discussed the future.

"He's a good man, and he loves Gwen very much," Beth admitted. "I wish I could find someone to love me half as well."

Patience laughed. "You will. Just be patient. There's no need to rush into a lifelong commitment."

"I'm hardly rushing," Beth now murmured as she headed home. "I'm twenty-three. Half my life is already gone."

Hadn't Justice Halbrook said as much in her latest read, *The Copper Canyon Renegade*? He was battling the regret of a life only half lived, and he was no more than twenty-five. Surely a year or two wasn't important when it came to such matters. Beth could certainly share regret and frustration—even if she wasn't a gunslinger.

Beth pulled her thoughts back to the road as the sound of an approaching rider caught her attention. There had been talk about highwaymen—less-than-savory characters who took advantage of poor travelers. Lacy had suggested she carry a gun with her, but Beth knew she could never shoot another person, even if he was threatening her life.

Glancing over her shoulder, Beth easily recognized Simon Lassiter's dark brown gelding. She breathed a sigh of relief. Simon was, no doubt, headed home, as well, and thought to accompany her the rest of the way. Beth smiled and waved.

Simon reined up as he pulled even with Beth's wagon. "Howdy, Beth. Headin' home?"

"Yes," she said, smiling. "Looks like you're doing the same."

"Yup. I was over at the Vandercamp Ranch, helping to do some fencing. I guess you're on your way back from the Shepard place."

Beth nodded and stretched awkwardly. Her shoulders were stiff from the drive. Simon instantly noticed. "Say, how about I tie up Moe to your wagon and drive you the rest of the way?"

"That would be wonderful. I think I'd like that very much." She pulled the horse to a stop and waited for Simon to join her. He made quick work of seeing to his horse, then bounded up into the wagon to squeeze into the seat beside her. Simon was a broad-shouldered man who stood at least six feet one. His presence made Beth feel safe, but he also forced her thoughts steadily on Nick.

"I nearly forgot. Happy birthday," Simon said as he urged the horse forward.

Beth laughed. "I think a lot of folks forgot, so don't you think anything of it. Thanks, though. I've had a better day than I figured. Patience gave me gifts and cake, and we talked for hours. It was a lovely way to spend the day."

Simon smiled. "She's a good woman. I think Jerry Shepard is one of the luckiest men in the valley."

"I agree. Whenever I miss my mother too much, I just go to Patience. She always makes me feel welcome and loved."

"I think there's someone else who'd like to make you feel . . . well . . . both those things," Simon said rather sheepishly. "I suppose it's not my place to talk about such matters, though."

"What do you mean?" Beth looked at him oddly. She knew he wasn't sweet-talking her. Simon had eyes for little Ellie Martindale at Rafe's place, and Beth seriously doubted he even thought about other women.

Simon laughed. "I wasn't going to say anything because I don't think it's right to interfere in other people's lives, but I care too much about Nick not to."

Beth felt her heart skip a beat. "Then speak your mind."

"He cares for you."

Simon said nothing else for a moment, and Beth had no reply to offer. She was relieved when Simon finally continued.

"He thinks you care for someone else, though. Is that true?"

Beth shook her head. "I don't know who else he thinks I'd care about." Suddenly she remembered Adrian Murphy's very public kiss a few months ago. "Oh, I suppose he's still thinking on Mr. Murphy, but I thought we'd straightened that out."

"I can't be sure, but I'm supposing he still thinks Mr. Murphy holds your affections. I know you and Nick haven't talked much all winter, and to my way of lookin' at it, Nick might wonder if you're mad at him."

Beth felt a little irritation at this statement. "He's the one who's been avoiding me. I've seen him go out of his way to avoid me at church and at the store."

Simon nodded. "I know. He's just trying to guard his heart, Beth. If you don't have feelings for him, then just forget everything I've said. I don't want to see him get hurt worse in all of this."

"But I *do* have feelings for him," she blurted, surprising herself. "I'm just not entirely sure what those feelings are all about. I miss him when he's gone. This winter has been hard, since he never came around for lunch or just to chat. I mean, I knew Millie was taking care of you boys, but we . . . I . . . still missed his company."

She paused and looked away, embarrassed by her declaration. She'd never in her wildest imaginings thought she'd be sitting here talking to Nick's brother about her heart.

"But do you really care about him?" Simon asked softly. "You know . . . do you . . . well, maybe . . . love him?"

Beth laughed in a nervous manner that she hoped Simon wouldn't question. "I don't know. I'm not sure I know what love is or what it requires. I think Nick is a wonderful man. I thought so even before he got right with God, but I especially think so now that he knows Jesus as his Savior and doesn't go to Rafe's anymore." She stopped and fidgeted with her skirt. "I'm sorry, but it seems really strange to be having this conversation with you."

Simon laughed. "I know. I sure never planned it this way. I apologize if I've made you uncomfortable. I just care about Nick, and I know he's head over heels about you."

Beth looked at him in surprise. "Do you really think so?" She thought back to her beloved romance books and all the tales she'd read over the years. Most men in the books were happy to confess their love. They were dashing, noble souls who easily swept the heroine off her feet. Had she expected no less from Nick?

"I know so," Simon said. "Just don't let him know I told you. A fellow ought to be able to speak those words on his own."

They were nearing the house now, and Beth was almost sorry. "What about you, Simon? I know you've been sweet on Ellie for some time. Do you have plans for her?"

Simon frowned. "I spend as much time with her as I can afford."

How could he talk so casually about paying for Ellie's affections? She cleared her throat. "I think Ellie's a wonderful young woman. I feel so sorry for her having to end up in such a position, just because her husband died."

"Not everyone has family to turn to," Simon replied.

Beth knew most of the prostitutes were either orphaned or deserted. "If it's any consolation, she's never wanted to be . . . well . . . working for Rafe."

Simon halted the horses in front of Gallatin House. "I know. It tears me up inside, and as soon as I can do something about it, I intend to see her freed."

Lacy came bounding out the front door, eager to help. "I see you got extra milk," she said, reaching into the wagon to take up a wooden crate of eggs.

"I'll get this stuff inside," Simon said as he jumped down from the wagon. He reached up to help Beth down and lowered his voice. "Don't be too hard on Nick. He's had a lot to overcome in the past. He's not proud of some of the things he did back then. But he's a good man now, and you can depend on him to be honorable in every way."

Simon hurried off to unload the wagon, giving Beth no chance to ask what exactly he meant. She sighed, tucked her presents from Patience under her arm, and followed him into the house.

"Surprise!" multiple voices cried out as Beth stepped through the door.

She could see that nearly everyone, short of Rafe and his bunch, had gathered in her front room. Words escaped her until she finally simply said, "I . . . I don't know what to say." Beth looked at the smiling faces of her family and friends and felt like crying.

"We've been beside ourselves trying to plan this and keep it a secret," Gwen said, coming forward to hug Beth. "We have musicians and a cleared dance floor. We're going to have a regular party."

"And there's a lot of good food," Lacy added. "Patience even sent extra with the eggs. That's why I hurried out to get it." She grinned.

"Oh, but Patience should be here, too." Beth instantly felt a sense of sorrow that the Shepards should miss the party.

"They'll be here," Gwen assured. "They were heading over just behind you. They wanted to give you enough of a lead that you wouldn't suspect anything."

Beth laughed. "Well, I have to say you've planned it all just perfectly. Thank you!" She hugged Gwen again and then gave Lacy a tight embrace. "Here I was feeling sorry for myself, and you've humbled me completely."

"I say we start the music," Forrest declared. "I didn't bring my fiddle over to have it just stashed in the corner. Come on,

Evan." The two went to get their instruments—Forrest taking up a well-worn violin and Evan grabbing a guitar. Together they began a jaunty tune that soon had everyone clapping.

"May I have this dance?" Nick whispered in Beth's ear.

His breath was warm on her skin and Beth couldn't help but give a shiver. She turned and found him very close. She smiled. "I thought you'd never ask."

He took her in his arms and began to move her around the room along with the other couples. Beth hardly noticed anyone else, however. She could scarcely draw a breath for the very nearness of Nick's handsome face.

"Happy birthday," he said, his expression quite serious. "I came over this morning to tell you, but they'd already sent you on your way."

"Yes, I guess they wanted to keep me busy. I really had no idea that anyone but Patience even remembered my birthday, so this was definitely a surprise. Oh, look—here they are!" She let go of Nick long enough to give a little wave in the direction of Patience and Jerry.

Patience waved back and gave Beth a knowing nod. Beth couldn't believe she'd been in on the plans all along and never once slipped up. "I'm no good with secrets."

"What?" Nick asked.

Beth turned her attention back to him. Goodness, but he was dashing. He was dark and handsome—just like Justice Halbrook, the gunslinger in her book. Maybe Nick was full of regrets, too. Maybe he had secrets that haunted him. She shook the thought aside. "I was just saying that I have trouble keeping secrets. I'm always blurting out things when I shouldn't." She gave a sheepish shrug. "Guess that's just one of my many faults."

"I don't think you have many faults, Beth Gallatin."

She laughed. "Oh, yes you do. You've called me stubborn and pigheaded, nosy, too bold . . . hmmm, let me see what else."

He chuckled and gave her a quick turn to the music. "All right, so maybe you aren't perfect. But that hardly matters. I'm sure not perfect."

Beth studied him for a moment and thought of the things Simon had said. "You haven't been around much."

Nick looked away and nodded. "I know."

She waited a moment for him to expound on his answer, but when he said nothing, Beth continued. "I missed you. I was just telling Simon that we all missed you both coming over to share meals with us. I know Millie is taking good care of you, but you really shouldn't be such strangers."

Nick looked at her, and his expression seemed pained. "We've been busy trying to help Evan and Millie get their house built and to set up places for his business at our stables. We've even expanded to have a proper livery."

"I know. Millie has told us what great strides you've all made this winter. Hopefully with the spring and newcomers to the area, you'll be profitable and able to keep expanding. I know business is important to you."

"It's no more important than the people in my life," he said softly. "I'm starting to see that a lot of those things aren't quite as important as I might have thought at one time."

"What is important, Nick?" Beth asked, suddenly serious. "What's important to you?"

Beth considered it for a moment. "A lot of things. Family. Love. Stability. Reliability. Trust. Faithfulness. God above all."

He nodded. "Those are important to me, too. In fact,

they probably would have been the very things I would have chosen."

"Stability figures heavily into what I want out of life. I want to know that I can put down roots and stay in one place. Pa had us moving all the time—all over the country. I don't want to do that anymore." She hoped he understood the seriousness of her words. If he really did love her as Simon had told her, then he needed to know that she had no desire to leave Gallatin Crossing.

"I think roots are important. A man can hardly be successful at a business if he's always moving from place to place. Still, I think a fellow needs a reason to stay put. If he can't make a good business or have his other . . . well . . . needs and expectations met, then he can't very well continue to go for broke."

Beth frowned. What exactly was he saying? Did he mean that if his business didn't make a lot of money, he'd want to move away from the area? The music ended and Beth dropped her hold on Nick, while his hand lingered on her waist. She liked the way he touched her in that possessive way. It made her feel weak in the knees.

"I guess it's my turn to dance with the birthday girl," Hank said, stepping up. He pointed to his red shirt. "I wore this just for you. I thought it might make you smile."

Beth remembered only too well dying the shirt out of spite. "You should just toss that away. We agreed to let bygones be bygones. I'm going to feel less than forgiven if you keep throwing my mistakes back into my face." She grinned and let him lead her in a jaunty reel.

"I've come to be quite fond of this shirt," he told her as they danced. "Along with my blue ones. I've often thought

I should have had Gwen keep at least one of them lavender instead of dying them all blue."

Beth laughed. "It does suit you. Still, I'm sorry for the trouble I caused and I'm glad you're my brother-in-law. I liked Harvey well enough, but you're a much better match for Gwen. You're what she needs. Someone strong. Someone who will endure and go the extra mile."

Hank glanced across the room, and Beth's gaze followed to where Gwen was busy dancing with Cubby Reynolds. Somehow the boy had managed to sneak over for the celebration, but that really didn't surprise Beth. Where there was food, Cubby Reynolds could be found.

"I never thought I could love anyone as much as I love your sister." Hank looked back at Beth. "She means the world to me; how could I not go the extra mile?"

"Well, a lot of men wouldn't. Not only that, but you care about what she needs. Pa was a good man, but he never seemed to put Mama or us first. It was always about what worked well for him. I know Gwen appreciates that you give her needs consideration. That's important to a woman."

"I'll keep that in mind, little sister."

After everyone had danced and shared turns singing a song or two, Gwen announced it was time to eat. They all moseyed into the dining room, where Gwen and Lacy had worked to put out a spread that rivaled the previous year's Christmas and Thanksgiving celebrations.

As they finished with the hearty fare, several gifts were presented to Beth, much to her surprise.

"I don't know what to say. This is all so sweet—so wonderful."

"Well, open your presents, then," Lacy admonished. "Don't make us keep wondering what's inside."

Beth nodded and did exactly that. She smiled at the new books given to her from Hank and Gwen. She hadn't read either one, so this was a special treat. Next came Lacy's present of new hair combs.

"Hank helped me get them," Lacy told her sister. "They were a special order from New York City."

"Oh my," Beth said, fingering the delicately carved pieces. They were beautiful, trimmed in gold scrolling and tiny rhinestones. "I'll always cherish them."

Millie was next. She handed Beth a rather large bundle. Pulling back brown paper revealed a beautifully knitted shawl of the softest yarn Beth had ever known. "It's beautiful, and I love the creamy color. I have nothing like it."

"I'm so glad. I talked to Gwen about what color might be good. She said you were wanting something in ivory, and this was as close as I could get."

"It's perfect and it feels so soft. Thank you."

"Well, I probably won't have a chance to make another for a while," Millie announced. "I'm going to be devoting myself to baby things for a time."

"What?" Beth and Gwen both exclaimed.

Millie laughed and flushed red as she reached for Evan's hand. "We're going to have a little one. I've just been waiting for the right time to let everyone know, and this seemed a good time."

"A perfect time!" Forrest declared. "I couldn't be happier. I'm going to be a grandpa."

"When will the baby arrive?" Beth asked.

"I figure September," Millie said rather shyly, as if the impact of the moment had caught up with her.

"That will give us all summer to make little outfits and blankets," Beth said, nodding. "And give you time enough before the heavy winter comes to get some fat on the baby. It's a perfect month."

❧

Gwen tried not to be jealous of Millie and Evan. She was happy that they were going to be parents, but she fervently wished she could be making a similar announcement. She'd thought of nothing but having a child since marrying Hank the previous year.

*I shouldn't be so impatient,* she told herself. She pulled on her nightgown and prepared for bed, hoping that her frustration and sadness wouldn't betray itself to Hank. She didn't want him to think her petty or selfish.

"I think the party went very well," Hank announced as he came into their bedroom. He locked the door behind him and turned to face his wife. "Don't you?"

Gwen forced a smile. "I do. Beth never suspected the surprise and she had such a nice time. Thank you for all your help." She quickly slipped into bed while Hank started to undress.

"And it was great news to hear about Millie and Evan having a baby, don't you think?"

Gwen bit her lip. She wanted to answer quickly, but the words stuck in her throat. Hank turned down the lamp and slid into bed beside her, but she remained stiffly on her side.

"Did you hear what I said?"

"Yes. Yes, I think . . . it's a . . . I'm happy for them." She turned to put her back to Hank and fought to keep from crying. *This is so silly. I'm acting like a child. What in the world is wrong with me?*

Hank was undeterred. He reached out and pulled her snugly against him. "What's wrong?"

"Nothing. I'm just tired."

"You're also a liar."

She smiled to herself. Relaxing against his warmth, she knew it was futile to try to keep anything from him.

"I want a baby."

He chuckled against her ear. "Well, sulking about it isn't going to get you one."

She laughed and turned in his arms to face him. "I'm sorry. I'm very happy for Millie and Evan. I'm just feeling sorry for myself. I figured I might have news like that by now."

He gently stroked her face and kissed her lips with tenderness. "I'd love nothing better than to hear such news from you. But I know it will come in time. God's timing is just right. Look at how long it took for Him to bring us together."

"Goodness, but I hope He's a little quicker about this matter," Gwen said rather boldly. "I don't want to be an old woman like Sarah in the Bible before I have my first baby."

Hank snorted in laughter and pulled her even tighter. "You're a long ways from being an old woman, Gwen Bishop. A long, long ways."

# CHAPTER NINE

"Well, Pa, it isn't much, but I thought you might like these," Lacy said as she placed a few wild flowers on her father's grave. She stared down at the patch of land that only now seemed to be blending back into the rest of the ground. New grass had grown where once there had been only mounded, barren dirt. It seemed nicer now, more natural.

"You've been gone a year," Lacy said. Major came to stand beside her and gave a whine as if to confirm her statement. "Hardly seems that long, but I know it's true."

She frowned and looked away from the grave to the range of mountains to the east. "I never meant to let it go on this long, Pa. I was determined to see your killer behind bars."

Memories from that fateful night still gave Lacy nightmares.

Rowdy cowboys at Rafe's had been shooting it up, and a stray bullet had caught her father. At least that's what everyone said. Lacy had never been convinced. It seemed too convenient that her father had been the only one to be harmed with so many others nearby.

A chilled breeze blew across the cemetery, and Lacy hugged her jacket close. Major leaned against her leg and waited patiently for her to conclude her visit. He no longer seemed as lost and saddened by Pa's death; Hank had filled that void for Major. But there was nothing and no one who could fill the emptiness for Lacy.

If only the law would find the one responsible for her father's murder. Lacy just knew that would ease her mind and relieve the hurt that threatened to overwhelm her heart. She had promised Pa she would seek justice, yet Gwen had interceded and made her promise to dismiss such ideas.

"Well, I can't," she said firmly. "I can't just let it go. No one else cares, and it's obviously not going to get done unless I do something about it."

She glanced toward the river and began to walk away from the graveyard. Major followed eagerly, happy to leave the quiet behind him and barking incessantly at some of the birds that mocked him from the trees.

Lacy, however, paid little attention to her surroundings. She had to make a plan. A woman had no hope of getting a confession from a man unless she found a way to be smarter than he was. She knew a half dozen names of men who had been at Rafe's that night, but they were a tight bunch. And Rafe, of course, would offer little help in the matter.

*Cubby.* She thought of the boy and wondered how useful he might be. She didn't want to take advantage of his feelings for her; ever since his declaration in December, Lacy had been uncomfortable with saying or doing anything that might be misconstrued by the boy. Still, if she explained the situation, maybe he could be her eyes and ears at the saloon. Someone was bound to talk about the incident sooner or later.

Lacy paused for a moment to look around. She liked Gallatin Crossing well enough, but in truth, she had never felt it was a real home. No place had ever felt permanent, and sharing your home with a new set of strangers every few nights made Gallatin House seem even less so.

Sometimes Lacy wished her sisters would just agree to let Rafe buy them out so they could all move to Bozeman. She liked Bozeman and figured she might even live there one day. After all, she was twenty years old. There was nothing that said she had to stay with her sisters and run Gallatin House. *Maybe once I get Pa's death settled . . .*

But even as she thought of it, Lacy knew her opportunities were limited. Women simply didn't gallivant around the country, living on their own. She was handy with repairs and domestic chores, but she could hardly expect to make a living at either one. She was very good with horses, but again, who would hire a woman? Maybe she could talk to Hank about learning how to mind a store.

Major began to growl, drawing Lacy's immediate attention. It wasn't like the dog to get upset, but the hair on his neck seemed to jut straight out as he focused on a thicket of brush by the river's edge.

"What is it, boy?"

Just then, a black bear charged out from the coverage. Lacy couldn't stifle a scream as the dog rushed forward to meet his opponent. The bear stopped abruptly as if he hadn't realized anyone else was there. He watched for a moment, swaying back and forth.

Lacy froze in place and watched the entire thing as if she were sitting in a theater watching a play. Major barked and rushed at the bear, distracting him from Lacy and drawing him farther toward the south.

The bear was unusually aggressive. Black bears weren't known for much more than curiosity and being a nuisance, but this bear seemed determined to stir up trouble. He swiped at Major, making contact. The dog gave a painful yelp. This pulled Lacy from her shock. She glanced around and picked up a dead branch, knowing that it would offer her little protection.

"Get out of here!" she yelled at the bear.

This only served to draw the animal's attention. The bear turned from Major and started back toward Lacy. She took several steps backward, only to stumble on a tree root and fall. She hit the dirt hard as Major rushed to intercept. The bear bit into Major's hip, then whipped his head to one side, tossing the dog as he did. Lacy couldn't suppress a scream. What was she to do? She had foolishly left her gun at the house.

She scooted back as the bear started toward her once again. A commotion to her right caused Lacy to turn her attention only momentarily away from the animal. Rafe and Cubby halted a short distance away while Dave Shepard raised a rifle and fired a shot at the bear, barely missing the beast. The blast startled the animal enough that he took off, back into the brush, and disappeared down the river.

"Cubby, go get my gun—the big one. I'm going bear hunting," Rafe announced. "Seems that fellow would make a right good coat."

Heart still pounding, Lacy hurried to Major's side. The

dark stain of blood was saturating his coat, especially near his chest and hip, but from what Lacy could tell, the wounds didn't seem too debilitating. She tried to lift him in her arms but soon found Dave at her side.

"Lead the way. I'll bring him." He gently lifted Major.

Lacy nodded and headed for the house. Soon Gwen and Beth appeared on the steps.

"We heard shots," Gwen announced.

"That bear is back," Lacy said rather breathlessly. "He attacked Major."

"He was trying to attack Lacy," Dave said, coming up behind her.

"Dave fired at him, but he got away," Lacy added.

Beth hurried ahead of them to put an oiled tablecloth down on one of the trestle tables. "Put him here," she directed.

Major whimpered but lay perfectly still as Dave inspected his wounds. "The cut on his chest is worse than the bite on his flank. Still, I don't think it's too bad. The bleeding has stopped."

"Poor Major," Lacy said, pressing her face against the dog's. "You saved my life, boy. Such a good dog."

"Sounds like Dave did his part, too," Gwen said, bringing water and a rag to clean Major's wounds.

Lacy turned to Dave and nodded. "Yes, thank you. I'm glad you showed up when you did."

"I was talking with Rafe when we heard you scream. I knew it couldn't be good." He smiled. "You're not given to screaming."

"He caught me off guard when he charged us," Lacy admitted. "I was visiting Pa's grave and didn't think to take the rifle. We must've startled him when we headed home." Lacy felt rather dizzy and reached for the back of the chair. She supposed the excitement had just caught up with her.

"We'll take care of Major," Gwen told Lacy. "Why don't you go rest a bit."

"Yeah, come on. Let's go sit on the porch while you get your breath," Dave told her. He took hold of her arm and led Lacy through the house.

Lacy didn't protest. She hated to appear vulnerable to anyone, least of all Dave Shepard, but at this point she knew it was futile to fight. Easing into a rocker on the front porch, Lacy drew a deep breath and steadied her nerves.

"That was a close call," Dave said, leaning back against the porch railing.

"Yes." Lacy said nothing more.

For several minutes, neither one spoke. Dave broke the silence with a surprising comment. "You really hate it, don't you?"

Lacy looked up at him. He was watching her intently. "What are you talking about?"

"Having to take help. Letting someone else be in control."

"Does anyone like it?" she asked, trying hard not to let anger get the better of her emotions.

"I don't know. Sometimes it's nice to have help—to have someone at your side."

"That only works if the person is trustworthy, and you can count on them to do what they say they'll do."

"I suppose there's something to that. Still, I know you hate taking help. I guess it makes you feel vulnerable."

"You guess that, do you?" Lacy's temper began to flare. "Well, you're right. I don't like being vulnerable. I've been vulnerable all of my life. You never had to put your mother in the ground. You never had to sit alone in a house in the middle of nowhere while your Pa and sisters were elsewhere and wonder if they would ever come back home. No, Dave, vulnerable isn't a state I enjoy one bit."

"I'm sure it was hard." The timbre of his voice was low and hushed.

His soft-spoken answer surprised Lacy. She had expected him to give her a hard time about her confession. Almost against her will, Lacy continued. "You think I'm wrong for being self-determined and trying to take matters into my own hands, but all of my life, that's the only choice I had. You don't know what it's like."

"You're right. I don't."

Lacy felt uncomfortable with the tenderness in his voice. She stiffened. "Sometimes I think men like to keep women vulnerable so that they can feel better about themselves. But out here women can't afford it. It isn't a luxury that can be had. It'll just get you killed. Could have gotten me that way today. Next time I won't be so stupid. I'll take the rifle with me."

Lacy got to her feet. "I have chores to do." She headed for the door and stopped. She looked back at Dave, who continued to watch her. "Thanks again for what you did."

Dave said nothing as Lacy entered the house. He wanted to hold on to the sensation, the knowledge that he'd connected with Lacy . . . at least in some small way.

"I didn't know you were still here."

Gwen's voice caught Dave's attention.

"Yeah, I guess I've been thinking."

"I was just going to take Hank some lunch at the store,"

she said, holding up a covered plate. "You're welcome to eat something with us."

He shook his head. "No, I ought to be getting on my way. I have some things to take care of."

"I'm certainly glad you were here to ward off that bear. Hopefully Rafe will track him down."

"My guess is food is scarce, or else the grizzlies have taken over his territory. He didn't look to be sickly."

"Well, he's been around too much," Gwen countered. "I heard from Hank that he's been wreaking havoc with the livestock. I'm surprised no one has caught him yet, but now that he's getting bolder about his attacks, someone is sure to."

Gwen started down the steps, and Dave followed. "I've never seen Lacy quite like that."

Dave stopped as Gwen turned. "What do you mean?"

"Well, it's just that she was more like I'd expect a woman to be. She is always so headstrong, so to see her in need . . . It was different to see her that way."

Gwen nodded. "Lacy wants everyone to think she's capable and strong, but if she were able to admit it, she has a great deal of fear inside."

"I'm seeing that for the first time," Dave said.

"Well, now that you have, I hope you'll be . . . well . . . careful with her. Watch out for her."

"What are you saying, Gwen?"

Gwen glanced back at the house and frowned. "She's got it in her mind again to go after the man who killed our father. I thought I had her talked out of it, but she's stirred up again, with it being close to the anniversary of his death. I'm afraid for her, Dave."

He clenched his jaw. Lacy was convinced he'd failed to

do his job where her father was concerned. If only she knew how hard he'd worked to learn the truth—how he was still working on the matter.

"She told me a while back that she couldn't keep her promise to me any longer. I expect she'll be sneaking around Rafe's again and getting herself into harm's way."

"I hope not. I'd hate to have to arrest her for trespassing." Dave found himself in an impossible situation.

"Look, I believe you care about what happens to her—to all of us," Gwen offered, "but you have to understand that Lacy has never seen our father's death as an accident."

"I know that, and I understand her position."

"You do?" Gwen looked at him oddly. "Do you believe it was something more than a mishap?"

"Possibly," Dave admitted, "but I'd rather you not say anything about it to anyone else. There are things going on around here that I'd like to uncover and get to the bottom of, but if too many people are looking into it, I won't have as much luck."

Gwen nodded. "I suppose that makes sense. Lacy won't understand, but I think I do."

"I'll try to keep Lacy out of it as much as possible."

"Be kind to her, Dave. She's fragile. She doesn't want anyone to know it, but she is."

Dave slowly smiled. "I'll look after her. Don't worry."

# CHAPTER TEN

With spring roundup concluded, Rafe opened his saloon to the inevitable celebrations and festivities that appealed to many of the local ranchers and their hands. Gallatin House filled up fast with men seeking a good hot meal, bath, and shave before they headed out for a night of debauchery.

Beth had experienced this routine since they'd first taken on the place, but she'd never gotten used to the noise and senselessness of it. Besides, this year it only served as a painful reminder of their father's death.

With dozens of men loitering around the stage stop, there were continuous demands for food, coffee, and, of course, female attention. Though the cowboys sought the ladies of the night at the saloon, they seemed starved for female companionship of any kind. The men loved talking to Beth and her sisters—it didn't even matter to them that Gwen was now married.

Returning to the kitchen to make a new pot of coffee, Beth remembered her father's comment last year about the danger of pretty girls and rowdy men. Worried about their safety, he'd decided to run an errand to the Lassiters' himself, rather than letting Gwen go. He'd been protecting his girls.

*Perhaps that was why Pa had wanted to move again. He knew this place was going to continue to draw rowdy cowboys and newcomers who might be a danger to us.* She gripped the handle of the coffeepot so tightly that her hand ached. How selfish she'd been in her thinking! Maybe their father knew how bad things would get as time went by. Maybe it had little to do with his wanderlust.

A woman's scream cut above the noise from outside, followed by laughter. Beth cringed and went to close the kitchen window. She had no desire to hear any more of the affairs next door than she had to.

"How soon before the coffee's ready?" Lacy asked, bringing in an empty tray that had once been filled with sandwiches.

"Sorry, I haven't even put the pot on. I just can't bear much more of this noise."

Lacy nodded. "I feel the same. And I can't help thinking one of the men out there might have been the one who shot Pa."

"Oh, Lacy," Beth said, reaching out to embrace her. "I thought of that, too." Beth paused. "I can't stand knowing those men are going to be over at Rafe's all night, drinking and . . . well . . . you know." Beth quickly prepared the coffee and put the pot on the stove. She checked the fire and added another couple of pieces of wood to the cook fire. "I wish we had a way to stop them."

Just then Beth remembered the case of laudanum they had tucked away. She looked at Lacy, who seemed to have the same thought in mind as she began to smile rather mischievously.

"At least we wouldn't have to carry them up the back stairs to their room," her sister murmured, referencing the time they'd drugged Hank.

"But there are so many of them," Beth said, looking around the room nervously. "And if Gwen or Hank caught wind of the idea, they'd be livid."

"Gwen's already upstairs lying down, remember? And Hank's over at the store, getting us more supplies."

Beth remembered that her older sister had complained of a headache, and Hank had insisted she go to bed and rest. "But how can we get everyone to take it?"

"We can put the laudanum in the coffee." Lacy motioned to the pot. "Did you make it strong? That will mask any bitterness."

"It *is* strong." Beth looked at the cupboard where the laudanum was hidden on the top shelf. "Do you think we dare?"

Lacy shrugged and went to retrieve a chair from where it stood by the back door. She quickly climbed atop, despite being in a skirt, and glanced over her shoulder. "It's the only answer. We can give coffee to everyone, and once they're asleep, it will be too late for them to do anything about it."

Beth frowned. "What about the others—the ones already over at Rafe's?"

Lacy took down several bottles of the medicine and placed

them on the counter before answering. "Maybe we can put it in their liquor."

"How?"

Her younger sister smiled. "Cubby. We'll get him to help us. He's not had a quiet moment since that bunch arrived, and he's bound to be exhausted. We'll tell him what we're doing and why. I'm sure he'll help. After all, most of the men pass out at some point. No one has to be the wiser." Lacy shrugged. "I'll hide this on the back porch, and after we deal with our fellows, we'll head next door."

Beth bit her lip. "But Rafe won't let us on his property. And even if he did, we're not allowed in the saloon. If he saw us there, he'd know something was going on."

"Then he can't see us."

Beth looked at Lacy's confident expression. "What do you have in mind? We have to be able to at least get the laudanum to Cubby and explain how to use it."

"Leave that to me. We'll just borrow some of Pa's old clothes from out in the shed. We'll braid our hair and tuck it up under a hat and rub our faces with dirt. No one will know the difference in the middle of all their partying."

"But what if they do?"

Lacy shrugged. "It's not well lit at Rafe's, on account that it's not as easy to cheat folks when they can see clearly. Plus, it'll be smoky, and they've already been drinking for a spell and that clouds a man's vision. I don't think anyone is going to even notice us."

Beth could see the possibilities in Lacy's plan. It was daring, but frankly, she was willing to risk it. She couldn't bear to think of Ellie and the others being used throughout the night.

"Hey, where's the food and coffee?" a cowboy demanded. He filled the entryway to the kitchen, grinning. "You two are cuter than baby bobcats. Wanna dance with me?"

Beth shook her head. "I'm making the coffee, and Lacy has to make more sandwiches." She glanced to where her sister stood, blocking any view of the bottles on the counter.

"It'd sure be nice to dance," the man persisted. "I think we need to have a dance."

"There's no one to play any music for us," Beth reminded. "Now, just go on back, and we'll have everything out for you in a few minutes."

The man begrudgingly complied, but Beth knew it would only be a matter of time before the men became more demanding. She looked at Lacy and nodded. "Let's get to it."

Half an hour later, Lacy teased and smiled as she poured coffee for each of the dozen men who were still at Gallatin House. "This is our special coffee," she told them. "We only make it for our very favorite customers."

"Then pour me two cups," one of the men said and patted his lap. "I'll drink 'em both while you sit here and tell me how come you're so pretty."

Lacy laughed. "One cup per man for now. I wouldn't want anyone to miss out on getting a chance to try this."

Beth delivered a tray of sandwiches and one of cookies. Generally, they didn't allow for eating in the front room, but she and Lacy had decided earlier it would be simpler to meet the men where they were, rather than try to herd them into the dining room.

Waiting for the men to nod off seemed like a painfully long affair, though in reality it didn't take that much time. She was glad Hank had returned earlier with the needed supplies.

He'd hurried upstairs to check on Gwen and had reported she was sleeping peacefully before he returned to the store once more. With any luck at all, Beth and Lacy would be free to do what was needed.

One by one, the men yawned or rubbed their eyes. They would look uncertain for several moments, then nod off. Where once-rowdy conversation and loud voices had reigned supreme, now only snoring interrupted the silence of the room—that and the ongoing party at Rafe's.

"Well, this went well enough," Lacy said, stepping carefully over one cowboy who'd stretched out in front of the fireplace. "We'd better go change and get next door."

It was nearing ten o'clock when Beth and Lacy walked into Rafe's place. As Lacy predicted, the heavy smoke and dim lighting allowed them to pass unnoticed through the room. With their hats drawn low and their long coats disguising their figures, no one even took note of the newcomers.

Lacy walked up to the bar as though it were something she did all the time. Beth marveled at her sister's composure and glanced around anxiously to make certain all was well.

In the far corner Rafe was dealing cards to a number of scruffy-looking, half-sober cowboys. On the opposite side, Wyman held court with his own group of rowdies. Beth had no idea what game they were playing, but the men seemed quite worked up over it when Wyman turned a card over and presented it for their consideration.

"Cubby," Lacy said in a low, husky voice.

Cubby was just returning with a new crate of whiskey. He looked at her oddly, then put the case down. "You fellas want a beer?"

Lacy nodded and put several coins on the bar. Beth's jaw

dropped, but she quickly recovered and hunched over the bar as some of the other men were doing. Cubby drew two beers and practically thrust them into their hands.

A couple of the prostitutes came up and began sweet-talking the men to Beth's right. When they moved off from the bar with the women, Beth breathed a sigh of relief and stared down at the beer. For just a split second, she gave consideration to taking a long drink to steady her nerves.

Lacy made quick order of things. "We need your help," she told Cubby and smiled. "A little adventure." She offered the last without attempting to disguise her voice.

He stared hard at her and blinked several times. "Miss—"

"Never mind. Come in the back room with me." Lacy went around the bar and took hold of Cubby's arm. "You wait here," she instructed Beth.

Feeling the blood drain from her head, Beth couldn't believe Lacy was just leaving her alone to face . . . well . . . whatever happened to come her way. She held the beer and tried to figure out what to do next.

Minutes seemed like hours. Beth longed to bolt for the door but knew she couldn't just leave. Lacy wouldn't know where she'd gone or what had happened to her.

A ruckus broke out behind Beth, and she turned, beer in hand, just in time to avoid a glass being hurled her way. She ducked to one side and was just coming back up when Simon and Nick Lassiter made their way into the bar.

Beth felt a sense of dread and disappointment at the sight of the men. Nick had claimed he no longer came to Rafe's to drink, but here he was. She kept her head down and wondered what she should do. If they took a table or joined one of the card games, then she'd be all right—at least for a time.

The fight intensified as two more men got in on the action. Rafe bellowed at them above the din, but the men ignored him. They were feeling their whiskey and had no thought for anything but their altercation.

Simon and Nick moved deftly around the fight and headed closer to the bar. Beth froze in place, watching and waiting to see where they would go. She was just about to turn away and follow Lacy into the back room when Nick met her gaze. The recognition was immediate.

Beth dropped the beer, and liquid and glass sprayed across the dirt floor. Uncertain of the layout of Rafe's Saloon, she skirted the opposite side of the fight and rushed for the front door. She didn't have to look behind her to know that Nick would follow. The thought of him catching her and demanding to know what was going on only served to fuel her steps.

But she had no idea where to go once she'd made it outside. There were several men milling about and a great many horses tied to the posts just off Rafe's porch. Beth hurried to put the horses between her and the door to the saloon, hoping that if Nick couldn't see her, he'd give up and go back inside. Never had she prayed for Nick to head into Rafe's den of iniquity like she did just now.

She knew she couldn't simply go home. That would be what Nick would expect. So without giving it any more thought, Beth cut a path to the forested area across the road. The night hid her well as she slipped into the thick new foliage.

Beth was panting by the time she reached the far edge of the forest, where the roadway made a bend. It hadn't been all that far to travel, but nervous excitement caused Beth's heart to race.

Cautiously, she peered out of the trees to examine the

situation. The Lassisters' livery and stables were just across the road. A dim light shone from the front room of the house. A lamp had probably been left burning for Simon and Nick, as Millie, Evan, and Forrest were, no doubt, already in bed.

A thought came to Beth. Her father used to joke about how most of the things he lost were found hiding right in plan sight. Beth noted there was light coming from the open stable door. Maybe some of the cowboys had secured their mounts with the Lassiters, and the stables had been left in such a way for easy access. If Beth could make it to the barn unseen, she could hide there. Nick would never expect her to be in his own stable.

She smiled to herself. It was the perfect plan—one that even Lady Effingham or Justice Halbrook could be proud of. Looking back toward Rafe's, Beth couldn't tell if Nick was still among the men outside or not. She hoped he'd given up pursuing her.

Creeping toward the stable, Beth crossed the road. She climbed over the fence and crossed the corral, where the horses stood ready and waiting for tomorrow's noon stage. They moved to the far end of the pen as if to show they'd have nothing to do with her escape plans.

It didn't matter. Beth hurried in through the side door and quickly made her way to a hiding place behind a stack of hay bales. Prepared to wait out the situation as long as was necessary, Beth breathed a sigh of relief.

Without a watch, Beth had no way of knowing how long she remained hidden. But when no one appeared in the stable and sufficient time passed uneventfully, Beth decided to make her way home. Surely Nick had gone back to the bar. The thought irritated her, but now was not the time for contemplation.

She looked around the corner of the bales to see if the way was clear. She'd thought about returning the way she'd come but figured that might be more dangerous. If Nick had followed her, he might still be out there. No, she'd slip around behind Rafe's, closer to the river. There might be the additional danger of meeting up with that rogue bear, but even that failed to frighten her as much as confronting Nick Lassiter and explaining why she'd been in the bar.

Beth took a deep breath and headed for the stable door. She'd only made it about five feet, however, when she felt someone crash into her back, forcing her to the ground. She tried to fight, but it was useless. Her hat fell away and her hair tumbled out around her.

Even before being rolled over, Beth knew her captor was Nick. However, she wasn't prepared at all for the anger in his expression as he held her in place.

Nothing seemed to make sense in her mind, but Beth— ever willing to stick her foot in her mouth—matter-of-factly said, "I didn't think you went to Rafe's anymore."

# CHAPTER ELEVEN

"Have you lost your mind?" Nick bellowed. He hauled Beth to her feet but held her securely, though he noticed she wasn't even trying to fight him. "I can't believe this. What in the world are you doing dressed like this—and at Rafe's!"

"If you yell loud enough, maybe Rafe will come over to investigate, as well," Beth replied.

When Nick had first seen her in the saloon, he'd thought his heart might actually stop beating. Why would she have ever ventured to put herself in harm's way like that?

Still, she had a point. He had to calm down or he'd say something he'd regret.

"This has got to be one of the most dangerous nights at Rafe's, and yet there you were . . . dressed like a cowboy—a man—and with a beer. What got into you, anyway? Do Gwen and Hank have any idea where you are? Do you know what would have happened to you if Rafe figured out who you were?" He barely took a breath before continuing. "I'll tell you what would have happened. He would have given you over to those cowboys, and you would have lived out your craving for danger and adventure. I think you need a new philosophy, Miss Gallatin."

He stared hard at Beth, hoping she might be intimidated by his strength and anger. Better he scare her out of such stupidity than someone else who cared nothing about her.

"Are you going to tell me why you were there tonight?" he asked.

Beth raised her chin ever so slightly. "I can't see that it will help the matter at all. You're just going to keep ranting and raving at me."

She tried to pull away, but Nick tightened his grip and held her close against him. "You aren't going anywhere until I get some answers."

"Then we might be here a long time."

Nick couldn't deny that he enjoyed their closeness. Her body was pressed against his, and a million thoughts raced through his mind. Right at the head of the pack was his desire to kiss Beth Gallatin soundly. He resisted the urge, however. He'd been worried about her being compromised by other men, and the last thing he wanted was to take unfair advantage of her.

"I've got all night," Nick finally replied in a barely audible voice.

Beth glanced toward the open stable door. "Don't you

think folks are going to be surprised to find us like this? Seems rather . . . well . . . intimate, to my way of thinking."

How could she talk like that? How could she just stand there, all calm and collected, and talk of intimacy? Nick let go of her hands and stepped back. "If you run, I'll just come after you."

"It's not like I'd go all that far," she said. Beth took off the kerchief around her neck and wiped at her face. "I'll tell you why I was at the saloon if you'll tell me first why you were there."

Nick knew he had nothing to hide and shrugged. "I was helping Simon. Ellie sent word that something was wrong, and she needed to talk to him. Simon knew Rafe would never let them slip off together—especially tonight with all those customers. So I was going to keep Rafe preoccupied while Simon found Ellie."

"So you weren't there to drink or . . ." She let the words trail off as she met Nick's gaze.

"You were the one holding a beer, as I recall," Nick countered. Even dirt-smudged and wearing her father's old clothes, Beth Gallatin was still the most beautiful woman he'd ever seen. Her nearness was intoxicating. Why couldn't she see how much he'd come to care about her?

"I was just trying to look like the rest of the crowd so no one would notice me." She tucked the dirty cloth into her pocket but didn't attempt to leave. "I certainly wasn't there to drink beer, however. I'm surprised you'd even think that of me."

"I'm surprised you were even *in* Rafe's Saloon. I think that tops your thoughts on the matter."

Beth shrugged and her reddish brown hair rippled down

against her shoulders and arms. "I didn't know it was a competition."

Nick shook his head. "I've told you why I was there, and it was nothing more than that, Beth. I've given up living like that, and I don't intend to start with it again. You have my word."

"I'm glad, Nick. I really am. I hated that you went there. I wish Rafe's business would dry up and blow away. I can't bear . . . well . . . knowing what's going on over there. It just breaks my heart."

Her soft voice was nearly Nick's undoing, but he held himself in check and pressed for more explanation. "If you don't like the place, why were you there?"

"Well, I don't suppose you can get much madder than you already are," she said with a halfhearted smile. "We went there to drug the cowboys."

"What?"

She gave a nervous giggle. "Lacy and I just wanted to put an end to the night's activities, so we drugged the men who were still at Gallatin House by putting laudanum in their coffee."

"You did *what*? Are you out of your mind?" Nick couldn't help but raise his voice. "That stuff can kill a man."

Beth bent down and picked up her hat. "If you plan to keep yelling at me, I'm going home."

"You're going home, all right, but not until I hear the rest of this story." Nick crossed the distance to where Beth toyed with her hat. "So you went to Rafe's to drug the cowboys. How did you plan to accomplish that? Slip laudanum into each of their glasses?"

Beth shook her head. "Lacy was working with Cubby to put it into the liquor when you saw me."

"Lacy went with you?"

"Yes." Her face paled all at once. "Oh no. She's still there, and now she's alone. I left her when I knew you'd found me out."

Beth moved toward the door, but Nick pulled her back. "Wait. You can't just go barreling in there again."

"But I can't leave her to deal with Rafe alone. He already hates her."

"I'll go in and get her out, but you aren't going anywhere near the place."

"Just try to stop me," Beth said, pushing hard to get away from him.

Nick easily reclaimed his hold on her and pulled her against him. "That's not a difficult task." The feel of her in his arms made it difficult to keep his mind on the matter at hand. "Look, the more time we spend arguing about this, the more time Lacy will be alone."

Beth stilled and looked up at him, her lips only inches away. Worried about what he might do, Nick released her abruptly. "If there's trouble, I'll need you to go for help. You can hardly do that if you're in the thick of things."

This seemed to make sense to her. "All right, we'll do it your way." She tucked her hair back up and pulled the hat down tight over her head. "Let's go."

They walked the short distance to the saloon. A jaunty tune from the old piano could just be heard from beneath the loud voices and revelry.

"Stay here," Nick said as they came around the back of Rafe's.

"Nick?" a voice called out.

Nick instinctively grabbed Beth and pulled her close, then relaxed as he saw it was Simon and Ellie. "We've got problems," Nick told his brother.

"What's going on? Who's he?"

"*He* is Beth Gallatin," Nick replied.

"Beth?"

"I'm afraid so."

Beth tilted her chin up so they could see her features more clearly. Ellie giggled. "You're a sight."

"I'm sure I am," Beth admitted, "but that's not important right now. We have to find Lacy."

"What's happened to Lacy?" Simon asked.

"It's a long story," Nick replied. "I'll tell it to you as we go. You ladies stay here."

"Now, wait just a minute," Ellie said, hands on hips. "If Lacy's in trouble, I want to help, too."

"He doesn't like getting help from women," Beth told her.

Nick shook his head in frustration. "It's dangerous. Beth and Lacy snuck into Rafe's dressed like this. They had plans to drug the cowboys with laudanum and put them all to sleep for the rest of the night. I saw Beth, and she took off running. I followed her. Lacy was left behind, and now we need to find her and get her out before Rafe recognizes her."

"Then you need my help," Ellie said matter-of-factly. "Rafe won't think twice about my being there, and I can get into places you can't."

"She's got a point," Simon agreed.

Nick conceded the point. "But Beth stays here."

"That wouldn't be all that safe," Ellie said, glancing over her shoulder. "There are men everywhere, and those who aren't looking for a good time with the ladies are itching for a fight with the men. Someone's likely to try to pick a fight with Beth, just because she's small and they figure they can take her."

"All right, then she can go home and wait for us," Nick said. "But time is getting away from us while we stand here arguing."

"I'm going with you, and that's final," Beth said, starting for the door. "You can either come with me or go back to what you were doing."

"Wait," Ellie called. "Let me go in first. I'll go in the back door and check with Cubby. You three wait there, and I'll come back and let you know what's going on."

"That's probably the best way," Simon agreed. "We can just wait and keep watch."

Nick gritted his teeth and nodded. He wasn't at all happy with the way things were going, but there was nothing to do about it. He'd deal with Beth later, but right now it was most important to get Lacy out of danger.

The foursome walked past the rooms where Rafe's girls handled their affairs. Nick hated that Beth should be in the midst of such debauchery. He wanted to blame Lacy for the events of the evening, but he had a sneaking feeling that Beth had probably masterminded a good portion of their actions. What had ever possessed them to make such a daring play?

He was still contemplating this as Ellie motioned them to wait off to one side. "You boys stay here, and I'll get us a bottle," she said, playing her role quite well.

Simon leaned toward Beth. "Did you really imagine you could put them all to sleep?"

She shrugged. "It seemed reasonable enough at the time.

Lacy figured Cubby could slip it in the beer and whiskey, and no one would be the wiser. We both figured men pass out all the time from their drink, so this wouldn't be all that different."

"It's different, because you're in the middle of it," Nick hissed. "And there's the fact that if a man chooses to drink himself unconscious, it's his choice and no one else's. You took matters into your own hands and robbed him of that."

She crossed her arms in defiance. "Seems like a stupid choice to me. Maybe I was actually helping them not to drink so much."

"You could have killed someone, too. How will you deal with it if Ellie comes back to report men are dying in there because of what you did?"

Beth's expression lost its smugness. "You don't really think that could happen, do you?"

"I know it can. Laudanum is nothing to fool around with."

"I don't want anyone to die, Nick." She looked at Simon. "I really don't. I just wanted to save Ellie and the others. I just wanted them to stop drinking and doing harm to themselves."

"It was admirable enough of you, Beth," Simon admitted, "but Nick's right. That stuff is deadly. You should never do anything like this again."

"I intend to see that she doesn't," Nick said before Beth could reply. He'd already determined that no matter what it took, he was going to see that Beth gave him her pledge on the matter. "I'm sure Hank and Gwen will be surprised to hear about this."

"Not nearly so much as you might imagine," Beth muttered.

Just then Ellie returned with a bottle of whiskey in hand. "She's not in there. I don't know what's happened to her. Cubby said he hasn't seen her since she gave him the laudanum."

"Where could she be?" Beth asked anxiously. "You don't suppose that Rafe has her, do you?"

"No. He and Wyman were still dealing cards," Ellie said, reaching out to touch Beth with her free hand. "She probably just went home. Why don't you head over there and see. If she's not there, we can keep looking for her."

"Ellie's right. That's the best place to start," Simon agreed. "We can check in over there, and if she's not back, we can get Hank's help, as well."

Beth grimaced. "He's not going to be happy about this."

Nick gave an exasperated sigh. "He's not the only one."

# CHAPTER TWELVE

Beth rushed into Gallatin House with Simon, Ellie, and Nick right behind. She rushed from room to room, finding numerous snoring, smelly men, but no sign of Lacy. Hurrying to the kitchen, Beth found it empty. A strange sense of remorse settled on her shoulders. She'd left Lacy to face the dangers on her own, and now her sister was nowhere to be found.

Her breathing quickened. Beth pulled the long coat close to avoid tripping over it as she raced for the stairs. "I'll go upstairs and see if she's there."

As if summoned, Lacy appeared at the top of the stairs. She was dressed quite appropriately in a brown skirt and yellow blouse. She smiled down upon them and spoke as if nothing were amiss.

"I wondered where you were, Beth. You look a sight. Evening, Nick. Simon. Ellie. It's awfully late for you to come visiting."

"We've been half sick looking for you," Beth announced. "I ran out of Rafe's because Nick spotted me. I knew the whole thing would be for naught if he caught me there."

Lacy laughed as she came down the stairs. "I'll bet that was the shock of your life, seeing my sister dressed like some kind of drover."

"To say the least," Nick replied.

"What's going on?" Hank called from the top of the stairs. He took one look at Beth and shook his head. "Why are you dressed like that?"

Two groggy cowboys stumbled in through the door behind Beth. They pushed past her, dragging a third man. They didn't seem aware of their clumsy actions or the people surrounding them, and instead pressed on to struggle up the stairs. They narrowly avoided Hank as he descended.

Hank looked at them rather oddly for a moment, then turned his attention on Beth as he joined them on the first floor. He glanced at Lacy, who was smiling. "So who's going to tell me what's going on?"

Beth felt nervous being confronted by her brother-in-law. His piercing blue eyes held her captive. "Well, it's nothing all that bad."

"Let me be the judge of that." Hank eyed her suspiciously. "I've come to learn that when you or Lacy tell me something isn't that bad, it's probably just the opposite."

"But . . . well . . . I suppose it's all in how you look at it," she answered with a nervous giggle. "I mean . . . well . . ." She looked to Lacy for help.

"How's Gwen feeling?" Lacy asked.

"She's sleeping. Now, don't change the subject. Tell me why it's after midnight and you two are standing here with visitors, and Beth is dressed like she's ready to drive a herd to market."

Lacy folded her arms. "I hardly think it's wrong of me to ask after my sister."

Hank raised a brow and turned to Nick. "It's that bad, is it?"

"It's bad."

He looked back to Beth. "You might as well tell me, or he will."

Beth licked her lips and cast a quick glance at Nick. Hank was right. Nick would be only too happy to explain it all.

"Well, it started out as a good thing," she began. "Lacy and I wanted to help Ellie and the others. So you see, it wasn't that we were just selfish or trying to cause harm to anyone. In fact, it never dawned on me at all that someone could die from it."

"What?" Hank lowered his voice quickly. "What do you mean someone could die?"

"It's just that . . . I didn't know that the effect could be that deadly. It hadn't been before," Beth muttered, looking at her hands and wishing everyone would just go away.

"Beth, I don't understand at all what you're talking about. Tell me right now what happened tonight."

There seemed no easy way out. Beth bit at her lower lip for a minute, then leaned close to her brother-in-law and whispered, "Don't drink the coffee, Hank."

For a moment, he looked even more puzzled, and then

realization dawned. "You didn't." He looked again at Lacy. "Please tell me you didn't."

"We had to. They were making such a ruckus, and some-one could have gotten killed," Lacy explained. "And we hate the business that goes on next door with the women."

"So you took it upon yourselves to . . ." His words faded as he seemed to notice the snoring for the first time. He stepped into the open area of the front sitting room. Hank shook his head and walked back to where the others stood.

"As you can see," Nick began, "they did, indeed, take it upon themselves. I don't know where they're getting the laudanum, but I would suggest you find it and get rid of it before they do it again."

"I don't plan on doing it again," Beth quickly threw out. "I didn't think about how it could kill a person. I never wanted anyone to die."

"A little late to worry about such things now, don't you think?" Hank looked at her and rolled his eyes. "Didn't you learn anything from before?"

"Before?" Nick asked. "You mean she's done this before now?"

Beth felt a wave of humiliation rush over her. "Never mind."

"No, since we're making confessions, why not come clean?" Nick asked, gazing at her intently.

Beth met his dark eyes. Goodness, but he was handsome. She thought of all of the heroes in her books and decided none were as courageous and dashing as Nick Lassiter.

When Beth said nothing, Lacy interjected, "Not that it matters now, but we once did the same thing to Hank. We didn't like him then."

"Oh, well, that makes it all right," Nick said sarcastically.

"Exactly," Lacy countered. "He was being rather obnoxious and mean to Gwen."

"And we didn't just leave him on the floor to sleep it off," Beth said, as if that made it somehow better. "We put him in bed. Well, sort of, anyway. He was in his room."

"Only after bouncing my backside up every step they could find." Hank blew out a heavy breath. "My behavior toward your sister was rather appalling, but it doesn't dismiss the wrong you did in drugging me. Nor does it excuse drugging them." Hank motioned over his back at the sleeping cowboys.

"Well, what's done is done," Lacy said. "It's very late, and I'm going to bed. We can discuss this further in the morning. Oh, and, Beth, I left hot water for you in the bath."

"She's right. There will be plenty of mouths to feed come daylight." Hank turned to follow Lacy up the stairs. "Groggy men who will no doubt want a cup of coffee to help them wake up. Do you suppose you two can manage that?"

"We'll manage it just fine, Hank," Lacy replied. "We were managing it before you came here, and we could handle it if you went away. Coffee really isn't all that difficult to make."

Beth couldn't help but giggle at her sister's comment. But then she looked at Nick and saw the disapproval in his eyes. Her smile faded, and she longed for a way to win back his favor. Beth pulled off her hat, and her hair spilled down around her shoulders. She noticed Nick's expression soften.

Beth wished Ellie and Simon weren't in the room. She wanted to say something to let Nick know that she appreciated his concern—that she had never meant to cause him grief. She wanted to tell him thanks for caring and coming after her, despite the problems she'd created. But most of all, she felt the most compelling desire to kiss him. Lady Effingham would have simply done the deed, but Beth was starting to realize her novels were far removed from the events that made up her daily life.

"I'm sorry for worrying you, Nick." It seemed a rather lame apology, but Beth couldn't think of anything else to say.

"Look, I need to get back," Ellie announced. "If Rafe finds me missing, he's going to be mad."

"Here, take this," Simon said, handing her several dollars. "He won't think so much of it if you have money to show for your time with me. I'll walk you back." Simon turned and smiled at Beth. "That look really doesn't suit you, Beth."

Beth frowned and turned away. She waited until he was gone, then shook her head. "I don't know how he can just do that in plain sight of other people."

Nick looked confused. "What are you talking about?"

"Paying her . . . for . . . well, you know what for." The disgust in her voice was clear and Beth didn't try to hide it.

"Do you?"

"Do I what?" She frowned. "What are you talking about?"

"I wanted to ask you the same thing. You're so quick to judge Simon for something that he hasn't even done."

"But he just paid Ellie—"

"No, he gave her money out of the goodness of his heart and his love for her. Rafe will know she's been absent most of the evening, and he's going to expect she's been making him a tidy sum during that time. Simon gives Ellie money whenever he can in order to keep her from having to share her bed."

Beth looked out the door Simon and Ellie had exited. "You mean he wasn't paying her for . . . well . . . services rendered?"

"Does that disappoint you? Honestly, Beth, you can't just sit here passing judgment on the rest of the world. Sometimes things look bad, but they aren't always what they seem." He headed for the door. "Just like you're not what you seem."

He was gone before she could reply, and Beth's heart tightened with regret. She hated that he thought her so heartless. She wanted to go after him and explain—plead his forgiveness and make things right.

Beth held on to the door handle for several minutes, then released it with a heaviness in her soul that she had never before known. Once again, she had failed to do the right thing—say the appropriate words. She had rushed to judgment and had earned the scorn of the only man whose opinion really mattered.

"There's nothing to be done about it tonight," she told herself aloud. Her words lacked the comfort she had hoped to feel. Climbing the stairs, Beth felt as if she'd let everyone down tonight. The only one who wasn't mad at her was Lacy.

*Oh, what a mess I've made of everything.*

Beth made her way to the bath, anxious for the hot water that Lacy had arranged. The desire to wash away the events of the night and all of its disappointments compelled Beth to hurry.

Stripping out of her father's clothes, Beth gave a sigh of relief. She didn't know how Lacy enjoyed such outfits. Beth found them rather awkward, if not thoroughly embarrassing. She left the clothes piled beside the tub and slipped into the water. The previous hours played out in her mind as she slid beneath the water's surface.

Nick's touch still seemed so real to her. She had wanted him to kiss her—badly enough to instigate it herself. But, of course, she hadn't. She had stepped far enough outside of the bounds of propriety. There was certainly no sense in adding to her list of sins.

With that thought, guilt began to creep in. She had totally gone against all that she knew to be right. They had drugged the men, risking the possibility that one or many might die.

She eased against the back of the tub. "But I never thought about how dangerous it might be. I just wanted them to stop drinking and causing trouble."

Still, that didn't pardon her actions. Beth grimaced. They had also trespassed and tainted Rafe's liquor supply. Who knew where Cubby put all the laudanum? The effects could go on for days, simply because no one would be the wiser as to what their drinks contained.

Then, of course, she had caused Nick problems. He had been there to help Simon and Ellie. Thinking of that couple caused Beth even more remorse. She had so wrongly misjudged the situation.

*And of course I couldn't just keep it to myself. I had to speak it all out loud and embarrass myself in front of Nick. Now he probably thinks me a horrible hypocrite, all judgmental and hardhearted.*

Those thoughts plagued her throughout her bath. They followed Beth into her bedroom and sat as a constant companion as she dried her hair in front of the fireplace. And by the time Beth climbed into bed, they met her there, unwilling to leave her for even a moment.

Beth reached under her pillow and pulled out the novel she'd been reading. She looked at the book for a moment, then glanced to where her Bible lay on the nightstand. Once again, feelings of remorse and inadequacy flooded her heart. She had long been negligent when it came to communing with God. At first, she'd just cut short her Bible reading and time in prayer in order to read her various novels. As time went by, however, she'd given less and less time to God. Now, after all this time, a simple "sorry" seemed insufficient. With a heavy heart, she put the book back and reached for the Scriptures.

She opened the Bible and thumbed several pages to Psalm 51 and read the first three verses. *Have mercy upon me, O God, according to thy lovingkindness: according unto the multitude of thy tender mercies blot out my transgressions. Wash me thoroughly from mine iniquity, and cleanse me from my sin. For I acknowledge my transgressions: and my sin is ever before me.*

Beth read the words over and over. It had been David's prayer after sinning with Bathsheba, and now it was hers. She longed for the cleansing that David spoke of. Nothing seemed more important than being free of the guilt that threatened to consume her heart and soul.

"Oh, God," she prayed, "I am so full of sadness for the things I've done—the things I've felt. I need your forgiveness, and I need to start anew. Please show me how to let go of my fairy-tale ideals and desires and to focus instead on the way you would have me live my life."

The burden lifted from her heart almost immediately. Beth drew in a long, deep breath. She read on through several chapters of the Psalms until her eyes grew heavy. Morning would come too soon, she knew, but for now it felt good to rest in God's Word and feel His presence.

Beth woke up feeling surprisingly rested, though she'd only had a few hours of sleep. She dressed quickly, having already decided that the final step to cleansing herself completely was to talk honestly with her sisters.

It wouldn't be easy to admit to her selfish thoughts, but it seemed the right thing to do. This past year since their father's death had been difficult; Beth wanted to set it aside and look to the future.

"Now I have something else I want to think on," she said, putting the final pin into her hair. Nick's face came to mind. She hugged her arms around her body, pretending he held her tight.

*He cares for me.* She smiled and let go of her hold. *Maybe he even . . . loves me.* Beth couldn't help but giggle. What a wonderful thought. It practically sent her singing down the stairs as she hurried to join her sisters in the preparations for the day. Today would be the start of something new and good. She knew God had forgiven her and that He would help her to set her path straight.

"I've felt so guilty," Beth admitted. "I didn't want anyone to think that I wanted Pa to die. I just wanted a home." Beth looked to Lacy. "You've been so good to care about what really happened—to get justice for Pa. And, Gwen, you were so worried about being cursed and causing Pa's death. It was something I could understand because I worried that my own resentment toward Pa about moving had somehow brought it about." She paused. "I just want your forgiveness for being relieved that Pa couldn't move us again."

"There's nothing to forgive," Gwen declared. "You can't help that you wanted a home. Pa loved us all very much, but he didn't always think about what was most important to us."

Lacy had been silent throughout most of Beth's confession. Beth worried that her younger sister might not be willing to forgive her the past as easily as Gwen. "Lacy," Beth began, "are you mad at me?"

Lacy looked confused for a moment, then shook her head. "No. I really do understand. I'm mad at myself. I keep thinking that if I could just find Pa's killer, this would be put to rest once and for all. I think we've all had to deal with our guilt and frustration over Pa's dying."

"But it isn't your place to find Pa's killer," Gwen countered. "Honestly, Lacy, what purpose will it serve?"

Beth was surprised at the anger in Gwen's tone. Their sister seldom lost her temper—especially with one of them.

Lacy got to her feet. "I don't expect you to understand. You never have. Let it be enough for you to know that it's something I feel God would have me do. If you have a problem with it, take it up with God." She stormed from the room, knocking over one of the dining room chairs as she went.

# CHAPTER THIRTEEN

"I'm so glad you're feeling better," Beth told Gwen. The last of the cowboys had exited the house and now the cleanup had begun. Gwen seemed like her old self, working alongside Lacy and Beth, her eye on every detail.

"I think I just overdid it," Gwen admitted. "We were cooking so much yesterday to accommodate everyone that I didn't even take time out to eat. By evening, I felt completely spent. I'm just fine now."

"It's a good thing, too," Lacy said, dumping a pile of laundry at the bottom of the stairs. "We have a lot to do if we're going to be ready for the stage tonight."

"I'll start washing the bedding," Beth offered, "but first I'd like just a minute to talk to the two of you privately."

Gwen eyed her oddly. "Is something wrong?"

"No—I mean, not really. In fact, maybe it's more accurate to say it's a good thing." Beth motioned to the still-cluttered dining room table. "Let's sit for a moment."

They went to the nearest table, and Beth quickly sat and pushed back the dirty dishes. Once her sisters had taken a seat, she began.

"I need to make a confession about the bad thoughts and feelings I've harbored this last year."

She drew a deep breath. It was going to be hard to admit her feelings about Pa's death, but after her time of prayer last night, she knew it was the right thing to do.

"You both know I loved Pa dearly. He was a good father, and he always made me laugh. He taught me so much, even how to play tricks on people." Beth smiled at the memory, then sobered. "But in truth, when he died . . . well . . . I hate to admit this." She fell silent for a moment and bowed her head. "I felt a sense of relief."

"Relief?" Gwen questioned in disbelief.

"What do you mean by that?" Lacy asked.

Beth squared her shoulders and met their gazes. "I knew Pa was thinking about moving us again. I overheard him talking about it. He thought the area—because of Rafe's—was becoming dangerous, and he didn't want us to be troubled by it. When I realized that he was considering another move, I was so upset. I didn't want to go."

She folded her hands and considered her words carefully. "We'd been moving around all of our lives. All I wanted was a home, but it seemed just the minute we settled in somewhere, Pa would up and move us again."

"That's true enough," Gwen admitted.

"I guess I felt the same way," Lacy said, looking to G "It was never easy to pack up and leave, just when we getting comfortable."

"It made me bitter. I blamed Pa, even though now see that it was often a simple matter of necessity. There always work for Pa or a good place for us to live. Still, I l for a home." Beth wiped a tear from her eye. "I wanted here at Gallatin House, even if Rafe's business made more difficult."

Her tears flowed more freely. "I didn't want Pa to d have to understand that. I honestly figured to go a to him about the situation. Gallatin House was mal a good living, and Rafe's Saloon seemed like a smal to endure. Then Pa got shot." A sob escaped her, ar fought for control.

Her sisters remained silent, waiting for Beth to re composure. They seemed to sense that she needed hear her out, and for this, Beth was grateful.

"I couldn't believe he was dead. I wanted to wak find that it was all a bad dream. I loved him dearly.'

Gwen reached out and took hold of Beth's hand. "( you did. No one doubts that."

"But then I thought, with Pa gone," Beth said her head, "we wouldn't have to leave. We could sta run Gallatin House. When you even suggested the of selling out and moving, I was heartsick. I want here. I still do. It doesn't have to be here in Galla but this area is home to me. I love the people—I fi friends."

Gwen nodded. "It's all right, Beth. I think I perfectly."

The loud clatter of wood upon wood resounded in the otherwise silent room. Beth dried her eyes on her apron and drew a deep breath. "I feel like I caused that. I'm sorry."

"No, it wasn't your fault. She told me the other day that she can't keep her promise to leave off with the search for Pa's killer. Even if it was just an accident, as everyone believes, Lacy thinks a name needs to be given to the culprit. I'm worried that she'll end up getting hurt."

"Well, we can pray."

Gwen reponded with a smile. "Yes. We can pray."

By noon the house was back in order and ready for the evening stage. Hank marveled at the efficiency of the Gallatin sisters while enjoying his lunch.

"You three never fail to amaze me," he said, giving his wife a smile. "How in the world you managed to put everything right in such a short time is a mystery to me."

"Well, the laundry isn't finished just yet," Beth said, digging into the meat pie her sister had made. "The sheets are drying outside and then I'll have to iron them. That will take me the better part of the afternoon."

"Still, my hat is off to each of you."

A knock sounded at the front door, causing Lacy to jump up. "I'll see who it is." She left and momentarily returned with a well-dressed man. He carried a leather satchel in one hand and a black bowler hat in the other.

"Ah, Mr. Bishop," he said in greeting.

"Mr. Weiserman." Hank got to his feet and extended his hand. "I didn't expect to see you."

Weiserman juggled the hat and satchel and shook Hank's hand. "I know. I had the Vanhouten papers ready and wanted to bring them to you straightaway. I know you're anxious to move forward."

"Would you care to join us for lunch?" Gwen asked. "We have plenty."

Weiserman smiled. "I'd like that very much."

Gwen motioned him to take a seat. "Would you like coffee, as well?"

"That sounds equally good." Weiserman took his place beside Hank and placed the satchel on the floor.

"I'll take your hat," Lacy offered.

Soon Mr. Weiserman was settled in, enjoying the meal alongside them. He complimented Gwen on the meat pie and gravy.

"It reminds me of my mother's *bierrocks*," he declared. "She arrived in America from Germany, and her cooking is full of memories from the old country."

"What a poetic way of putting it," Gwen said, smiling. "Does your mother also live in Bozeman?"

He shook his head. "No. She and my father live in Illinois. When I brought my family west, they were quite grief-stricken, but they understood the necessity. Our youngest son has breathing difficulties and needed the drier air."

When the meal concluded, Hank suggested they go next door to the store to review the papers.

"There will be a stage through here this evening, and the ladies have further preparations to make," Hank told Mr. Weiserman.

As they walked to the store, Hank pointed to the road.

"The stage comes through here on a regular basis. It's a good place for a town, especially with the railroad coming in."

"I hate to be the bearer of bad tidings, but it's my understanding that the railroad is going in to the north of this area."

Hank frowned. "Are you certain of that?"

"I have it upon good authority that the route was easier to build by going north. It will come through Bozeman and head directly west. My law firm is already dealing with some of the details, although I would ask you to say nothing about it until the railroad is ready to announce it."

"That *is* bad news," Hank said. "But not a complete tragedy. We still have the stage route."

Mr. Weiserman entered the store as Hank held open the door. "It's hard to predict," he told Hank, "but my guess is that the stage stop will relocate to the towns along the tracks. Supplies and services will be easier to obtain, and many passengers will seek to debark and continue their journey on the train."

"So you believe this is the beginning of the end for our little town."

"I hate to say so, but I've seen it happen before."

Hank nodded. "Still, I've committed to this land. The deal is complete, as you very well know."

"Perhaps you will be able to sell it in whole to a rancher. That would be the best solution." Weiserman pulled the papers from his satchel and presented them to Hank. "Why don't you look them over."

Hank felt little excitement in doing so. He had hoped this area would boom to life with the railroad. Now it seemed as if those dreams were fading into impossibility. There was always a chance that Weiserman was wrong. Hank considered that for a moment. Adrian Murphy had wanted the line to come through the area, and he had a great deal of influence over his superiors. At least that was what he had told Hank. Maybe Adrian was nothing more than a blowhard—a braggart who had no power to direct the choice at all. And of course, Weiserman had mentioned that his law office was already working on details for the railroad.

Still, the news was not to Hank's liking. Maybe the purchase of the Vanhouten land had been a mistake. Perhaps he should have asked for Gwen's thoughts on the matter before jumping into an agreement.

"Everything looks to be in order," he said as he glanced over the papers.

"I'm glad you find it so. Mr. Vanhouten was quite eager to be reunited with his wife. I know that weighed heavy on him," Weiserman said.

"Yes. I know it, too."

The bell over the front door sounded as Rafe Reynolds swaggered into the store. "Howdy, Bishop."

Hank nodded. "Let me know if you need anything." He turned his attention back to the papers. "Do I need to sign?"

"Yes," Weiserman said. "On the fourth page, you'll see two places that I've marked for your signature. After that, the land will be yours. I have two other copies for you to sign, as well. I'll keep one to file and one will go to Mr. Vanhouten."

"What land are you buying from Vanhouten?" Rafe asked, frowning.

Hank hadn't realized the man was listening in. The last thing he'd wanted was to explain his transaction to Rafe. The man would be livid. He'd long been after Vanhouten to sell him additional land so that he could expand his business. Still, Rafe was right here, and there was no hope of keeping the news to himself for long.

"I bought him out. He's moving east."

"You *what*?" Rafe looked at the lawyer, who apparently figured that since Hank had offered this much, he was at liberty to share his thoughts on the matter.

"Mr. Bishop is now the proud owner of the Vanhouten ranch lands. With exception to the house and ten acres. That has gone to Mr. Shepard."

Rafe threw down a can of beans in anger. "Vanhouten knew I wanted land. I offered to pay him twice what it was worth so that I could build my own hotel and expand the saloon."

"Perhaps that's why he didn't sell to you, Rafe," Hank countered. "The Vanhoutens are temperance people."

The barkeeper's face reddened a deep crimson. Hank had never seen Rafe quite this angry. "You do-gooders think you'll ruin me. Well, you've got another think comin'. I'm not one to be pushed around and forced out." He stomped out of the store, slamming the door behind him.

Hank looked at Mr. Weiserman apologetically. "I'm afraid Mr. Reynolds is going to be less than happy with my purchase."

"There's nothing he can do about it now."

"I wish you were right, Mr. Weiserman, but you don't know Rafe Reynolds. He won't give up so easily, and I fear we'll all pay the price before he's through."

Hank sat in his office until even after he'd heard the stage pull in. He knew Gwen and her sisters would easily manage Gallatin House and the customers, and frankly, he just needed time to be alone and think.

If the railroad route truly was settled and would go in eight miles to the north, he wasn't at all sure what they would do. Weiserman was probably right about the stage line changing its stop, as well. No doubt it would be less than convenient to stop both here and another eight miles down the road. Many folks would be happy to change over to the train for the speed and comfort of an easier mode of transportation. Those who couldn't afford the train could just as easily journey on without ever making a stop at Gallatin House.

He frowned. It seemed to be just one more reminder of how ill-equipped he was to deal with Montana and the life he had here. What would be best? Should they try to get a fix on where the railroad would be and move their businesses north? At least that would get them away from Rafe. Maybe he could even sell a portion of Vanhouten's land to the saloon owner.

"Lord, I don't know how to find the answers," he prayed. "I'm just as new to you and seeking your direction for my life as I am to Montana." For the first time in a great long while, a sense of failure niggled at the corners of his mind. All he wanted to do was be a good businessman and husband.

He looked at the contract on his desk once again and shook his head. "What am I supposed to do with all this land if we don't set up a town?"

# CHAPTER FOURTEEN

"Ellie is pregnant," Simon told Nick as they prepared for yet another day. They were alone in the forge area when he blurted out the news.

Nick eyed his brother sternly. "Is the baby yours?"

Simon shook his head. "I've never . . . well . . . you know. I haven't been with Ellie that way."

"I'm glad. You know what trouble it can cause."

"Doesn't much matter. This has caused trouble enough. If Rafe finds out, he'll make her get rid of the baby. She told me he made Marie do the same thing last summer."

Nick cringed at the thought. "What are you going to do?"

"Well, I want to get Ellie out of here."

"Sounds reasonable. Where will you send her?"

"That's the problem," Simon told his brother. "I can't just send her off. I plan to go with her. I want to marry her and take care of her and the baby."

Nick was surprised by this announcement. He knew his brother was sweet on Ellie, but for him to just pick up and leave was an entirely different thing. "You'd go?"

Simon looked torn by the question. "You know I wouldn't want to desert you, but . . . well . . . Ellie needs me, and I need her."

Nick laughed. "I wasn't worried about myself. I just wondered what you'd do about the business—about your livelihood."

"I'll take my share of the tools with me and start over. There's always a need for a good smithy."

"Rafe will come after you. You know that, don't you? He'll put the law on you unless you buy out Ellie's contract."

"I've already tried to do that. He told me even if I had the money, he wouldn't let me pay off her obligations." Simon pumped the billows as Nick stoked the fire. "He doesn't want her happy. Rafe seems to love knowing that people are miserable on his account."

"I know. No matter what you choose to do, it won't be easy. You know the problems that come from making the wrong decision." Nick knew only too well for himself. His mind overran with painful memories based on his poor choices.

"Can you manage without me? You'd be welcome to join us, but I'd hate to run off and leave Uncle Forrest and the others."

"I can manage. I wouldn't leave. We've got the stage contract, and well, you know how I feel about Beth. I plan to put more effort into our relationship. I don't know if she'll be as interested, but that's my plan."

Simon smiled. "I think Beth Gallatin is happy for your attention. You need to get in there and stake your claim before someone else does."

"I'll take care of things with Beth—don't you worry. What we need to do is figure out how you're going to make this work with Ellie."

"I've been thinking on that. We need to be able to leave as soon as Rafe is settled in for the night. That will give us a good ten- or twelve-hour head start. I had thought about taking the stage out one morning, but that would only give us a few hours before Rafe would wake up and know that she was gone."

"And it would be better if no one could say they saw you leave," Nick said thoughtfully. "You know, we should probably talk to Hank about this. He'd have a better idea of how to handle the situation. Maybe he could even talk Rafe into letting you buy out Ellie's contract and then you wouldn't have to worry so much about it. You could even stay here. With Evan and Millie's house nearly finished, we'd have the room for you to set up here."

"It's worth considering, I suppose. I just don't know what to do." Simon ran his hand through his hair. "There are times I want to call Rafe out into the street and challenge him to a fight for her. Other times, I think about what Pastor Flikkema says about turning the other cheek and doing good, even when people mean to do you harm."

"Yeah, but Rafe is someone who delights in causing others pain. He won't care that you've been good to him. He'll just find a way to corrupt it and make everyone miserable. Let's leave this for now and go talk to Hank." Nick pulled off his leather apron. "The sooner you get this resolved, the better things will be for you and Ellie."

⚬⚬⚬

Hank considered the situation and rubbed his jaw. "I don't think Rafe deserves much consideration in this matter. Ellie's the one who needs our protection and care."

"So you wouldn't try to buy out the contract?" Simon asked.

"I can't see that God would want us to give money to benefit Rafe's evil causes," Hank said. "Besides, Ellie's only real debt with him is that he brought her out here and has kept her fed and housed. And even then, it's been a poorly done job. No, I think you should just take her and go. I'll even give you money to help your cause."

"That's mighty good of you, Hank, but I can't just take your money," Simon declared. "I have a little bit set aside and saved. I think it would get us through until I could set up business for myself elsewhere."

"How soon will you go?" Hank asked.

"The sooner, the better. Ellie's suffering from morning sickness already. She's afraid one of the other women will find out."

"Simon thought they'd maybe head out after Rafe and Wyman go to bed one night," Nick added.

"Where will you go?"

"I'm not sure," Simon replied. "I had thought about going west. Maybe California."

"Then you should head south to Corrine," Hank offered.

"The railroad goes through there. If you were to take the stage south, you could be there in no time at all."

Nick shook his head in agreement. "That's a good point, Simon. The weather's been unseasonably dry, so you could probably get over the mountains without any problems."

"And if you wait and go on Thursday, you'll not only have the overnight stage leaving in the morning, but you'll have the noon stage come through heading north. Once Rafe realizes you've taken the stage, he won't know if you've gone north or south. If we plan it out right, we can even make it look like you've gone to Bozeman. Maybe Nick could take the wagon and head over there as a diversion."

"I think Hank's right. That just gives you one day to make your plans, but it will give you the best advantage for keeping your whereabouts secret. By the time Rafe figures out which way you really went, you should be on the train and bound for California."

Simon nodded. "It all makes good sense. I'll get word to Ellie."

That night as Hank prepared for bed, he felt good about the advice he'd given Simon. He relayed the story to Gwen and waited for her praise and approval. Instead, she frowned and turned away.

"What's wrong?"

"Hank, I don't think God would want you to encourage Simon to lie and cheat. Even if it is Rafe to whom he's lying and cheating."

Hank shook his head. "I don't think God wants us to give

over good money for bad causes, either. Besides, Simon would buy out her contract, but Rafe won't let him. He doesn't want to let Simon have her."

Gwen faced him. "Hank, the Bible says we're to render unto Caesar that which is Caesar's. Jesus said we're to honor the law and those in positions of authority. Rafe is Ellie's authority. She placed herself under his care and made a contract with him. He deserves to be paid, even if he does use it for evil."

With his pride amply pricked, Hank threw his boots across the room in anger. "It doesn't make any sense to honor men who are evil. I think you're wrong about this, Gwen. Rafe has made it clear that he won't let Ellie go for any amount of money. Do you honestly think that God would have us just leave her in prostitution?"

"No, I don't think God wants that, either."

"Well, now that you've established what God doesn't want, why don't you tell me what He does want?"

"I don't pretend that I know everything God wants or doesn't want," Gwen said, her feelings clearly hurt. "I just know that someone could get in trouble for this—even hurt. You surely don't want that."

"Leave this to the men, Gwen. We'll see it handled. Don't you worry about it." He punched his pillow and rolled away from Gwen's side of the bed.

Even after he felt the bed move as Gwen joined him, Hank refused to acknowledge her. He felt foolish and frustrated. Would he never be able to offer advice and solutions that met with her approval?

*But it isn't her approval that's in question here*, he thought. *She's only pointing out the Bible and what Jesus directed.* That bothered him most of all. She knew the Bible better than he did.

*Well, whose fault is that? If I spent more time reading the Scriptures, I'd be able to know these things.* Hank felt his hardheartedness begin to fade. He heaved a sigh and rolled over to face his wife.

"I'm sorry. I have a wonderful education, yet when it comes to God and the Bible, I am so lacking in wisdom and knowledge. I didn't mean to take it out on you. You didn't deserve my anger."

Gwen reached out and touched his face. "I know you're only trying to help. I'm sorry I made you feel bad."

He pulled her into his arms, relieved to have the matter resolved between them. "Sometimes I don't think Montana is the place for me."

Gwen pulled back just a bit. "I didn't know you were feeling that way."

"I didn't want you to worry about it," Hank admitted.

"But maybe I could help."

He hugged her closer. "I don't know. I can't figure out how to help myself. It seems the choices I make are wrong and that the ideas I come up with aren't useful."

"I certainly don't feel that way," Gwen countered. "I find your ideas quite useful. Like the idea that we should be married, and the idea that we never let anything or anyone come between us." She wrapped her arms around his neck and kissed him gently. "I love you, Hank."

He sighed and felt the last of his anxiety melt away. "Ah, Gwen. You always seem to know just how to calm my spirit."

"So we'll leave day after tomorrow?" Ellie asked in a whisper.

"That seems best," Simon told her. He glanced around. "We'll take the morning stage south and then catch the train to California."

"If Rafe gets wind of this, he'll kill us," Ellie said fearfully.

"He won't know a thing about it. He sleeps until past noon. By that time, we'll be long gone and the noon stage will have come through and gone, as well. He won't know which direction we've gone, and that will give us the time we need to get out of his reach."

"What if he sends the law after us?"

"He can try, but no one will know for sure where we'll be." Simon gently pushed back the hair from her face. "I love you, Ellie. I intend to take good care of you. Nothing will ever come between us, if I have any say."

"I love you, too, Simon. I can hardly wait to become your wife. I have such hope just knowing that we'll be together."

"You get on back, now. Don't worry about anything. Come out to the stage Thursday morning, and I'll have everything arranged."

She leaned up and kissed him on the cheek. "Thank you. Thank you for saving me from this life." She pulled her shawl close and hurried off in the darkness, while Simon made his way quickly back to his house.

Marie watched the two lovers part company and shook her head. They were fools. Fools to think they could steal their happiness, and fools to think that Rafe would let them go without a fight.

Jealousy ate at her heart as she made her way to find

Rafe. She wasn't about to let this happen, either. Happiness was an elusion, and while Ellie might have found a man who truly loved her, she had an obligation to Rafe. Marie knew that if she simply let Ellie slip away to be married to Simon, the rest of them would pay a hefty price. And who knew— maybe Rafe would even reward her for her information and give her some time off. The thought of having a few days to herself appealed in a great way to Marie. Maybe she'd strike a bargain with him.

She smiled to herself and felt no remorse for what she was about to do. Ellie knew better than to cross Rafe. Whatever happened would fall entirely on Ellie's shoulders.

# CHAPTER FIFTEEN

Simon paced back and forth in front of Gallatin House as the other passengers filed into the stage. There had been no sign of Ellie, and he was starting to get worried.

"I'm sorry, Simon, but we're going to have to get moving. I've got to keep to my schedule," the driver said, climbing atop the stage.

There was little Simon could say or do. He nodded and watched as the man released the brake. "Maybe next time," he called down to Simon.

The dust from the stage hadn't even cleared before Simon was making his way to Ellie's room at the back of the saloon. Something was wrong; otherwise, she would have been there.

He knocked on the door. When no one answered, Simon pushed the door open.

"Ellie?" She sat on the edge of her small makeshift bed, face in her hands. "Ellie, what's wrong?"

"You're what's wrong, Lassiter." Rafe stepped between Simon and Ellie. "So you thought you could steal from me, eh?"

"I love her and want to marry her," Simon declared. "I asked you to sell me her contract, but you wouldn't even consider it."

"And you thought that gave you the right to just step in and take what you wanted." Rafe crossed his arms. "I could have you hanged for this."

"No, please," Ellie cried out. She came to Rafe's side and took hold of his arm. "Please don't hurt him. He didn't do it to cause you problems. He did it because he loves me."

Simon stepped to the side, allowing light into the otherwise shadow-filled room. Ellie's face was bruised and swollen. She had an ugly gash over one eye. Simon had seen men who'd been pistol-whipped look better in the aftermath.

"Why, you—" Simon stepped forward, ready to throttle Rafe in the same manner he'd treated Ellie, but the barkeeper raised a pistol and pointed it at Simon's head.

Ellie screamed. "No, Rafe." She clung to his arm. "You can't do this!"

"I can and I will if you don't shut up." Rafe turned back to Simon. "If you ever set foot on my property again, I'll put a bullet in your head. Understand?"

"I understand that you're a coward who beats up women. In a fair fight, you wouldn't win."

"You're the only one who cares about it being fair. I fight any way I can. No one ever worried about treating me fair."

"Just go, Simon," Ellie begged.

"I want to marry Ellie," Simon told Rafe again.

Rafe laughed. The action distorted his features, making him look almost demented. Simon figured he had to be half crazy to treat people the way he did.

"I don't care what you want. She belongs to me. That's all there is to it."

Ellie put herself between Rafe and Simon. She looked at Simon with such pleading that he couldn't help but take a step back. He hated that she'd suffered a beating because of something he'd instigated.

"I'll go, but—"

"You'll go, and that's it. If you try this kind of stunt again, I'll sell Ellie to a friend of mine in Seattle, and you'll never see her again." He pushed Ellie aside and lowered the gun to Simon's chest. "Now get out of here and don't come back."

Simon backed out of the door. He could see the terrified look on Ellie's face, and the last thing he wanted to do was cause her more pain. "This isn't over, Rafe."

"It better be," the man countered. "Unless you want me to make good on my threats."

⚭

Nick knew something was wrong when he saw Simon return to the house with his tool chest on one shoulder. Simon said nothing after tossing his belongings to one corner, but Nick recognized the rage in his brother's eyes.

He followed Simon into the barn and braved the question. "What happened?"

"Rafe. He found out about our plans and beat Ellie. He

threatened to kill or sell her if I ever come on his property again."

"How did he find out?" Nick shook his head. "Who could have told him?"

"I don't know, but he found out, just the same." Simon pounded his fist against the wall. "Her face was swollen and bleeding. He'd taken out his anger on her when it should have been me."

Nick felt his own temper rise. "Well, let's go deal with him."

"You have no idea how much I want to do exactly that, but Ellie will be the one to suffer." He paced the room, hands balled into fists. "I would have taken care of it right then and there, but he had a gun on me."

"Rafe's getting a little too dangerous for polite society if he's pulling guns on his neighbors. If we can't beat him physically, then maybe we can outsmart him. Why don't you talk to Dave about it? He could probably let you know if there's something legally to be done."

"It wouldn't do any good. Rafe said I was trespassing, and I was. He said I was planning to steal from him, and I can't honestly say that I wasn't. The law sure as shootin' won't be on my side." Simon sat down on one of the log stumps and shook his head. "It's useless to go to the law."

"I'm sorry, Simon. I wish there was something I could do."

When Simon turned to face him, there were tears in his eyes. "It isn't her fault, but he's making her pay the price."

Nick tried to think of something that might help, but short of killing Rafe, nothing came to mind. He knew Simon loved

Ellie and wanted to make a good life for her, so why hadn't God interceded to allow for their escape?

For all of Nick's life Simon had been there to protect and encourage him, yet now that he had the opportunity to do the same for his brother, Nick couldn't think of a single thing.

"We'll think of something, Simon," Nick finally murmured. "I promise you we'll think of something."

A couple of hours later, however, it was Nick's own love life that took the uppermost place in his mind. He knew Beth was washing bedding behind Gallatin House, but he hoped she might have time to go for a ride with him before the noon stage arrived.

He found her hanging sheets on the line. The sun made her auburn hair seem even redder as it illuminated the strands. Nick felt his chest tighten at the sight of her. He had cared about her for so long, and he wanted only to make a future with her.

"Beth?"

She looked up and smiled. "Nick! What brings you over here?"

"You. I wondered if you'd have time to go with me for a ride. I know there's a stage due in at noon, but I wanted some time to talk with you privately."

She smiled rather shyly. "I don't have enough time for a ride, but we could take a short walk. Would that be all right?"

Nick felt a sense of relief that she hadn't said no. He grinned. "I'll take whatever I can."

Beth pointed to the rifle. "We'd best take that along, as I understand no one has managed to catch that bear."

"Hopefully he's taken himself up into the mountains, but

you're right." Nick went and picked up the rifle. "Better safe than sorry."

They walked out away from Beth's house and meandered toward the cemetery as if by silent agreement. Nick tried to think of exactly what he wanted to say.

"Did you hear about Simon and Ellie?" Nick asked nervously. He thought he could at least fill the silence with talk of his brother.

Beth lifted her skirt ever so slightly as she stepped over several large rocks. "I don't think so. What's going on?"

"They were going to run away this morning and get married, but Rafe heard about it."

"Oh no." Beth stopped and turned to face him. "Are they all right? Did Rafe do anything to cause them harm?"

"He beat Ellie and threatened Simon."

"Oh, Nick, that's terrible. Is there anything we can do?"

He could see the genuine concern in her eyes and hear it in her voice. "I don't know. I'd like to, but Rafe said he'd sell Ellie to someone in Seattle."

"He's an awful man." Beth shook her head. "I wish he would see the harm he's caused and cease at once."

"Rafe Reynolds enjoys causing harm."

"But Simon obviously loves Ellie or he wouldn't want to marry her. Surely that means something, even to Rafe."

Nick loved the passion and fire in Beth's eyes. She cared so deeply about the people in her life. He only wanted her to care as much about him.

"It makes me so angry. I want to march over there and tell him exactly what I think!" She let out a heavy sigh. "Poor Ellie. Poor Simon, too."

"I didn't know what to say to him or how to help." Nick drew a deep breath. "But it got me thinking about things."

"What kind of things?" Beth asked.

She didn't look away from him, and Nick felt bolstered by her attention. "How short life is and how we only get a certain amount of time to accomplish the things that are important."

"It's true," Beth said, suddenly seeming rather shy. She looked at the ground as if embarrassed.

Nick knew it was now or never. He had to know how she felt about him—had to tell Beth how he felt about her. "I'd like to marry and have a family of my own one day. I think a man needs a woman to complete him."

"You do?" Beth asked softly.

"I do. Furthermore, I'd like a chance to prove myself to you. I feel confident that you are the woman who can complete me."

Beth's head snapped up and her eyes widened. "You *do*?"

He smiled and, despite the rifle, pulled Beth into his arms. She didn't resist. "I do. You know I've cared about you for a long time. I've asked you to court me before, but there was always something that stood in the way."

"I see nothing there now," she said in a whisper.

"Are you sure?"

She lifted her gaze, and her cheeks grew red. Nick felt her tremble in his arms as she whispered, "I'm sure."

He leaned forward to hear her, but Beth closed her eyes as if he meant to kiss her. How tempting it was. He looked at her lips and then back to her closed eyes. She was so willing to let him take his pleasure.

"Beth, look at me."

She opened her eyes and appeared confused. Nick reached up and ran his finger along her jaw. "I really want to kiss you, but I also want to wait."

"Wait?" She frowned. "What are you waiting for?"

"Our marriage," he replied.

"But we're just at the place where you want to court me."

"I've been at that place for a long while, Beth. I was just waiting for you to get to that same place." He put his hand to her cheek and felt the warmth of her skin. "When Adrian Murphy kissed you, I thought for sure I'd lost you."

"That kiss meant nothing to me."

Nick nodded. "I know, and that's why I want to wait. I want my kiss to mean a great deal to you. I want it to be the token of a love that will last forever."

Beth sighed and smiled. "You've turned into quite the romantic, Mr. Lassiter."

He gave a low laugh and released her. "Miss Gallatin, you have no idea how romantic I can be, but I certainly intend to show you."

∞

Beth fairly floated on air the rest of the day. The noon stage came and went, and she couldn't have told anyone how many passengers they had or what they ate. She gathered the sheets and took them to the dining room to iron, but she couldn't remember the task or if she'd burned her fingers even once.

All that was on her mind was Nick Lassiter and his very stirring request to court her. She could still feel his arms around her and closed her eyes to imagine him standing there. It was truly better than any romance she'd ever read.

"You seem quite happy."

Beth opened her eyes to find Gwen watching her. "I am happy. Nick has asked to court me."

Gwen's face lit up with a smile. "That's wonderful news. Before you know it, we'll be having another wedding. Oh, Beth!" She embraced her sister with great enthusiasm.

"I can hardly believe the way I feel. I think I could actually fly if I tried hard enough." She giggled and added, "But I don't really mean to try." Beth pulled away and twirled. "I feel like it's a dream, to tell you the truth. I'm just so . . . so happy."

"I hope I have something to do with that happiness."

Beth stopped in midstep and turned. Adrian Murphy stood hat in hand at the door. The look on his face told Beth that he was quite serious.

"I had to come back, Beth. I'm determined to change your mind about me—about us."

"Adrian . . . I . . . uh." She couldn't think of a single thing to say and looked to Gwen as if for an answer.

# CHAPTER SIXTEEN

Beth found it impossible to sleep that night. She tossed and turned, and when dawn finally touched the skies in hues of faded pink and yellow, she gave up the battle and dressed for the day.

Why had Adrian come back? Why now? Didn't he realize the kind of problems this could cause for her? It was exactly like one of her romantic novels. Just when the heroine figured out what she wanted out of life, lo and behold, a complication would arise.

"Of course, Adrian doesn't have to be a complication," she told herself as she loaded wood into the cookstove. There was the tiniest bit of warmth left from the night before, and the embers, once stirred, quickly ignited the dry fuel.

*But what am I going to tell Nick?*

Adrian had taken a room in Gallatin House the night before and would soon join them for breakfast. She could hardly avoid him as she had the earlier evening, when she'd made her excuses and hid in her room.

Beth hadn't wanted to snub him, but she honestly hadn't known what to say to Adrian. He was still the kind and soft-spoken man he'd been before leaving last December. He was handsome and he certainly seemed to care for her. Still, since Nick had asked to court her, Beth had thought nothing of Adrian Murphy.

"I hadn't thought that much about him even before Nick asked to court me."

"What did you say?" Gwen looked at Beth oddly as she pulled on an apron. "Are you feeling all right?"

Beth pressed her hands to her warm cheeks. "I'm fine. I'm just a bit perplexed."

"Because of Adrian?"

"Yes." Beth reached for a bowl in order to start mixing bread dough. "I didn't expect to see him like that. It was rather shocking."

"Especially since you just settled things with Nick."

Beth stopped and looked at her older sister. "I don't want to hurt Adrian. I mean, he's very nice and all, but I thought I'd made it clear to him last winter that I wasn't interested in courting him. Now I've said yes to courting Nick and . . . well . . ." She let the words trail with a heavy sigh.

"Do you have any regrets about saying yes to Nick?" Gwen asked. "If you care more for Adrian, you shouldn't lead Nick astray and make him think otherwise."

"I don't. I mean . . ." Beth waved her hands in the air and

went to the cupboard for flour. "It's just a very awkward situation. I've waited all this time to find someone I could care about, and now this."

"Beth, just explain to Adrian that things have changed. If he's the gentleman you believe him to be, he will understand and gracefully bow out."

"It didn't stop the duke's evil brother from interfering with Lady Effingham," Beth murmured.

"What are you talking about?"

Beth brought several ingredients from the cupboard and deposited them on the counter. "It's not important. I just know that some people cannot take no for an answer. Sometimes they try to interfere and cause problems. Adrian has come all this way and I don't want to be cruel. I worried for part of the winter that I'd hurt him, but when he showed up here yesterday, I realized I hadn't hurt him at all. He must have thought I was playing coy with him, or he wouldn't have come back."

Gwen shook her head and began to measure flour into a bowl. "What if he truly loves you and came back because his hope that you might return his feelings was too strong to ignore?"

Beth felt absolutely horror-stricken. "You don't really think so, do you? I mean, what would I do?"

Gwen studied her for a moment. "You would have to be honest with him and let him know that you have feelings for Nick. You mustn't let this matter go without resolution. It wouldn't be fair to either man."

"I know how I feel, I just don't want a scene." She thought of Lady Effingham once again. There was a horrible scene between her and the duke's brother when Lord Wodehouse found out about the man's intentions. The duke's brother had demanded a duel and Lord Wodehouse was wounded. Of course, the duke's brother had cheated, but what if Adrian cheated and Nick got injured? "What if Adrian refuses to leave or somehow challenges Nick?"

Gwen shrugged. "I don't know. I've never had that problem."

"I wish I didn't," Beth said in a moan. Suddenly without willing it at all, she had more adventure on hand than she could have ever imagined.

"I've heard it said," Hank began as they gathered for lunch, "that the railroad has decided to go to the north of this area."

Adrian nodded. "Sadly enough, I believe that has been the decision, although it's not yet common knowledge. Of course, many people have been certain that this choice would be the best. There are fewer obstacles and better water sources."

Hank stared at his coffee cup for a moment. "That doesn't bode well for us as a community that would like to be a town."

"If the railroad goes in miles away from us, what will happen to the stage route?" Gwen asked.

Hank looked to Adrian and waited for him to speak. The younger man shrugged his shoulders. "It's hard to say. Even though they narrowed the distance to five miles north of here, it might cause the stage company to rethink their stop here."

"That's what I would suspect," Hank said, looking rather apologetically to his wife. "I've had my concerns."

"Why didn't you say anything?" Beth asked.

"I'd just recently heard of the new railroad plans and I didn't want to worry anyone," Hank admitted. "After all, we have no reason to believe our lives will change overnight. Even if the railroad goes north, there isn't a town, proper, in place. We could consider moving our businesses to accommodate the railroad. Other towns have done just that and with more at stake than we have here."

Beth frowned. "But I don't want to move."

"It wouldn't be all that far," Adrian said with a smile. "And just think of the adventure."

Beth got up from the table, shaking her head. "I'm beginning to think adventure is too highly esteemed."

She made her way out to the front porch and leaned against the rail. She loved it here. The mountains surrounded the valley and made her feel safe and protected. Except for Rafe and his saloon, Beth thought it absolutely perfect.

A gentle breeze touched her face, and the air smelled of pine and wild flowers. She sighed and wondered how she could remain if everyone else moved north to accommodate the railroad.

"I didn't mean to upset you," Adrian said, apologizing as he joined her on the porch.

Beth turned and met his sympathetic gaze. "I just don't want things to change. I love it here. I love the life we have here at Gallatin House."

"But you could have just as good a life elsewhere—especially with the right person at your side." He moved forward. "I know you told me you wouldn't wait for me, but I see you're still here and not attached to anyone else." He grinned and reached for her hand. "Can I dare to hope I still have a chance with you?"

Beth shook her head and drew her hand away. "I'm not yet betrothed, but I have been asked to court someone."

"That Lassiter fellow?"

"Yes." Beth glanced toward the Lassiters' property. She looked back at Adrian and saw his frown. "I'm sorry if that comes as a surprise. Nick and I have known each other for quite a while now."

"So you won't even give me a chance? I came all the way back here because I couldn't get you out of my thoughts. You aren't engaged to this fellow, so why not let me try to prove myself to you?"

Beth felt such a sense of frustration. Her well-planned thoughts from the night before fled her mind and left her feeling worse than ever. She hated hurting anyone, especially someone who had been as nice to her as Adrian. He had been so very kind and attentive. He enjoyed talking to her and always said such complimentary things. Still, she wasn't interested in courting him. While at one time she had pondered such an idea, even daydreamed about the possibilities, she now only held thoughts of Nick.

"Adrian—Mr. Murphy," she began, "we are much too different. You told me yourself that you love the life you lead, moving from place to place, living out under the stars. I need a home—a stable place that won't change every few days or weeks."

"But with the right person, you might very well enjoy living as I do."

She shook her head. "What kind of life is that for a lady?"

"Then what if I told you I would give up my job? I could find something else to do with my life and settle in one place."

Beth wished he would just give up. She wanted to tell him to go away—to forget about her—but how could she do it in a polite manner that wouldn't seem cruel?

The sound of a wagon approaching drew Beth's attention. They weren't expecting a stage, yet one was clearly making its way around the curve of the road.

"Oh dear," she said, hurrying for the door. "Gwen, we have a stage." She rushed inside. "I don't know how many people are on board, but there's at least the driver and his shotgun."

Gwen jumped up from the table. "Lacy, put on some more coffee, then get out the leftover roast and we'll slice it for sandwiches. I'll get some more bread." She glanced over her shoulder. "Beth, you greet the visitors and show them to the table."

"Can I help?" Adrian asked.

Gwen shook her head. "I believe we'll have everything under control shortly."

Beth went back to the front porch just as the driver set the brake and jumped down from the stage. "Howdy, Miss Beth. Guess you're surprised to see us."

"I'll say. We weren't expecting another stage until evening."

"We had so many passengers heading to Butte, we had to make the extra run."

"Well, we're making ready for you. How many passengers do you have?"

The driver opened the door. "Six. Two are staying on here."

Beth turned back to the house and called out to her sister, "Gwen, there are eight total for lunch."

An older man handed a young boy down to the driver. Beth thought the child looked to be nine or ten. He wore a suit of brown serge and looked quite uncomfortable. The man followed after the child and looked around him as if trying to figure out where they were.

Beth smiled sweetly. "Welcome to Gallatin House. We have a meal just about ready for you."

"I'm looking for someone," the man stated rather curtly. His expression betrayed a heavy burden. Dark smudges circled his eyes, making the man look sickly.

"I know most everyone in the area," Beth answered with a smile. "Perhaps I can help."

The man shook his head. "I'll need a room for the night."

"Would you like separate beds for you and your son?" Beth asked.

"The room is for me. The boy will be staying with his father."

Beth looked behind the man as the others debarked the stage, tipping their hats as they passed her. They were sweaty and dirty but still saw to the proprieties. None stopped, however, to claim the child. Beth turned back to the man and boy. The child was watching her as if to judge her importance in his life.

"Hello. What's your name?"

He frowned. "Justin." He pulled on his collar and looked away.

Beth smiled. "Are you hungry? We have some applesauce cake for dessert. Of course, you would have to eat something more substantial first, but at least it would give you something to look forward to."

The boy's frown faded. "I like cake."

Laughing, Beth nodded. "I do, too." Beth looked to the older man and then back to the boy. "Why don't you come on inside? You can introduce me to your father. We'll make sure he doesn't mind if I cut you an extra-large piece of cake."

The boy's frown reappeared. "I don't know my father. He's a no-account, and I hate him."

"Justin!" The older man's exclamation immediately quieted the boy.

Beth looked at the man in confusion. "I'm sorry. I presumed the boy's father was onboard the stage."

"No," the old man said, shaking his head. "His father is Nicholas Lassiter. He's the man I seek."

# CHAPTER SEVENTEEN

"We've got trouble," Simon told Nick.

Nick joined his brother at the open door. "It's just an unscheduled stage. It won't be any problem. I'll get the team unhitched and you bring up the fresh horses."

"It's not just the stage." Simon took hold of his brother's arm. His expression left Nick feeling suddenly cold inside.

"What is it?" Nick turned and looked across the road to Gallatin House. The first thing he noticed was Beth. She stood speaking to a man and small boy. But it was the man who stood directly behind her that caused Nick to drop his jaw.

"What's he doing here?"

"I was just wondering the same thing."

Nick shook his head. "He's got some nerve, coming here."

Simon turned to his brother. "What are you doing to do?"

"Well, hopefully Beth will have told him the truth about us." Nick felt a wave of concern. Beth had assured him she didn't have feelings for Adrian Murphy. Surely his appearance here wouldn't change things. But what if she told Murphy and he didn't listen? *Then I'll just take things into my own hands and tell him my own way,* Nick decided.

"Did you hear me?" Simon asked, looking at Nick oddly.

"I . . . uh . . . I guess not. What did you say?"

"I asked you why Beth should have anything to do with this."

"Well, she did just agree to court me. If Adrian Murphy thinks he can just waltz in here and steal Beth away, then he's going to have a fight on his hands."

"What are you talking about? What does Adrian Murphy have to do with this?"

Nick looked at Simon and shook his head. "You're the one who saw him first."

"I wasn't talking about Murphy." Simon turned Nick around and pointed across the road just as the man standing in front of Beth moved to face them. The distance closed in, and Nick felt a band tighten around his chest.

"Claude Foreman."

The past came rushing at Nick like a winter storm blowing over the mountains. In his mind, he was sixteen again and Annie Foreman was telling him that she was pregnant.

*"I'm sorry, Nick."* He remembered her eyes had been red-rimmed from crying. *"I'm so scared."*

Nick had taken her in his arms. He longed to give her the reassurance that everything would be all right, but he had no hope of that for himself. Her father and brothers would be livid when they learned the truth, and he'd be lucky if they didn't come gunning for him.

Shaking the memory away, Nick saw the child turn to stare at him. He was the spitting image of his mother, with his own coloring. Nick's breath quickened. This wasn't happening. It couldn't be happening. He looked to Beth, who held an expression of complete confusion.

Nick ran his hand through his hair. "I have to explain this to her. I should have told her a long time ago."

"I think you're going to have to deal with Foreman first," Simon said. "He's coming this way."

Nick could see that much for himself. Annie's father looked so much older than he remembered. The years had obviously been difficult for him, and he walked with a slight limp.

The boy—his son—trailed behind his grandfather. He didn't appear pleased to be here, nor even remotely interested in meeting Nick. In fact, he looked quite angry, but how could Nick blame him?

*I've never been a part of his world. He's never known me, and I can only imagine what his grandparents have told him.*

But knowing how the Foremans felt, Nick couldn't understand why Claude would suddenly come to Gallatin Crossing, much less bring Justin.

"Do you want me to go?" Simon asked.

"No. Stay. I'm not sure I can do this alone." Nick drew a deep breath and blew it out slowly. "Pray."

Nick gave one last glance to where Beth stood. But she was gone. So, too, was Adrian Murphy.

Claude Foreman halted some five or six feet away and looked Nick up and down. He then glanced over to Simon.

"I'm certain this is a surprise to both of you, but I had no choice in the matter."

"Would you like to come in the house and sit?" Simon asked.

Nick could see that the old man wasn't well. "We could offer you something to eat and drink."

"No. I think I'd rather stay right here and have my say."

The boy peered around his grandfather at Nick and Simon. He seemed to be sizing them up—maybe even trying to decide which one was his father. Nick noted again how much the boy looked like his mother. He had Annie's mouth and nose—a rather pert nose that would hopefully take on a more masculine look as he aged. It was the boy's dark eyes that pierced Nick's heart, however. It was like looking into his own soul.

"Regina passed on a few weeks ago," the man began. "Just before her death, the doctor told me I have a cancer. He gives me a couple of months at the most." He looked at the boy. "Regina and I talked it over before she died and decided it would be best for Justin to come and live with you."

"Why?" Nick asked. He felt a rise of bile along with bitterness. "You threatened my life because of what happened with your daughter. You wouldn't let me marry her, even though I wanted to make things right. You said she was ruined—that there was no way to make it right." Nick narrowed his eyes. "We weren't the first ones to make a mistake—to give in to temptation. Yet when she died giving birth, you put her brothers on me like I was some kind of common thief."

Justin looked at Nick but said nothing. It was clear he was considering the conversation, however. Nick had no desire to cause his son pain by relaying the issues of the past, but he felt confident the child had never been told the truth.

"I loved Annie," he continued. "I might have only been sixteen and her fifteen, but we loved each other with all our hearts."

"You were children."

Nick raised his hand. "We might have lacked the years of experience you would have preferred we have, but we knew what we felt. We had great hopes for our future, but instead of being happy for us and working with us, you were against us. If you hadn't caused us so much grief, Annie might not have died."

"You have a right to be angry," Claude said, surprising Nick. "We did you wrong."

The boy looked to his grandfather. "What's he talking about, Grandpa?"

The man looked down at the boy and shook his head. "There's too much to explain just now. In time, though, I hope you'll come to understand. Your grandmother and I did what we thought was best for your sake. But we didn't handle things very well at all. In fact, we led you to believe your father was no good, but that was a lie."

"You *lied*?" The boy looked back at Nick. "Why would you lie to me?"

The old man looked to be in pain. "You're too young to understand. We did what we had to do—what we thought was best for you."

The boy refused to take this as an answer. "But you lied?"

"I'm sorry, Justin," his grandfather said, shaking his head. "It seemed right back then. You were a baby, and Nick was just a boy. We'd lost your mother, and our grief was too great to deal with."

"But that's no good reason. You said my father didn't want

me. You said he ran off." The boy's eyes were wide in challenge, daring his grandfather to correct him. "Why did you
do that?"

Nick felt his anger ebb. The old man was sick and looked so
sad to have upset his grandson. Teachings from the previous
Sunday's sermon came back to haunt Nick. The verses had
been from Matthew and spoke of forgiveness. Nick couldn't
remember exactly where they'd been, but he knew the heart
of the passage had been about reconciliation. For the sake of
his son, Nick would attempt to do just that.

"They wanted to protect you," Nick said softly. They were
the first words he'd addressed to his son since leaving him in
the care of his grandparents.

"We went about it all wrong, but your father is right,"
Claude Foreman said, taking hold of the boy's shoulder. "We
did want to protect you—to love you. I wanted to talk to you
about it on the trip out here, but there never seemed to be the
right time. I'm sorry, Justin."

"I hate you," the boy said, wrenching away. "I hate you
both!" He ran back in the direction of Gallatin House.

"Justin, wait!" his grandfather called after him.

"Let him go." Nick shook his head. "This isn't going to be
easy for either of us." He considered the complications this was
going to cause between him and Beth, but worse still, he thought
of the little boy who had come into the world upon the death of
his mother. The boy Nick hadn't seen since his birth. His son.

◦⁀◦

Beth felt as if she'd had the wind knocked out of her. Ever
since learning that Justin was Nick's son, she'd not been able

to draw a real breath. Seeing that Gwen and Lacy had the meal under control, Beth excused herself and went for a walk. She hoped she could avoid having to deal with anyone else, but instead found herself face-to-face with Justin.

"Looks like you're in a hurry," she said.

The boy stopped in his tracks and regarded her for a moment. "I wish I could fly."

"Me too. I think it would definitely help when I just want to get away and not have anyone bother me. I'd fly up into a tall tree and just sit there and think things through."

Justin considered this and nodded. "I'd fly up even higher. Way up into the mountains. Maybe into a cave."

"There are bears in the caves around here. Sometimes mountain lions, too." Beth pointed to the span of trees that lined the river. "You want to walk with me?"

He shrugged. "I guess so."

"My name is Beth Gallatin," she told him and they began to amble along. "I live here with my sisters, Gwen and Lacy. We run the stage stop."

"Do you really have bears here?"

"Yes, I'm sorry to say. There was one particularly mean one that attacked our dog. They've been trying to hunt him down, but most of the menfolk believe he's gone up into the high country to fatten up on berries and such."

"Did he hurt your dog?" The boy sounded gravely concerned.

"He did, but it wasn't too bad. Major is back up and running after rabbits."

"I'm glad. I had a dog back in Kansas. He was really old, though. He died last year. My grandma died, too."

"I'm sorry to hear that. My father died last year," Beth said.

"Where's your mama?"

Beth looked at the child and smiled. "Heaven. She died when I was a little girl."

"Mine's in heaven, too. She died when I was born."

"I'm so sorry. She missed out on knowing a wonderful young man."

Justin said nothing until they reached the river. Beth thought perhaps he was done talking, but instead, he turned to her and stunned her with his question.

"Do you know my pa?"

What should she say? She could hardly tell the boy that she fancied herself to be falling in love with Nick Lassiter. Nor could she tell Justin that she was as confused and upset with his arrival as he seemed to be.

"I do know your father," she said, picking her words very carefully.

The boy frowned. "I don't. I thought he was a bad man, but I just heard my grandfather say he lied about that."

Beth's heart broke for the boy. He sounded so lost and confused. "That must really hurt. I've had people lie to me before, and it didn't feel at all good." She thought of Nick and how, in all her wildest dreams, she'd never considered that he might have a child. And while it wasn't exactly a lie, he hadn't told her, just the same. Had he thought she wouldn't understand? Had he ever planned to tell her?

Justin pursed his lips as if to keep his mouth closed. After a moment, he seemed to relax. "It doesn't feel good."

Beth walked a little ways and took a seat near the edge

of the river. "If you want to sit and talk about it, I'm a real good listener."

"My teacher says sometimes it's good to talk about things." Justin walked to where Beth sat and joined her.

"It's pretty warm out here. Maybe you'd like to take off your coat so you'll be more comfortable. It's quite all right with me."

He threw her a look of gratitude and quickly ripped the coat off and tossed it aside. He was undoing the top button of his collar when Major joined them. Justin startled, but when Beth took the dog to her side and allowed him to settle his head in her lap, the boy relaxed.

"This is Major. He's the one I was telling you about—he was very brave to face the bear and keep my sister from being attacked."

Justin reached out his hand. "Can I pet him?"

"Of course." Beth smiled. "Major would love to have a new friend. Wouldn't you, boy?" As if to answer, Major turned and licked Justin's hand in welcome. "See there? He's already decided to make you his friend."

Justin smiled for the first time since Beth had met him. For several long moments, they just sat there, petting Major and watching the river run. Spring thaw gave added depth to the river, and Beth found comfort in the rippling water splashing over the rocks.

"Do you think my father is a bad man?"

Beth had almost expected the question, but still it caused her a bit of discomfort. She only knew who Nick was now— she had no idea of who he'd been.

"Well?" Justin pressed. "Is he bad?"

"Not at all. I'm quite fond of your father. I think he's a very good man."

The boy appeared to think on this for a time. "He left after I was born. My grandparents always told me he was a no-account. That he wasn't good enough to be my father."

"Maybe they were just sad because your mama had died. Maybe they didn't want to lose you, too."

Major shifted from Beth to Justin. He snuggled up against the boy and maneuvered his head under the boy's arm. Even this didn't break Justin's concentration on the conversation. "I suppose they were really sad. But they shouldn't have lied to me."

"No," Beth agreed. "They should have told you the truth."

Major perked his ears and lifted his head at the sound of rustling in the brush behind them. Beth tensed and got to her feet as quickly as she could.

"Get behind me, Justin. It might be the bear."

The boy hurried to do as he was told. He clung to Beth's skirt and peered around her to see what was happening. Beth held him behind her and prayed that God might protect them both. When Nick appeared around one of the cottonwoods, Beth breathed a sigh of relief.

"I'm sorry if I'm intruding." He looked apologetically at Beth, and she got the distinct feeling his expression was on behalf of more than just his interruption.

"We were worried that bear had come back," Beth said, letting go her hold on Justin.

"You must be hungry," Nick told his son. "Your grandfather is at the Gallatin House, having lunch. Would you like to join him?"

Justin looked at Beth and she smiled. "There's still cake."

"I'll go then." He looked at Nick for a moment longer, then ran off toward the house.

Beth noticed he'd forgotten his jacket and walked to where it had been discarded. She picked up the garment and handed it to Nick. "You'll want to take this with you."

"Beth . . . I . . . don't know what to say."

She met his gaze. "Just don't lie to me. I can withstand a lot, but I can't abide lies."

"I wouldn't lie. I haven't lied to you. I told you there were things in my past that I wasn't proud of. I wanted to tell you all about it, but I was waiting for the right time."

Beth couldn't discount the confusion, and even a bit of hurt, over the secret Nick had kept from her, but in all honesty, she couldn't be mad at him.

"Look, I just need for you to know that having Justin here doesn't change how I feel about you, and I hope it doesn't change your feelings for me." He took hold of her hands. "Beth, I can't lose you now."

"This isn't about us anymore," Beth said softly. "You have a son who very much needs to get to know you. I think you have to give him time."

Nick pulled away and shoved his hands into his pockets. "I know you're right. I just . . . I . . ."

Beth put her finger to his lips. "I like your son very much, and right now he needs you more than anyone." She felt tears come to her eyes and fought against her emotions. Life certainly wasn't anything like the romantic stories she'd read. There, the problems seemed so easily solved. But Beth knew her courtship would simply have to wait, despite the cry of her heart.

Nick finally nodded and blew out a long breath. He turned and walked away, his shoulders bent as if carrying the weight of the world. As Beth watched, tears trickled down her cheeks.

# CHAPTER EIGHTEEN

"We love the new cabin," Millie told Beth and her sisters. "It's wonderful to have space for everyone."

Spreading a basted quilt out between the four girls, Millie smiled. "Thank you so much for helping me provide for the house."

"It's the least we can do," Gwen said, gently smoothing the quilt top. "I love this pattern."

Millie smiled. "My mama made part of it and sent me instructions on the rest. She calls it Journey to the Mountains."

"I like the star in the center," Gwen commented. "And the colors. The deep greens work well with the brown calicos."

"Mama always had a good eye for such things," Millie replied. "This quilt is for Forrest's bed. I'm going to make him curtains to match in the darkest of the greens."

"I suppose you heard about the robbery the other day," Lacy threw out to change the subject.

"The highwaymen?" Millie asked. "I heard from Forrest. He said three people were held up on the trail to Virginia City."

"One man was hurt," Lacy said. She took up a needle and threaded it. "One of the thieves hit him in the head. He was trying to keep the man from stealing his watch."

Gwen shook her head. "Hank said we will have to be extra cautious. He doesn't want us traveling alone on the road."

"If we had a decent legal system around here," Lacy said, "these kinds of things wouldn't happen."

"That's hardly fair to say," Gwen replied. "Bozeman has plenty of crime, and they have the sheriff right there in town."

"And larger cities have all sorts of violence and crimes," Beth offered.

"I suppose," Lacy said, but she didn't sound at all convinced.

"So how have you been feeling?" Gwen asked.

Millie laughed. "Fat. I feel very fat. Here it is only June, and I feel as big as a barn." She patted her growing abdomen. "Evan teases me about having twins."

"What does the doctor say?" Beth asked. She worked on making tiny stitches on the inside edges of the pattern.

"The last time I visited him in Bozeman, he said I looked normal to him. He reminded me that in three months I'll have a baby, and for that to happen, the baby has to grow." She put her hand to her stomach again. "He kicks all the time."

"So you've decided it's a boy, have you?" teased Beth.

"Evan says it is. He rants about it all the time, telling me all the things he's gonna do with his son. Personally, I don't care. I'm so excited about being a mother, it doesn't matter in the least to me."

"Ah, here are all the valley's loveliest ladies gathered in one place," Hank said as he bounded into the room. "I see you are all hard at work." He kissed Gwen on the top of the head.

"Hard at work and deep in conversation," Gwen replied with a smile.

"And what has captured your attention today, besides quilting?"

"We were talking about the highwaymen, for one thing," Lacy said, struggling to keep her thread from knotting.

"Funny you should mention that. I've been talking about it, as well. That's why I'm here. I'm going to ride over to Bozeman to speak with the sheriff. I'm hoping to convince him to allow Dave to work from here. I think with all the problems going on, we need a full-time officer in the area."

Lacy frowned. "I doubt it would matter much."

"Now, Lacy, that's hardly fair. You are too hard on Dave."

She shrugged. "I just don't see that having him around is going to help much. He'll just spend all of his time chiding me about how I dress or what I work at. I'm sure he thinks I ought to just sit around and quilt all the time."

Hank laughed. "Somehow, I doubt that. Anyway, I need someone to handle the store while I'm away. Would you like to do that, Lacy?"

She quickly discarded her needle and thread. "I'd love to."

Gwen laughed. "She's never cared for sewing. You've given her a reprieve from a fate worse than death."

Lacy got to her feet. "I can't help it if I'm no good at this kind of thing."

"And you'll never get any better if you don't practice," Gwen countered.

"Well, for now, I'm going to practice running the store." Lacy turned to Hank. "Let's go."

Hank leaned down and kissed Gwen again. "I probably won't be back until late. Don't worry about me."

"You really shouldn't be on the road at night, what with the robberies. Maybe you should just plan to stay the night in Bozeman."

"If Dave can't come back with me, I'll do just that."

Lacy dusted off the canned goods at Bishop's Emporium while Rachel Bradley inspected the selection of fabrics. The Bradleys were fairly new to the area and had set up a cheese shop in their home. They owned a small herd of sheep and six large milk cows and produced some of the finest cheese Lacy had ever tasted.

"Hank usually trades me supplies for cheese," Rachel said, finally deciding on a blue-and-white gingham material. "I suppose you can just list what I bought and let him figure it up later."

Putting aside the duster, Lacy nodded. "I think that would be best. I'll just tally your selections and put it on your account. He can let you know what's still owed or on your credit."

Rachel smiled. "That works for me. Oh, I also need a package of pins."

Lacy retrieved them and added the item to her list. Once she'd managed to write everything down, Rachel loaded her purchases items into her basket and headed for the door.

"Oh, tell Gwen that I'll have some curds for her tomorrow."

"I will."

When Rachel had gone, Lacy went back to work straightening the shelves. She rather liked running the store. It suited her being her own boss. Still, once the work was done, she grew bored. Customers were few and far between, and the day was dragging by at a painfully slow rate.

She tried to busy herself by glancing at several of the books Hank had for sale. Two were on animal husbandry, one was a biography of English kings and queens, and another three or four were novels. None held her attention, however.

By five that evening, Lacy was more than ready to close up shop a bit early and assist her sisters with supper. Perhaps if there had been more people, it wouldn't have been such a long day. It might have even helped if Hank hadn't been so completely efficient. At least then Lacy could have spent her day rearranging and cleaning. Her brother-in-law, however, was a very meticulous shopkeeper. He liked order, and Lacy admired him for that.

She locked the cashbox and was just preparing to put it in the office safe when the bell over the door sounded. "I'm closing up, but if you hurry, I'll wait for you," she called from the back room.

There was no comment, and Lacy straightened to listen for some sound. "Hello?"

She made her way to the front of the store but found no one there. How odd. She started to turn and in an instant the hairs on the back of her neck seemed to crawl. Without warning, someone grabbed her from the side and clamped their hand over her mouth.

"Keep quiet, and you won't get hurt," the man growled.

Lacy tried to fight his hold and realized he was too strong. She tried to kick him, but her legs only managed to tangle in her skirt.

"Hold still, you little wildcat." He dragged her into the back room and started to take his hand from her mouth. "Where's the money?"

Lacy started to scream, and he tightened his hold. "I said be quiet. I don't particularly care for beating up women, but I will if need be."

He dragged her to Hank's desk chair and threw her against it. This time Lacy didn't attempt to call for help. Instead, she dared to look at the man. He'd covered the lower part of his face with a red bandana and wore his hat down low over his eyes.

"Now, where's the money?"

Lacy knew that once he started looking around the room, he'd spy the open door of the safe. Still, in the dim light she hoped he wouldn't see it.

"It's up front," she lied. "I'll get it." She started to get to her feet, but the stranger pushed her back down.

"Tell me where. I can get it myself."

"Under the front counter in a cashbox. We don't have a cash register." She fought to keep calm. If the man went up front for the box, she could easily slip out the back and run for help.

"You stay here," he said, moving toward the front of the store. "And keep quiet or I'll gag you."

Lacy nodded, watching and waiting for her chance. Once the man had cleared the threshold, she made a dash for the back door. Her heart raced, beating so hard she could hear it like a drum in her ears. She slid the lock back and had just opened the door when she came face-to-face with another masked man.

"And where do you suppose you're going?" He grabbed her by the hair and pushed her back into the office.

Just then the first man returned. "I don't see—" He stopped short as he took in the situation. "Tried to escape, eh?"

"She was just heading out the back."

The first man nodded and motioned to the chair. "Tie her up and gag her."

Lacy tried to pull away from the man, but he held her fast. The first man began to search the office and spied the safe. He sauntered over to it as if they were long-lost friends.

"Here's what we need." He took up the cashbox and rifled through the other contents of the safe. Finally satisfied, he turned back to Lacy. "You could have saved us all a lot of time and trouble if you'd just pointed this out to begin with."

"You won't get away with this," Lacy said, struggling as the man tied her to the chair.

The man laughed. "You know, folks have been telling me that since I was knee-high to a grasshopper, and they ain't been right yet." He motioned to the man. "Now gag her so she can't yell for help, and let's get. We've been here too long already."

With Lacy tied up, the man had very little trouble silencing her. The smelly rag nearly caused her to vomit, but Lacy fought against the urge and watched as the men hurried from the back room. She tried to mark their height against the back door and paid attention to the detail of their clothes. At least this way, she'd have some kind of information to give the sheriff.

She felt foolish just sitting there, but Hank's oversized wooden chair was too heavy and awkward to maneuver in any direction. Lacy pulled against her bonds, but it seemed the material only tightened against her wrists.

Anger egged her on. She'd been robbed in broad daylight. It wouldn't be dark for hours. Surely someone would have seen something. But when minutes and then what was surely hours passed without anyone coming to check on her, Lacy knew no one had seen a thing.

She was just beginning to despair when she heard the front doorbell ring. She fought against the gag, trying to call out, but could only manage muffled moans.

"Lacy?"

It was Hank. Lacy kicked at the desk, hoping the sound would carry better than her struggles to speak. It worked.

"Lacy, what's wrong?" Hank called as he came into the office. In the muted light he couldn't see her until he struck a match.

"Lacy! What in the world happened?"

"What is it, Hank?" Dave Shepard called from the front room.

Lacy wanted to crawl into a hole and pull the dirt in behind her. The last thing she needed was Dave telling her she should have been home quilting instead of working at the store.

"It's Lacy," Hank declared, hurrying to light his lamp.

The soft glow quickly betrayed her situation. Dave hurried

to her side while Hank turned up the wick. Pulling the cloth from her mouth, Dave asked, "Who did this?"

"I don't know who they were. There were two men. They came near closing time."

"You didn't recognize either one?" Dave questioned as he untied her hands.

"I said I didn't know who they were," Lacy snapped. "They took your cashbox, Hank. I'm sorry."

"That's not important, so long as you're all right." Hank came to her. "You are all right, aren't you? They didn't hurt you?"

Lacy shook her head. "No, I'm fine. Just mad."

"Tell us what happened," Hank suggested.

Lacy recounted the story and concluded with her observations of each man's clothes and height. Dave made notes in a little book he'd pulled from his pocket. This rather surprised Lacy, but she made no comment.

"I didn't hear any horses, so I'm thinking they might have hid them in the trees," Lacy added, rubbing her sore wrists. "We could probably track them."

"It's nearly dark," Hank countered. "We can look in the morning. Let's get you home first. Gwen was worried about you and was about to come over here herself. Now I'm glad she didn't."

Lacy nodded. She didn't like to think of her sister being in danger. "I suppose you're right about waiting until morning. I don't like the idea, but I know it makes sense." She looked to Dave. "I'll plan to leave at first light."

"No you won't," he said. "I'm the law around here, and I'll go after them."

"It doesn't mean you can't have help," Lacy said, putting her hands on her hips. "You know I'm good at tracking."

"That doesn't matter." Dave put his own hands on his hips and faced off with Lacy. "You aren't going."

"I am."

"You both need to stop arguing about it," Hank said. "It isn't going to solve a thing. Let's lock up and get over to the house. We can figure out what's to be done after we have something to eat. Lacy, you must be half starved."

She calmed a bit and nodded. "I am hungry." She pushed past Dave and headed out of the store. Her mind whirled with all that had happened. She'd had plenty of time to think about the robbery while waiting to be found, but now in the cool evening air, her mind flooded with thoughts. Had the men known she was there alone? Had they planned this out, or was it simply a random robbery? Were they part of the same group of men who were robbing folks on the road?

"Well, there you all are," Gwen said as they came into the dining room. "I thought I was going to have to come get you. Beth and I just finished the last of the supper dishes, but we saved you a plate. Would you like one, too, Dave?"

Beth retrieved her sister's food and brought it to the table. "Where have you been?"

"Tied to a chair," Lacy told her, taking a seat. She immediately began to eat without even bothering to say grace. She wasn't exactly sure she felt grateful at the moment.

"*What?*" her sisters asked in unison. They looked at Hank and Dave as if for an explanation.

"There was a robbery," Dave explained.

"No!" Gwen's hand went to her throat. "You weren't hurt, were you?"

Lacy shook her head. "No. Just my pride. There were two men, and they got the cashbox."

"Who were they?" Beth asked.

"If I knew, I'd tell you," Lacy replied. "They were masked, and I didn't recognize their voices, but I will if I hear them again. We're going to track them in the morning."

"No, *we're* not," Dave said, sitting opposite Lacy. "*I'm* going to track them. This is a matter for the sheriff's department, not citizens of the county."

"I don't have the highest regard for our legal system," Lacy said, meeting his stern gaze. "As you well know, other crimes have gone unpunished. I mean to find those men and get Hank's money back. If I'd been better prepared, they wouldn't have gotten it in the first place."

"Lacy, the money isn't as important as your safety," Hank stated firmly. "I'd like you to leave this in Dave's hands. Now that the sheriff has agreed to let him work in Gallatin Crossing for a time, we'll have him right here to see to our needs."

"What? Why?" Lacy looked from Dave to her brother-in-law. "Just where is he going to stay?"

"In the other building," her sister replied. "We have plenty of room, and even if we fill up with stage passengers, there is still enough space for Dave."

"Couldn't he stay at the Vanhouten house? I mean, he just bought it."

"That's much too far away," Hank countered. "We need him here."

Beth smiled. "It will feel very safe having our own sheriff's deputy."

Lacy rolled her eyes. She focused on the meal, but

everything tasted like sawdust. A shudder ran through her as she imagined the robber's hands on her mouth again.

It was bad enough to have to deal with those thoughts, but when she looked up and found Dave staring at her, she knew it was going to be even harder to contend with him.

# CHAPTER NINETEEN

Beth retrieved a bucket of hot mineral water and headed toward Gallatin House. Her mind raced with thoughts of Justin and Nick, as well as Adrian. She even considered Lacy's close call and all that had happened in the community of late. It seemed her calm world had turned upside down.

"Can we talk?" Adrian Murphy asked.

His voice so startled Beth that she nearly dropped the pail. "I . . . well . . . I suppose."

"You seem to be avoiding me."

Beth shrugged. "I have a lot of work to do."

"It's not just that. You haven't been the same since Lassiter's boy showed up. I figure maybe it has to do with his breaking your heart."

"Justin didn't break my heart," Beth said, shaking her head. "What in the world would give you that idea?"

"I didn't mean the boy," Adrian said. "I meant his pa. I heard that you were all set to court Nick Lassiter. I figure this changes everything."

Beth put the pail down and gave him a stern look. "You should never presume to figure anything without a solid reason to do so."

"Well, it just seems the man already has a family. You surely don't want to have to take that on, now, do you?" He grinned. "You and I could court without the inconvenience of a child."

"A child is an inconvenience to you?" Beth asked.

Adrian shrugged. "Where romance is concerned, I think a child is a huge nuisance."

"I see."

"So, does that mean you'll give me another chance?" he asked hopefully.

Beth shook her head and picked the bucket back up. "No, Mr. Murphy. I won't. I happen to love children and do not believe them to be any sort of problem. I very much like Nick's son. Now, if you'll excuse me."

"But, Beth . . . Miss Gallatin," he said, coming alongside her. "You have to know I care about you."

She stopped and looked at him sadly. "But, Mr. Murphy, I do not have the same heart for you. I'm sorry."

"What are you doing?" Justin asked Beth later that day.

Beth straightened and smiled. She'd been washing windows

all morning and figured her job was pretty evident. "Just trying to get rid of the winter dirt." She got to her feet. "And how
are you this fine day?"

The boy shrugged. He was more comfortably dressed in
a simple cotton shirt and trousers. "I saw you over here and
thought maybe I'd come over."

"And where's your father?"

Justin pointed back toward the blacksmith shop. "He's
working."

"How do you like living here?" Beth asked. She really
wanted to drill the boy about whether or not he was happy
with Nick and how they were getting along, but she didn't
want to seem too forward.

"I guess it's all right." The boy frowned. "I used to go fishing in Kansas."

"Would you like to go fishing here? We have a river full
of trout. They make wonderful eating."

The boy's eyes lit up. "Do you reckon we could?"

"I tell you what," Beth said, getting an idea. "Let's have
a picnic. We'll invite your father to come, too. He can bring
the poles and show you how we fish up here."

"I know how to fish," Justin said defensively. He folded his
arms across his chest and fixed her with a determined stare.
"My grandpa taught me."

"I'm sure he did, but have you ever gone fly-fishing?" She
smiled at the confused look on the boy's face.

"Isn't all fishing the same?" Justin asked.

Beth shook her head. "No, fly-fishing is completely different. For one thing, you don't use live bait but instead have
a decorated hook. It usually has feathery pieces or strips of
bright material. And the poles are very different. They're quite

long and made of split cane. It makes them really lightweight and pliable."

"Why would the fish want to eat feathers?" Justin asked.

"They think that it's a bug or a fly. You bounce it back and forth on the water." She mimicked the casting motion. "It's completely different. I'm sure your father will be happy to teach you. You run on over there and tell him I'm packing a picnic lunch and, if he wants to join us, to be ready to leave in fifteen minutes. Meet me in back of the house."

Justin considered this for a moment and finally nodded. "I'll ask him, but if he doesn't want to go, can we still have a picnic?"

Beth laughed. "Of course we can. A fella's gotta eat, after all. And if all else fails, *I'll* show you how to fish."

Nick and Justin were at the back porch door with five minutes to spare. Beth handed Nick a picnic basket, then pulled on a large straw bonnet. She offered Nick a rather shy smile, feeling only a little awkward in seeing him again. Funny how the presence of one little boy could so clearly change their situation.

Beth grabbed a blanket and started down the back steps. "I'm glad to see you are so prompt."

"I heard there was to be food involved," Nick began, offering Beth his arm. "I knew if it was prepared by the Gallatin ladies, it would definitely be worth taking time away from work."

Beth smiled. "Justin started talking about fishing, and the thought of enjoying this day on the riverbank appealed to me. I'm glad you two could join me."

"I'm going to learn how to fish in the river," Justin declared.

He held up two fishing poles and a net. "Simon let me borrow his pole, but later we're going to make me one of my own."

"That sounds perfect," Beth declared.

They found a shady spot along the edge of the river, and while Beth spread the blanket, Nick went to work teaching Justin to fish Montana-style. Beth watched as they stood in the shallow water. Nick had given Justin a pair of rubber boots that were much too big for him, but they serviced the boy well. Nick, on the other hand, had decided to forgo waders and simply wore old boots.

Beth laughed at their antics. Nick easily caught a trout right away. Justin seemed amazed at the fight in the fish. He was more than a little excited about trying the sport himself. Nick calmly instructed his son, and the scene warmed Beth's heart. Nick showed such patience for the boy, genuinely seeming to care about Justin, and this pleased Beth for reasons she couldn't quite understand.

They seemed a natural fit, she decided. In this environment, neither seemed nearly as tense around each other as they had been. Nick pointed to the water, then up at the trees. She wasn't sure what was said, but the boy nodded enthusiastically. They continued to fish, now needing fewer and fewer words between them. Justin tangled the line more times than not, but after about twenty minutes, he seemed to get the hang of it, bouncing the line back and forth on the water's surface.

"I'm hungry," Nick announced. "Let's eat."

"I want to fish some more. Can't I stay here?"

"We'll start eating without you, if that's okay."

Justin nodded with a big grin. "I'm not that hungry. Go ahead."

Nick cast a quick glance at Beth and then back to Justin. The boy was again focused on the water and his line. Nick made his way to where Beth sat and he smiled as he noticed the food she'd spread out on the blanket.

"I'm so hungry my stomach's keeping company with my backbone." He plopped down on the ground and fixed Beth with a gaze. "Thanks for thinking of this."

"I'm glad you could join me."

"I wanted to come and talk with you anyway," he said, taking a sandwich from the plate.

Beth turned her attention back on the boy. She could only imagine that he would be the topic of their conversation. "How are things going between you two?"

Nick swallowed and frowned. "We're strangers, and neither of us quite knows what to think or do with the other."

"That's to be expected," Beth replied. "This has come to you both so suddenly."

"But it's not like we didn't know about each other."

"Still, you only knew about the *existence* of each other," Beth offered without looking at Nick. "You didn't know anything *about* each other—you haven't shared any memories or experiences."

"I suppose you're right."

"And I can't imagine it was very easy for Justin to see his grandfather leave again so quickly. I was surprised he didn't stick around for a while."

"He's sick. He told me he doesn't have much time and wanted to go back to Kansas to die." Nick shook his head. "I just keep thinking of how strange it's all turned out."

He ate in silence for several minutes, and Beth tried to think of how to tactfully ask him to share his past, with

Justin so thoroughly occupied. Beth finally turned to find Nick watching her rather thoughtfully. She cocked her head to one side and raised her brow as if to question his thoughts.

"I don't know how you'll feel about me after I tell you what I've come to say," Nick began, "but I hope you'll still care about me."

"My guess is that I will," Beth admitted, "but why don't you go ahead with your story, and then you'll know for sure."

Nick leaned back against a tree. "I'd known Justin's mother for much of our childhood. She was just a year younger than me. Her name was Annie. We always figured on marrying. I remember thinking, even at the age of twelve, how lucky I was. Most folks had to wait until they were adults to find true love, but I knew I had it already. Annie felt the same way."

Beth smiled, but the tug on her heart was bittersweet. "That must have been very comforting."

Nick nodded. "It was. Our folks were neighbors, and the families were close. Simon and Annie's brothers were best friends. It seemed perfect that we would be so much in love." He laughed. "Of course, I'm not sure that I really knew what love was at the age of sixteen, but I knew I wanted to spend my life with Annie."

Beth frowned and looked away. She didn't want Nick to think she was upset. "But something happened," she said, hoping he'd think her expression was nothing more than a deep thought about the matter.

"Yes. We hoped to wed as soon as she turned sixteen. We knew our folks wouldn't be all that excited about us marrying so young, but we didn't want to wait until later. We were alone one night, talking about spending our lives together, and well . . . one thing led to another. We found ourselves tempted beyond our ability to resist."

Beth grew uncomfortable but said nothing. She could hear in Nick's voice that he was just as uneasy. "I dishonored her. I should have been stronger. I planned to go and confess it all to her father, but her brother found us, and after that, no one would hear reason. Before I knew it, her brothers and father were threatening to kill me."

"But if you were willing to marry her, why should they have acted that way? It was a mistake for you to do what you did," Beth said, choosing her words carefully, "but you were willing to make it right."

"In their eyes, there was no making this right. My father finally suggested Simon take me and leave for a short time. He was certain that once things calmed down, Annie's family would see the truth of my sincerity and let us marry."

"So you left. What happened to keep you from going back?"

Nick's brown eyes seemed to darken. "Annie found out she was pregnant. That just fueled the anger her family had toward me. My father and mother tried to intercede, but it did no good."

"But what of her reputation? I would have thought they would have wanted her to marry. At least then the gossip would have been lessened."

"That's what my folks suggested, but her father was adamant. He kept saying that her shame had marked her for life, and that God would punish us both for our sin. Things just got worse and worse, and my family feared for my life." Nick turned to watch Justin for several minutes before saying anything more.

"I went back one night. I went to her bedroom window and woke her up. She was nearly eight months along, and I thought she'd never looked prettier. She was embarrassed and cried. I told her I'd come for her and that she should get her things and meet me behind the barn. She agreed."

"What happened?" Beth asked, completely engaged in the story.

"We were about three miles out of town when her father and brothers caught up to us. They threatened to kill me, and Annie went into labor. Things moved so fast after that, they kind of forgot about me temporarily. They hurried Annie back to the house. That was the last time I saw her."

"She died giving birth to Justin," Beth said matter-of-factly.

"Yes. Her father went to see my father. He told him that they would never allow me to be a part of the boy's life, and that if they ever saw me again, they would put a bullet in my head. My mother was terrified and begged me to stay away. That's when Simon suggested we head west. That was nine years ago. I've never gone back. After a while, I heard from my folks that Annie's parents had allowed them to be grandparents to Justin. I was glad about that."

"I'm so sorry, Nick. I can't begin to imagine how painful that must have been." Beth shifted uncomfortably and bit her lower lip. She didn't want to ask the question that plagued her, but she knew she had to. "Do you . . . are you still in love with Annie?"

When Nick didn't answer right away, she found she had no choice but to look at him. He was watching her with such a tender expression that Beth wanted to rush into his arms.

"Annie's gone. There will always be a special place in my memories for her, but—"

"Pa! Pa!" Justin yelled at the top of his lungs, cutting off anything further Nick might have said.

Nick jumped to his feet, as did Beth. She feared for a moment that the bear had returned to cause problems, but when Justin began laughing, she could see his cries were for an entirely different reason.

"There's a fish on my line. Hurry!"

Nick ran to the water and helped his son bring in the catch. "Good job, Justin! Just look at the size of him."

Beth watched and smiled as the father and son began to build new memories together. The past had wounded them both, but the future promised healing. She prayed that their future might also include her.

⬥

Gwen went to the front door for the fifth time. "I can't imagine what's taking the stage so long to get here. They're nearly an hour late."

"Maybe they broke an axle or wheel," Beth suggested.

Lacy pulled off her apron. "I'll ride down the trail and see if I can find them."

"No," Gwen said. "I don't want you to endanger yourself again. We'll just wait, or we'll send one of the men."

Lacy fumed. Gwen made it sound like her encounter at the store had been due to some fault of her own. "I haven't yet put myself in danger's way, so I resent that you should suggest I'd be doing it *again*." She marched off to the kitchen, determined to do exactly as she had suggested. Just let them try to stop her.

"The stage just pulled up to Lassisters'," Beth called from the front room.

"There, see," Gwen said, following Lacy into the kitchen. "No need to fret or send anyone out. They were simply running behind schedule."

But within minutes, it was apparent that something much more sinister had delayed the travelers' arrival. Dave Shepard helped the stage driver carry a man into Gallatin House, and his expression told Lacy all was not well.

"He's been shot," Dave said. "Where can we put him?"

"Take him upstairs," Gwen instructed. "The first room. Should I send Hank for the doctor?"

"No, I already sent Cubby," Dave announced as they struggled up the stairs.

Lacy and her sisters followed. Beth had thought to grab a pitcher of warm water and a couple of towels before joining them in the bedroom.

"What happened?" Gwen asked.

"Stage was held up," the driver said. "Two men with guns. My man here got spooked and fired a shot at them, and they returned fire. Caught him in the side."

Dave tore away the man's shirt to reveal the wound. "Bullet's still in there, and he's lost a lot of blood."

"Where'd it happen?" Lacy asked.

The driver glanced her way. "About four miles back. I thought for sure we'd have no trouble that close to Gallatin House. They waylaid us long enough to force everyone out of the stage and make us unhitch the team. Then they took everything of value and headed off, down the opposite way from here. I spent the next twenty minutes rounding up the horses while the passengers worked on Zeke, here."

Gwen went to work on the man's injury. "We'll have to get him cleaned up and see exactly how bad it is."

"Well, I think we should be out there tracking the men who did this," Lacy said, heading for the door. "There's still plenty of light."

"That's exactly where I'm heading, but I'm going alone," Dave announced. "This is my job, not yours."

Lacy started to say something flippant but held her tongue. Dave was doing the right thing. She watched him go, wishing that someone might go with him. There were, after all, two bandits. Two against one could prove fatal.

A quick glance over her shoulder told Lacy she'd never be missed. Her sisters and the driver were much too busy attending the injured man. She had no idea where the rest of the stage passengers were, but she'd leave that to her sisters.

Slipping out of the room, she hurried to her bedroom, tripping over Calvin as she went. The cat gave a yowl as if to raise the alarm for what Lacy had in mind.

"Sorry, Cal," Lacy said, not even stopping to see if he was hurt. She quickly closed her bedroom door and rid herself of her cumbersome dress, then pulled on her trousers. It felt good to wear the pants again. She didn't know why women had to suffer all the time with skirts. She found a well-worn cotton shirt and quickly donned it, stuffing the tails into the waistband. Lacy would need to hurry if she was going to be any use to Dave. If he got too far out and ran into the bandits alone, he might very well get himself killed.

A sense of urgency drove her onward. Her sisters would believe her crazy, but Lacy felt as if this was something she needed to do. She'd hated how helpless she'd felt during the robbery.

The driver had said there were two men who'd attacked the stage. There had been two men who'd held her up, as well.

"They're probably the same two," Lacy muttered and pulled on her boots. "And if they are, then I want in on their capture."

She hurried out the back door of the house, grabbing up her rifle as she went. Nick and Simon might protest letting her have her horse, but Lacy was prepared for them. If they asked, she'd merely say she was going to see the Shepards. She didn't need to tell them which Shepard she was hoping to see.

But as luck would have it, Nick and Simon were still busy working. Lacy slipped into the corral and caught her horse without any trouble at all. She had the beast saddled and out the gate in a matter of minutes.

So far, so good.

Lacy tried to judge the distance to the site of the robbery. She looked for signs of where the horses might have stopped when the robbery began. There would no doubt be multiple sets of prints all in one place, as well as the telltale signs of men's boots.

She finally came upon the location. She could see the hoofprints of Dave's gelding. It was the only set of horse tracks that had come from Gallatin House, so Lacy felt certain they must belong to the deputy. She walked the horse around where the stage had stopped and looked for additional prints. There were two sets besides Dave's, and they clearly led south on the road.

Lacy urged her horse to follow. She saw no other sign of Dave but knew he couldn't be too far ahead. She kept her mount moving at a slow pace so as to watch for any sign of the bandits deviating from the road. At one point, she saw a set of prints heading down a narrow path. They didn't look to belong to Dave's horse.

"Should I follow them?"

Glancing back down the road, Lacy made up her mind to check it out. Surely it wouldn't take that long. She moved her horse down the narrow trail, watching for any sign of the robbers. Pines and aspen rustled on either side of the path, causing her mount to spook.

"Easy, fella. It's all right." She patted the horse, reassuring him. Lacy felt a trickle of sweat run down her neck. *Maybe I should turn back*, she thought. After all, there wasn't any sign of Dave. For the first time, she wished she'd heeded Dave's command to stay home. She felt out of place and uncharacteristically frightened.

She had just stopped the horse to turn him when Lacy heard voices. She froze. Someone was coming down the path. For a moment, she wasn't at all sure what to do. Glancing around, she spied a small opening in the trees. She could hide there. Jumping from the horse's back, she pulled the beast with her and led him deep into the forest.

Lacy tied the horse off nearly twenty yards away, then crawled back to the path, rifle in hand, to see who was talking. The ground was hard and dry, and Lacy had to work carefully to make as little noise as possible. If she broke a single twig, they might hear her.

The horses passed by her in a leisurely fashion as the men spoke. She knew the voices immediately. They were the same men who'd robbed her at the store.

"Not as good a haul as I would have liked," one said to the other.

"You suppose we killed the shotgun?"

"Can't be sure, and I don't really care." This came from the man who'd first taken hold of her at Hank's place. Lacy got to her knees and aimed her rifle, but the men were already out of her field of vision.

She figured to head out to the path and get them from behind, but just as she tried to get to her feet, someone slammed her down to the ground.

"Be quiet," Dave Shepard whispered in her ear. "Don't move."

Lacy held still, barely able to breathe from the weight of Dave pinning her to the ground. When he finally moved away and yanked her to her feet, Lacy couldn't help but pant for breath.

"What in the world do you think you're doing? Were you just going to shoot them in cold blood?"

"They're the same ones who robbed me," Lacy declared. "And they were talking about having shot the man on the stage."

"I figured as much, but they're also part of a larger gang. One I've been trying to catch for some time now. I want the whole gang, not just part of it," Dave said, bending toward her. "And you nearly cost me months of investigating."

Lacy looked at him oddly. "I didn't know."

He rolled his eyes. "Of course you didn't. You must think I sit around and play checkers all day or read the paper. Actually, I'm not sure what you think I do all day, but I'm certain you wouldn't believe the truth if it bit you."

"You could try just telling me," she countered.

"I might, if you ever shut up long enough." He looked at her and shook his head. "Why must you always believe the worst about me? What did I ever do to make you so certain that I'm useless at what I do?"

He walked away, and Lacy was uncertain what he was doing until he reappeared, leading his horse. "I could have followed after them if you hadn't interfered," she said.

"Don't blame this on me. I was trying to help. It's not safe for you to go alone. You do realize if you'd gone out there, they would have killed you. They would have seen a boy aiming a gun and shot you dead." He shook his head. "Then I would have had to live with it."

He mounted his horse and rode off in the same direction as the bandits. Lacy stood, looking after him for a moment. Her sense of indignation was nearly overwhelmed by her guilt. Of everything Dave had said to her, the one thing that bothered her most was that he was right. She did always believe the worst about him. But why?

She retrieved her horse and continued to consider this. It wasn't like her to just harshly judge people. She supposed because of her father's death and Dave's inability to deliver the killer to her doorstep, Lacy had wrongly believed him incompetent.

Drawing a deep breath, she considered what should be done. Lacy mounted her horse and headed him in the direction Dave had gone. She couldn't deny the thought deep within her that she should apologize to Dave—ask for his forgiveness and hope that he would see how bad she felt for having disrespected him so completely.

She frowned. Was an apology absolutely necessary? She didn't want Dave getting the wrong idea. She definitely didn't want him to believe that what he thought mattered in the least to her.

Even though it did.

"Oh bother. Why should it matter?" she asked herself.

She didn't like the way it made her feel inside. She didn't want to care about him or his opinions. It was costly enough to care about her sisters.

Lacy spied Dave's horse up ahead. He hadn't gone too far and was no doubt going slow in order for her to catch up.

She trailed behind him even after they made their way back onto the main road. Finally, just before the bend that would lead them to the Lassiters', Lacy allowed her mount to catch up.

"Look, I'm sorry," she said, forcing the words to sound as sincere as possible. It wasn't that she didn't mean them, but she really hated saying them.

Dave looked at her in surprise. He actually stopped his horse and waited as if Lacy should say something more. She grew uncomfortable under his scrutiny.

"I didn't mean to cause trouble."

Still he said nothing. He just continued to look at her. What more did he want? Lacy tightened her grip on the reins and looked at her hands. "I just wanted to help." She finally looked back up at the silent man. "Well? Aren't you going to say anything?"

Dave pushed back his hat a bit. "I didn't know 'sorry' was even in your vocabulary."

Lacy squared her shoulders. "Well, when I'm wrong, I don't mind admitting it. Well . . . I mind, but . . ."

He laughed and shook his head. "You are something

else, Lacy Gallatin. God truly broke the mold when He made you."

He urged his horse on with those words, leaving Lacy to wonder if he'd just insulted her or offered her a compliment.

# CHAPTER TWENTY

When Beth saw Ellie hurrying over from the saloon, she smiled. "You look as though you feel a little better," Beth said, noting that her cuts and bruises were nearly healed.

The young woman nodded and helped Beth hang a sheet on the line. "I do. And the morning sickness has passed. I'm thickening a bit, too. It won't be long until I'll be showing and everyone will know about the baby."

"I wouldn't fret." Beth reached out to clasp Ellie's hand. "I know Simon and Nick are working on a plan."

Ellie brushed an errant tendril from her forehead, but Beth thought it was actually to brush aside a tear. "I've seen you with Nick and his boy. I'll bet that was a difficult surprise for you."

Beth noted the change in subject and smoothed out the sheet. "I suppose it was a shock, but I don't mind. Not really. Justin is a nice young boy."

"What of Mr. Murphy? I heard him tell Rafe he was mighty sweet on you," Ellie said.

"Adrian has gone—at least for the time being. Hopefully even if he comes back he'll respect my wishes and turn his attention to someone else. I've told him flatly that I have no interest in courting him."

Ellie moved closer. "Look, I need to get back. Can you get a message to Simon for me? Rafe watches me so closely. Just let Simon know I haven't given up hope, and I know that he'll figure something out."

Beth reached into the basket for one of Gwen's skirts and nodded. "I'll tell him."

"Thank you. Sometimes it's hard to keep going with things like they are, but I want to believe it will be better," Ellie said, edging away from the clothesline. "I'd best get back to the saloon. Rafe thinks I'm at the privy, and it won't take him long to send someone to find me."

"I'll be sure to give your message to Simon." Beth reached out to take hold of Ellie. "We'll just keep praying."

"I'm so afraid," Ellie said, her eyes welling. "I can't bear much more. I don't want to live if I have to live this way."

Beth took Ellie in her arms and held her while she cried. "Don't worry. We won't let that happen." The anger that always edged Beth's emotions when thinking of the abused prostitutes surfaced. She fought to keep her voice even. "I won't stop looking for an answer, Ellie. Don't give up."

Ellie pulled away. "I . . . Simon!"

Beth turned to find Simon slipping around the back of

Gallatin House. Ellie ran to his arms. Beth gave a quick glance at the back entrance to the saloon. There wasn't any sign of Rafe.

Simon ran his hand over Ellie's blond hair. "I just happened to see you and Beth out here talking. I had to chance it. Are you all right? Has he hurt you?"

"I'm scared, Simon."

"I know." He glanced past Ellie to Beth. His expression told her that he was just as worried.

"They watch me all the time," Ellie told Simon. "Rafe is always threatening me. He tells me he'll sell me, and I think he will."

"Not if I have anything to say about it."

Beth heard the back door of the saloon open and spun around. It was Wyman, and he quickly assessed the situation and crossed to where Simon and Ellie stood. Simon put Ellie behind him.

"Leave her be. This isn't her fault."

"I don't care whose fault it is." Without warning, Wyman threw a punch that landed squarely against Simon's jaw.

Ellie screamed, and Beth rushed forward to intercede. She grabbed hold of Wyman's arm. "Stop it!"

Wyman pushed her back and continued to strike out at Simon. "We warned you to stay away from her, Lassiter." He started at Simon again but was surprised when he countered and blocked the punch.

Simon hit Wyman hard and sent him reeling backward. Wyman staggered and blinked hard a couple of times. Beth took the opportunity to launch her own assault. As Wyman moved forward she grabbed the basket and threw it over his head. It wasn't much, she had to admit, but it slowed him down and gave Simon an edge.

Wyman growled and tossed the basket aside. He yelled a stream of obscenities and reached out for Simon's throat.

"What's going on here?" Dave Shepard asked.

"That's just what I was going to ask," Rafe said, coming to where the fight had just halted. He glowered at Ellie. "What are you doing? Get back to your room."

Ellie paled and Beth stepped forward. "She helped me hang a sheet, Rafe. Simon just happened to be passing by."

"I don't care. She has work to be doing for me, not you." Rafe pushed back his greasy hair and fixed his gaze on Dave. Eyes narrowing, he pointed his finger at Simon. "I want you to arrest Lassister."

"On what charge?"

Rafe looked at the man as if he were crazy. "He's trying to steal my property."

"I didn't witness him doing that," Dave replied.

"He was attacked by Wyman," Beth interjected. "Ellie and I were standing here talking, and Simon just happened by. Wyman came storming over and began hitting Simon."

Dave looked at Rafe and raised a brow. "Sounds to me like Simon could press charges for assault."

"Then I want to press charges for trespassing," Rafe demanded.

Beth shook her head. "This is Gallatin property, and he wasn't trespassing. I fully welcomed him here, just as I welcomed Ellie. If anyone is here illegally, it's you."

Rafe's face turned several shades of red as he balled his hands into fists. He raised his arm as if to strike Beth, but Dave quickly put himself between the two.

"I can take that as a threat to Miss Gallatin's well-being," Dave told the man.

Beth strained to peek around Dave's shoulder. "And I would press charges."

Rafe shook his head and turned to walk away. "Have it your way. I have other plans for making Lassiter pay for this. He knows exactly what I'll do."

∞

Despite Rafe's threats, the weeks slipped by and everyone was relieved to see that his anger had abated. Instead of sending Ellie away to his friend in Seattle, he kept her under constant guard. Ellie was still in residence, but it was clear she wasn't happy. The Gallatin sisters often spoke of how pale and thin she looked. No doubt the pregnancy was taking its toll, even though Ellie showed no visible sign of carrying a child.

The other topic of conversation had to do with the ever-increasing trouble from the highwaymen. They hadn't tried to attack any of the other businesses in the area, but twice they had attacked travelers, causing everyone to feel nervous and watchful.

"I think we've had enough gloom and trouble around here," Hank declared after church one Sunday. "It's nearly our Independence Day, and I think we should plan a celebration."

"That sounds like a wonderful idea," Patience Shepard declared.

Millie put her hand to her swollen abdomen. "We agree." Gwen and Patience laughed.

"What can we do to help, Hank?" Jerry Shepard asked.

Hank shrugged. "I came up with the idea. Everyone else

can plan it out." He put his arm around Gwen's shoulder. "I know my wife and her sisters have very little trouble planning these things. We'll have some fireworks, though—I had already thought of that, and they were shipped to me last week. There's not much, but we'll make do and have a great time."

"Of course we will," Forrest declared. "Evan and I will play a few tunes, and we'll have us a right good time."

Lacy looked up and found Dave Shepard watching her. She wasn't sure, but she got the distinct feeling he wanted to see her privately. She edged away from the gathering and made her way to the front porch. What did he want? Had she done something to upset him? Lacy smoothed her yellow gown and waited.

Within a few minutes, Dave joined her. He frowned and looked her over as if assessing an adversary. Lacy stiffened.

"I suppose I've done something to offend you," she said, unwilling to bear his scrutiny any longer.

He looked confused for a moment, then shook his head. "There you go again, thinking bad of me."

Lacy shook her head. "Sorry. What do you want?"

"I'm going to be gone for a couple of days. I want you to keep an eye open for anyone that shouldn't be around here. You know . . . strangers."

"You're asking for my help?" Lacy couldn't keep the surprise from her voice.

"It's not because I want to see you doing anything foolish," he said, looking quite stern. "I figure you might recognize them or at least their voices."

"And if I do?"

"Just pay attention to who they talk to," Dave replied.

"Nothing else. Just see who they associate with and let me know. That will help me a great deal. It could very well reveal to me the other members of their gang."

Lacy frowned. "Do you really think they'll come around here?"

"It wouldn't surprise me. They know folks will be looking for them on the road. They'll probably try to lay low for a little while, maybe even come to stay at Gallatin House, if they know I'm gone."

"All right. I'll do what I can."

Dave nodded with a hint of a smile. "Thanks. I hoped you would."

Dave walked away from Gallatin House feeling a sense of satisfaction. His plan was working. With Lacy thinking it important to stay close to home and observe the people who came and went, he wouldn't have to worry about her out there on the road, trying to find the highwaymen. With any luck at all, he'd be able to make it over to Bozeman, talk to the sheriff, and get back, and no one would be the worse for it.

He hummed to himself and mounted his horse. Glancing back at the porch, he gave a wave to Lacy.

⚯

"I like picking berries," Justin told Beth. "I like eating them even better."

Beth laughed and tousled his hair. "You'll like them even more when I bake them into a pie."

"My grandmother made pies, but she didn't let me have but a tiny piece. She said sweets weren't good for children."

247

Justin frowned. "She didn't think much of anything was good for children. She didn't want me climbing trees or playing in the creek. She just wanted me staying home all the time."

Beth leaned back on her knees. "She probably wanted to keep you safe."

"I suppose." Justin fell silent and turned his attention back to the berries.

"Did you live on a farm in Kansas?"

He nodded. "My grandpa and uncles worked really hard. I wanted to help them, but Grandmother wouldn't let me. She said it was too dangerous. Grandpa tried to change her mind, but she was always worrying. She didn't even like it when Grandpa took me fishing." He stopped and looked at Beth. "I always wished I had a mama."

"Me too," Beth replied. Memories of her childhood flashed in her mind.

"How old were you when your mama died?"

"I was just seven." Beth dusted off her hands. "I think we have enough berries. Why don't we go back to the house, and I'll fix you some lunch."

Justin gathered his things. "How'd your mama die?"

"She was trying to have a baby," Beth said, knowing that it would strike a chord with the boy.

"That's how my mama died," Justin said, his eyes wide.

"Sometimes that happens, and other times it doesn't."

"Was she a good ma?"

Beth smiled and took his bucket and poured it into her own. "She was such a good mother. She used to bake me pies like this. She taught me to cook and bake when I was younger than you."

"I wish I had a ma like that—like you."

Beth stopped and looked at Justin, feeling her heart swell. "What about a father? Don't you want him, too?"

Justin lowered his gaze to the ground. "I guess so."

"You guess so?"

He shrugged. "He didn't want to be my pa when I was born. He might not want to be my pa now."

"Justin, have you asked your father why he left when you were born?"

"My grandpa told me he was a no-account." Justin looked up, his lip quivering. "But Grandpa lied. Now I don't know what's right."

Beth put down the buckets and put her arm around the boy. "Ask your father, Justin. He's a good man. He'll tell you what really happened. He deserves to have a chance to tell his side of things."

"Do you really think so?"

"I know so."

Justin considered her words for a moment. "Did you have a good pa?"

Beth thought for a moment. "He was good, but I'm sorry to say I didn't really appreciate him until after I'd lost him. I don't want to see that happen to you. See, people make mistakes, Justin. Your father, my father—they're only human. Just like we're only human. You and I will make mistakes and hurt others, but hopefully they'll forgive us. Please think about forgiving your father, Justin. Forgive him, and ask him to tell you the truth."

∞

Nick had just finished hanging up his leather apron when Justin appeared. "You done picking berries already?"

Justin nodded. "Miss Beth is making me a pie. She said it might be a good time for me to come talk to you."

Nick sat down. "What do you want to talk to me about?"

Looking smaller than ever, Justin took several steps closer. "Tell me about my mama and you."

The boy looked so small, so vulnerable. Nick immediately felt awash in emotions. The past few weeks had been so hard. He'd longed to reach beyond Justin's protective walls and help him to feel loved and wanted.

"Well, that'll take a little time. You want to go for a walk so we won't be disturbed?" Justin nodded and turned toward the door. Nick took up his hat. "Let's just go up to the cemetery."

"Will the bears bother us there?"

Nick could see that the boy was concerned about the danger. Taking up his revolver, Nick smiled. "They can try, but I don't think we have to worry."

They walked out across the road and made their way toward the graveyard. The day had warmed considerably, and Nick felt beads of sweat line the rim under his hat. He found himself praying for wisdom.

"Is this where Beth's pa is buried?" Justin asked.

The question took Nick by surprise. "Yes. Why do you ask?"

"She told me she didn't appreciate him like she should have until after he'd died. She told me . . . well . . . she didn't want me to let that happen with you."

"I don't want it to happen, either," Nick said, making his way over to the shade of several pines. "Why don't we sit here."

Justin nodded and flopped onto the ground. Nick did

likewise and took off his hat to let the warm breeze blow through his hair. He looked at his son's hopeful expression and began to tell him about his mother.

"The thing was, we were young—too young to really know how much grief we were causing each other and the people we loved. I was wrong, Justin. I dishonored your mother. I loved her more than anything else in my life, but I lost sight of that love and took advantage of the temptation to do things that we knew were wrong."

"But she was wrong, too," Justin said, as if to defend Nick.

Nick thought about that for a moment. "Yes. We were both guilty of going against what God wanted for us, but as the man, I should have protected her. I should have waited until we were married to be intimate like that. Do you understand?"

"I think so," Justin said. "When you're a man, you should take care of other people."

"Yes. I should have stayed to take care of you, but I was afraid. I hope you'll forgive me for not being there, Justin." Nick felt tears sting his eyes. "I hope you'll give me another chance."

"Do you really want to be my pa?" Justin asked. His eyes never left Nick's face.

Nick smiled, feeling hope for the days to come. "I've never wanted anything more."

Justin grinned. "And can Beth be my ma?"

Nick started at the question. "Well . . . I don't know. Beth needs to make a decision like that."

"I told her I'd like her to be my ma," Justin admitted.

"And what did she say?"

"She said I needed to work things out with you first." Justin got to his feet and looked at his father with great expectation. "So now that we have, you can go ask her to get married so that we can be a real family."

Nick laughed and stood. "You think it's that easy, eh?"

Justin shrugged. "I think it will be real easy. You just walk up to her and ask her. She likes you—she's told me over and over how great you are."

Shaking his head, Nick put his arm out to touch his son for the first time. Justin was so like Annie, but also like Nick. He was the best parts of both of them, and Nick intended to spend the rest of his life seeing that Justin knew just how precious he was—how honored Nick was to be his father.

# CHAPTER TWENTY-ONE

Hank awoke anxious to share what he hoped to be the perfect solution to Ellie and Simon's problems. He maneuvered out of bed, hoping to keep from waking his wife. Lately, Gwen had been so worried about Ellie and Simon that she'd not been able to sleep. Hank knew she needed the extra rest.

Making his way in the early dawn, Hank was relieved to find the Lassiter brothers both awake and ready to start their day. "I hope you don't mind the intrusion," Hank offered when Nick opened the door. "I have something to discuss."

"Come on in, Hank. We were just getting ready to eat breakfast. Why don't you join us."

"No. You go ahead and eat while I explain."

Simon looked over his shoulder from the stove. "It wouldn't be any problem. We have some ham steaks and potatoes."

Hank shook his head. "No, but I will take a cup of coffee."

"Sure thing." Nick went immediately to pour him a cup. "Now, what's this all about?"

Simon brought two plates to the table and handed one to Nick. "Yeah, what do you need?"

"I'm hoping I have something that will work out this situation with you and Ellie."

Simon frowned and took a seat. He let his plate clatter a bit as it hit the table. "I don't know what you could come up with that the rest of us haven't already tried."

"Well, hear me out." Hank took a drink and put the mug on the table. "I honestly don't know why I didn't think of this earlier."

Nick joined them. "Maybe we should offer grace, and then you can explain."

Hank nodded. Nick gave a quick prayer, then both he and Simon looked to Hank for answers.

"Well, you and I know that Rafe never does anything unless it profits him. I think I've found a way to do just that and hopefully get him to release Ellie from her contract."

"How?" Simon asked. He hadn't even touched his food.

"Land." Hank smiled. "Rafe wants land. He was very angry that Vanhouten sold me his land without considering Rafe's desires. Rafe wants that piece that stretches out behind his property. I own that now."

"And you're thinking that if you offered to sell it to Rafe, he would give up his hold on Ellie?" Nick asked.

Simon frowned and he shook his head. "I doubt he'd do

anything that appeared helpful to me. Especially if it involves having to buy something."

"I'm not going to offer to sell it," Hank said. "I'm going to let him have it, free and clear."

"What?" the brothers questioned in unison.

Hank laughed. "It came to me in a dream. I'd been praying about it." He sobered a bit. "I was wrong to suggest you just steal Ellie outright. I'm about as new to this Bible and faith stuff as you are. To me, it made sense to defeat evil by taking Ellie out of Rafe's grasp, but now I can see that it's better to do it in such a way that he allows her to go. That way, you can stay here if you like and continue with your business."

"Hank, I could never hope to repay you. I don't have that much money," Simon said, looking worse than when Hank had started.

"You wouldn't need to repay me, Simon. It would be our wedding gift to you and Ellie. Gwen thinks it a fine idea."

"It's too much."

"Oh, stop it," Nick declared, pounding his fist on the table. "We've been praying for an answer, and now Hank comes with one, but you don't want to take it because of your pride?"

Simon looked rather sheepish. "I guess I hadn't thought about it that way. I didn't mean it to sound prideful. I . . . well . . . I don't like having to be in anyone's debt. Pa always said—"

"To honor your commitments and help those in need. Ellie is in need—probably in the worst possible way. You love her, and this is how you can help her."

"And you won't be in my debt." Hank downed the last of his coffee and got to his feet. "Surely your pa taught you that you don't owe for a gift."

"How do we go about this?" Simon asked, still looking doubtful.

"*We* don't. I'll negotiate the entire thing with Rafe this morning. He won't like being disturbed before noon, but I plan to use that to my advantage."

"Are you sure we shouldn't be there?" Nick asked. "At least Simon?"

"No. I think seeing Simon will only irritate the situation, and Rafe might decide to stand on pride just to spite us." He grinned. "Men can be like that, you know."

Nick laughed. "I think we've all been guilty of that." He punched Simon's arm. "What do you say? Are you going to take this gift from God and Hank?"

Simon nodded. "I won't let worries about my dignity stand in the way. I guess sometimes a man has to sacrifice that in order to better the lives of other folks. Ellie is worth it."

"Then we're agreed. I'll have Cubby wake his father and send him to the store to discuss the situation with me. I'll let you know as soon as I have Rafe's decision one way or the other, but knowing Rafe as I do, I feel confident he'll do anything to possess that land."

Hank strolled across the way toward Gallatin House. He could see Cubby chopping wood on the north side of the saloon—as if God had it all planned out. Hank chuckled to himself. He supposed God *did* have it all arranged—there was no "almost" to it.

"Don't you wish it would just cut itself?" Hank asked with a smile.

Cubby nodded. "I was just trying to think of a machine or something I could build to cut the wood for me."

"Well, if anyone could come up with something like that,

I'm sure it would be you." Hank glanced back at the saloon. "I don't suppose your pa is up yet, is he?"

Cubby snorted. "Nah, Pa doesn't get up this early. Even on slow nights like last night, he's up almost till dawn."

"Well, I need for you to wake him," Hank said. He could see Cubby's face contort in discomfort. "It's important. I want you to tell him that I'm willing to discuss a deal to get him the land he wants so he can build his hotel. Tell him to meet me in half an hour at the store if he's interested."

Putting the ax aside, Cubby nodded. "I guess he might be willing to get up for that. He's been powerful mad since you bought out all of that property."

"I know." Hank headed toward Gallatin House. "Tell him to be on time. If he's late, I very well may change my mind."

Half an hour later, to the minute, Rafe stumbled into Bishop's Emporium with a scowl on his face. He looked like a half-drowned rat with his wet hair plastered to his head. He squinted against the light and seemed to grunt thanks when Hank closed the shop door.

"This better not be a joke, Bishop," he muttered.

"It's not, Reynolds. Come into my office, and we'll talk."

Hank led the way and waited for Rafe to join him before pointing to a mug of coffee. "I brought this over from Gallatin House. Thought maybe you could use it."

"I don't intend to be awake any longer than it takes to find out what this is all about. Cubby said you were talking about the land I want."

"And he's right." Hank took a seat behind his desk and motioned for Rafe to sit in a wooden chair opposite him. "I have a proposition for you."

"All right, I'm listening." Rafe sat down and eyed Hank with contempt. "But it better be good."

"Oh, I think you'll be pleased. I propose that we each have something the other wants. I have the land that stretches out behind your place to the river and beyond."

"Yeah, and what do I have that you want?"

Hank smiled. "Ellie."

Rafe laughed out loud. "That little Gallatin gal giving you a bad time of it, Bishop?"

"Don't be crude, Rafe. I want her contract so that she'll be free to marry Simon. I want her released from your employment, and I'm willing to give you the land in return."

"You mean sell it to me, don't you?"

Hank shook his head and toyed with a pencil. "No. I mean give it to you, free and clear."

Rafe slapped his knee. "You'd give good land for that waste of womankind?"

"If she's such a waste, then it shouldn't be difficult for you to make up your mind about this."

"Why would you do this? That girl don't mean nothin' to you."

"She means a great deal. My wife and her sisters have taken a liking to her and worry about her well-being. Not only that, but they are complete advocates for true love." Hank shifted and looked Rafe in the eyes. "I can't see a smart man like you letting pride stand in the way of a good business deal, but I suppose I could be wrong."

"So if I tear up Ellie's contract and let her go, you'll deed that land over to me? How soon?"

"Let Cubby come over and help with the store, and I'll

go today and have the lawyer draw up the papers. With any luck, you can have them in a couple of days."

Rafe leaned back and rubbed his chin. "Seems you want this signed and done awfully quick. You need to give me time to think it over."

Hank shook his head. "No. This is a limited offer. You either decide here and now that you will agree to my terms, or I'll let Simon Lassiter have the land."

"What!" Rafe jumped up. "You no-good two-timer. I knew there was more to this than you were letting on."

Hank got to his feet and shrugged. "Rafe, I came to you and posed my proposition. Either you want the land or you don't. I'm not going to play games. Give me your decision."

∞

Lacy found Cubby watching her with such intensity that she stopped dusting the shelves of Bishop's Emporium and put her hands on her hips. "What's with you, Cubby? You keep staring at me like I've grown a second head."

"I was just wondering how I could win your heart, Miss Lacy."

"I thought we talked about this. I'm much too old for you."

He looked at her as if he'd just gotten a brilliant idea. "If I killed that mean ol' black bear, would you want to court me then?"

"No. It's not about seeing you perform heroic deeds." Lacy came to where Cubby was arranging a display of tools. "You are a sweet fella, Cubby, but you have to put this from your mind. I think of you as a little brother—not as a suitor."

"I'm not that young!" he protested. "You aren't that old. I could make a good husband for you. Besides, you'd marry me fast enough if I found your pa's killer," he countered as she turned to go back to her dusting.

Lacy whirled around and looked at him with barely contained anger. "That's not funny, Cubby. You shouldn't joke about something so serious."

"I wasn't joking." He smiled rather satisfactorily and crossed his arms against his chest. "I heard something."

She didn't want to give in to his smug enticement, but she couldn't help herself. "What did you hear?"

He grinned in full. "First tell me you'll marry me if I catch your pa's killer."

Lacy shook her head. "I can't marry anyone, Cubby. I don't love you or anyone else in that way. If you were as much a man as you claim to be, you would know it wasn't right to try to force a lady to do such a thing."

His face lost its joyfulness as he considered her words.

"Tell me what you heard, Cubby. Please."

He lowered his head. "I heard Pa and Wyman say something about what really happened the night your pa died. I didn't hear anything else 'cause one of the girls came to ask Pa a question. But I'm thinking that if I worked it right, I might be able to get them talkin' about it again, and maybe I could find out what they know."

"Are you absolutely sure that's what you overheard?"

"I'm sure. They were talking about all the problems they've had since that night. I'm sure they know plenty."

"I've always suspected they did," Lacy said, biting her lip to keep from saying more. There was no need to tell Cubby everything she thought. "So do you suppose you could get them to talk when another adult is in earshot? Maybe Dave or someone could listen in from the back room while you get them to talk at the bar?"

Cubby flailed his arms like a small child having a tantrum. "I'm man enough to overhear anything they got to say. I'm tired of you seeing me as a kid and nothing more."

He stormed out of the store, muttering and cursing all the way.

# CHAPTER TWENTY-TWO

Fourth of July Sunday started much as any other Sunday might have. Services were held at Gallatin House, and afterward, folks moved outside to set up for the regular after-church dinner. The warm weather made it a perfect day for Beth to don her new gown. She'd worked on it for weeks in between mending and other chores. Now, knowing what she planned to do, it all seemed perfect. A new gown for a new life.

She had taken such special care with the pattern. The dress was stylish and fit her like a glove, with its short, puffed sleeves and rounded neckline. The blue-green calico was a good color for her eyes. With a quick glance in the front-room mirror, Beth smiled. Her sun-kissed face glowed with health and happiness.

Beth thought back on the conversation she'd shared with Patience Shepard that morning. Jerry had been handling the sermon and reading over his notes when Beth took Patience aside for some advice.

"I'm in love with Nick," she told the older woman.

"That doesn't surprise me," Patience replied with a broad smile.

"Well," Beth said, drawing a deep breath, "I wondered if maybe I should tell him."

Patience laughed. "I suppose that would clarify the matter."

"I love both of them—Nick and Justin," she continued. "I just don't want to waste any more time. Nick thinks I expect to be courted. Do you suppose it would be all right to explain to him that I don't need the time to make up my mind? I know what kind of man he is, and I know my heart. I think the extra time would only cause Justin more heartache."

"If this is what your heart is telling you to do, I think you should talk with Nick. After all, folks on the frontier have little opportunity to stand on ceremony," Patience counseled.

Beth thought briefly of the bold and confident Lady Effingham and wished she could feel as capable. But Lady Effingham was just a character in a book.

Over the weeks, Beth had gradually lost interest in her books. Real life seemed far too interesting, and at night her mind was too full of questions and concerns to lose herself in anything other than her Bible reading. She hadn't expected the change to come so quickly, but in fact, she found she didn't really miss the romantic and intriguing tales at all. She had her own romance, and God was more real than ever.

Throughout the festivities that day, Beth observed Nick

and Justin as they joined some of the other men and boys at play. They seemed happy to participate in the makeshift baseball game and later teamed up against Simon in horse-shoes. Though she could still sense their hesitation around each other, Beth could clearly see that they were becoming a family. And she wanted to be a part of it.

By early evening the games gave way to dancing, singing, and, of course, more food. Beth danced with both Nick and Justin, as well as a bevy of others. She felt light as a feather and imagined that being at the grandest European ball could not begin to equal the joy she had in this simple celebration. It was nearly nine-thirty when Hank set off the first of the fireworks. The children were notably impressed and cheered for more. Silver ribbons cut across the skies, bringing even more approval from the observers. Over the next half hour, Hank arranged a display to rival that of Bozeman's yearly festivities.

"Are you having a good time?" Nick asked Beth.

She glanced up from where she sat on the ground. "I am. It's been a wonderful day."

Nick sat down beside her on the blanket. "I'm glad you're sitting back here away from the others. I had hoped to get a chance to talk to you privately."

Beth laughed softly. "I have to admit I had the same thing in mind when I chose this spot." She looked around. "Where's Justin?"

"He fell asleep, and Simon offered to take him back to the house for me." He reached out and brushed back a wisp of hair that had fallen down around Beth's cheek. "So what did you want to talk to me about?"

Beth knew the moment of truth had come, and she wasn't

about to play coy and timid. This matter was much too important. "I don't want to waste time courting you, Nick."

He looked momentarily confused and started to protest when Beth put her hand to his mouth. "I already know I love you," she said with a smile. "I just think for Justin's sake, we shouldn't wait to marry. If you and I need to get to know each other better, we can just do it as a married couple. Justin needs to have a family in full, and I want very much to be his mother." She paused and let her hand trail against Nick's jaw before adding, "And your wife."

Nick just stared at her for several moments. There was enough of a glow from the moon to make out his features. Beth thought him more handsome than any other man in attendance. When he took hold of her hand and pulled it to his lips, she thought she might very well forget to breathe.

"You know, I thought all day long about how I might convince you to marry me right away. I went through at least a dozen ideas, but none of them seemed just right. Then I come over here to bare my heart and soul, and you just propose to me, calm as can be." He laughed, and Beth could see the pleasure in his expression. "Someday I'm going to enjoy telling our children how you offered to marry me, just as bold as brass."

Beth laughed then. "For a moment I thought I'd offended you—that you were going to tell me you'd changed your mind, that you and Justin didn't need me in your lives."

Nick took hold of her hands. "That will never happen. I need you for more reasons than I can attempt to express."

"So what should we do now?" Beth asked.

"The pastor will be here in two weeks. Do you suppose

you can wait that long?" He leaned in close and pulled her to him. Their faces were only inches apart.

"Can you?" she whispered with a smile.

He shook his head and pulled away. "It won't be easy, but I've heard it said that good things are worth waiting for."

"Two weeks will seem like an eternity," she said finally, "but I suppose it will give Justin time to get used to the idea."

"If anyone's already used to the idea, it's Justin. He's asked me twice today if I intended to marry you soon so that he could have a mother."

Beth felt tears come to her eyes. "Oh, Nick. I already love him so much. He reminds me of myself—the pain and sadness. I just want to make it all go away."

"And I want to make it go away for you," Nick said, gently stroking her cheek, "and for me. I want it more than you can possibly know."

❧

The crew that assembled to eat breakfast at Gallatin House the next morning was a bit subdued after the previous night's festivities. Beth's announcement, however, changed that. "I'm getting married in two weeks to Nick."

Gwen dropped her fork. It clattered against the plate. "You're what?"

"I'm getting married," Beth said matter-of-factly.

"In two weeks," Lacy offered, and Beth nodded.

Gwen looked at Beth in disbelief. "When did you decide this? Does Nick know?"

Hank and Dave began to laugh. "With a Gallatin girl involved, he probably hasn't heard yet."

"Of course he's heard," Beth said, putting her hands to her hips. "I told him last night."

This only caused Hank and Dave to laugh all the more. Dave nearly fell off the bench as Hank punched him in the arm. "Do you . . . do you . . . hear this? She told . . . him," Hank stammered out between gasps for air.

Gwen looked at the men with clear annoyance. "Will you two settle down? I need to hear what Beth has to say."

"I think . . . she's . . . said . . . enough." Hank's blue eyes seemed to gleam as he waggled his finger at Beth. Dave clutched his side, and Beth thought for a moment tears might stream down his face from the sheer hysteria of the moment.

"Men." Beth rolled her eyes and looked at Gwen. "I know it's short notice, but we don't want anything fancy. The pastor will be visiting in two weeks, so we decided that would be perfect. We just think it's important for Justin. We want to give him a family, and the sooner, the better."

The shock had worn off her sister's expression. "As long as you're sure," Gwen said. "As long as you love him."

Beth nodded. "I do. I love him very much."

"Will you still be able to come over and help us with Gallatin House?" Gwen asked. "We still have most of the summer and fall, and we'll be busier than ever."

"I'll be here. Justin can come and help, too. Unless, of course, Nick wants his help with the horses." She considered that as a strong possibility. "I don't think there should be any problem."

"Just tell Nick what he'll be doing," Hank said, still snickering.

Beth picked up a dry piece of toast and threw it at Hank.

He dodged just in time, but it hit Dave in the face, causing Lacy to laugh.

"Well, this day is off to a great start," Gwen said, shaking her head.

⚬∞⚬

That evening Lacy was restless. She couldn't keep from thinking about what Cubby had said. A part of her wanted to march right over to Rafe's and demand answers, but she knew the futility and stupidity of such actions.

Her biggest dilemma was Dave. Should she tell him what Cubby had said? Since he'd had so little time to really investigate George Gallatin's death, maybe this would be the one lead he needed.

"But he's got the highwaymen on his mind," she murmured. She walked to her bedroom window and pulled back the curtain to see the sun setting in the west.

"Well, if I'm going to say anything to him tonight," she reasoned, "I'm going to have to do it right away." She knew Dave usually walked around the area at this time and then retired for the night.

Biting her lower lip, Lacy paced her room for another five minutes before deciding to go tell Dave what she knew. If he discarded Cubby's announcement or told her to forget about it, then Lacy would just handle things another way.

Knowing her sisters would be getting ready for bed, Lacy tiptoed to the back stairs and crept down, praying no one would hear her and come to investigate. She reached the kitchen and breathed a sigh of relief, then lit a lamp and made her way through the dining room, just reaching the front door when she heard the bathing room door upstairs open. She hugged the side of the stairs and turned the lamp as low as possible without extinguishing it. When no one came down the stairs or called out, she felt confident that she'd gone unnoticed.

The night air held a damp chill that suggested rain was soon to be upon them. The covered passageway to the addition where Dave was staying would keep her relatively safe from any light sprinkle, but a downpour would be a completely different story.

When Lacy entered the building, she could see a light coming from under Dave's door. Hopefully he was there and she could quickly pass on her news and be done with it. She knocked lightly and held her breath, noticing that her heart was racing. She heard movement in the room and squared her shoulders in preparation of what she would say.

However, when Dave opened the door wearing nothing but his trousers, Lacy's mouth dropped open. His muscular chest was all she could think about, and her reason for coming completely fled her thoughts. She wondered if the tuft of blond hair in the center of his chest was coarse or soft. The thought ran through her like a bolt of lightning, and her gaze snapped up to meet Dave's eyes.

"What are you doing here?" he asked.

"I . . . ah . . ." She stared down at the lamp in her hand. "You . . . ah . . . should put a shirt on."

Dave chuckled low. "I was getting ready to go to bed. I don't usually wear a shirt. But I suppose it would be prudent." He turned and walked back into the room, leaving Lacy at the door.

She felt strangely uncomfortable. Why did this man have to make her feel so cotton-mouthed and dull-witted? Lacy chided herself for being so silly. There was no reason for this. She'd seen men without their shirts before. Rafe and Wyman were often minus theirs.

When Dave came back with the shirt in place, she felt her senses return. "Look, I just came to tell you something I heard—something about my father's killing."

He frowned. "Have you been out risking your life again?"

She met his stern gaze. "No. This information came to me."

"Tell me about it, then."

"Cubby was helping me at the store when Hank went to Bozeman. He was trying to impress me and asked me . . . well, it's not important what he asked, but he told me Rafe and Wyman were talking and that they said something about what had really happened the night my father was killed."

"What else did he say?"

"Nothing," Lacy said. "But that's proof enough for me that Rafe and Wyman are hiding the truth."

"You said Cubby asked you something. What was it?"

"It's not important."

"I'll be the judge of that," Dave said, narrowing his eyes. "What did Cubby ask you that caused him to tell you something that could only lead to incriminating his father?"

Figuring Dave wouldn't take the matter seriously or help her if she didn't come clean, Lacy drew a deep breath. "Cubby wants to court me."

Dave grinned and leaned back against the doorjamb. "He does, now, does he? What is he, fifteen?"

"That's not important. He wanted to impress me—to do something that would make me love him, I suppose." She shook her head and looked up at the ceiling. "Don't ask me why. It's just not important."

"Of course it's important. It speaks of a young man who would sacrifice his own father for the woman he loves."

Lacy looked at him and noticed that he hadn't bothered to button his shirt. That tuft of hair was beckoning her again. She frowned. This was ridiculous. She looked at Dave's grin and steadied her nerves. "You can be as amused as you want about this, but Cubby felt confident that Rafe and Wyman knew what really happened. They might very well know who fired the fatal shot. I thought you should know. I suggest you get Cubby to set them up and position yourself in a place where you can overhear the conversation. Then when they reveal the truth, you can . . . well . . . do whatever needs to be done."

"And if they don't reveal the truth?" he asked. "Should I beat it out of them?"

Lacy considered this a moment, then nodded. "If need be."

Dave laughed and straightened. He surprised her by turning her around and pointing her toward the door. "Go to bed, Lacy. I have an early morning, and you do, too."

She turned in his arms, careful to keep the lamp from burning either of them. "I'm not ready to go anywhere until I hear you say you'll check into this."

Dave's eyes seemed to devour her as he leaned closer. "If you don't go, I'll kiss you again."

Lacy felt her own eyes widen. She turned and hurried for the safety of the door. Dave laughed heartily behind her, but she didn't dare stop to say anything about it. Stopping would be her undoing, because in that moment she very much wished he had kissed her.

# CHAPTER TWENTY-THREE

"Are you ready?" Gwen asked Beth.

Gazing at her reflection in the mirror, Beth nodded. "I think so. I'm nervous."

Gwen laughed. "That's to be expected. Every bride gets the jitters on her wedding day." She took hold of Beth and turned her from the mirror. "You look beautiful. The dress suits you quite well."

"Well, I wouldn't have it, if not for your help." She pulled at the folds of cream-colored silk and smiled. "I never thought I would have anything this grand on such short notice."

"I wasn't sure you would, either, but Hank was able to get the material in Bozeman. It was as if God just had the fabric there waiting for you." She smiled. "The sewing was the easy part."

Gwen fanned the skirt out behind Beth. "The simple lines suit you, and corseted in as you are, your waistline looks hardly bigger than a minute. Nick will be in absolute awe of your beauty."

Beth toyed with the piece of lace she was using for a head-piece. "I hope he'll like it as much as you think he will."

"It's been my experience that men really don't pay too much attention to such details anyway. Nick will see your face, and he will lose himself in thoughts of how much he loves you and how blessed he is to be your husband."

"Oh, I hope so. For so long, I've read stories about falling in love and marrying, and frankly, my story is nothing like them."

"Well, you've had your share of adventure," Gwen declared. "I thought for sure when Justin arrived that everything would change."

"And it did," Beth admitted. "But only for the good. I couldn't see being angry at Nick for the past. He was just a boy, and the problems he created made it hard for him to take responsibility. Even I can see that."

"But are you sure you're ready to be a mother and wife?" Gwen asked. Her gaze seemed to search Beth's face for the truth.

Beth smiled. "I love Nick with all my heart, and I already love Justin as much as anyone could love their own flesh-and-blood child. He's so . . . easy to care about."

"That doesn't mean there won't be hard times."

"I know. Pastor Flikkema mentioned that when he talked to me alone. He said that Justin would probably have some resentment—even anger toward me at times. I hope he won't, but if he does, we'll just do our best. I know God has brought me to this place, and He will surely be faithful to see me through it."

"I believe He will," Gwen replied. "Just know that I'm always here for you."

Beth looked around her bedroom. It was the last time she would be here—the last time she would call this room her own.

"Come on. Everyone is waiting." Gwen opened the bedroom door as Lacy approached from the other side.

"You getting cold feet?" she asked.

Beth laughed. "No. I'm ready."

"Here are your flowers," Lacy said, handing Beth a bouquet.

Beth took the wild flowers and looked first to Lacy and then to Gwen. "I love you both so much. I'm so glad you're here to share this day with me." Her sisters hugged her in unison, and Beth felt tears escape.

"Now, now. None of that," Gwen said, dabbing at Beth's eyes with a lace-edged handkerchief. "This is a day of joy. Save the tears for another time."

Gwen and Lacy led the way down the back stairs. Beth followed, whispering a prayer for God's blessing on her marriage. Her sisters made their way from the kitchen through the short connecting hall that opened into the large gathering room.

Beth drew a deep breath and waited for them to take their places near the fireplace. She smiled when Justin appeared and held out his hand.

"You ready to be my ma?"

"Are you ready to be my son?"

Justin grinned and took hold of Beth. "I was ready two

weeks ago, but Pa said you had to have time to get ready. You sure are pretty, but I think you could have gotten ready quicker than two weeks."

Beth suppressed a chuckle and allowed the boy to lead her forward. Her sisters had done a remarkable job in preparing the house for the wedding. There were flowers everywhere, and the entire house carried their sweet summer scent.

Walking down the makeshift aisle, Beth could see the happy faces of the well-wishers who'd gathered after church for the ceremony. Her attention didn't remain on them for long, however, when she caught sight of Nick's smoldering gaze. There was a smile on his lips and an expression that suggested he was quite satisfied with himself.

When they reached Pastor Flikkema, the ceremony began. Justin handed Beth over to his father, then stood beside Simon to bear witness.

Beth could feel the warmth of Nick's hands beneath her gloves. She felt such a flood of contentment—of sheer delight. Now she would have the family and home that she'd always prayed for. Now she would have the forever love she'd always dreamed of.

When the pastor announced that Nick could kiss his bride, Beth trembled. They had waited to share this kiss—to seal their marriage in this special way. Nick pushed aside the lace and gently swept Beth into his arms.

Gone were the people who had joined them. Gone were her sisters and his brother. Gone were all the romantic notions and stories that had filled her head for years. There was only now—there was only Nick.

His warm lips met hers in such a tender fashion that Beth couldn't help but sigh against him. She felt her knees weaken as Nick deepened the kiss. His touch was unlike anything she'd ever known. It gave her a sense of overwhelming pleasure—of love and of coming home.

The congregation applauded and cheered the union. As soon as Nick pulled away from their embrace, Beth's sisters flocked to her side and kissed her cheek. Next, Simon was congratulating her.

"I've never had a sister before," he told her. He kissed her cheek and smiled.

"It can be a real trial," she said, laughing. "I guess we're both in for a few changes."

"They will all be good ones," Simon promised. "I'm sure of it."

"What about me?" Justin asked, tugging on Beth's skirt.

She looked down and smiled. "You're one of the best parts of this day. See, I didn't just promise God that I would be a good wife to your pa. I promised I would be the best mama I could be for you." She opened her arms to him. "I love you, Justin."

He wrapped his arms around her waist and hugged her close. "I love you, Mama."

Beth's eyes welled with tears. She caught sight of Nick and realized that he, too, had damp eyes. The blessing of the day was upon them. They were now a family.

Lacy watched Beth for a few more moments before slipping out of the house. She was happy for her sister, but something about the day caused an aching in her heart that Lacy couldn't quite explain. Everyone had someone to love except for her.

*But I never wanted love,* she told herself. *I don't want to deal with the pain that comes when you love someone and lose them.*

She thought of the countless times she'd cried herself to sleep, longing for her mother. All of her life she had felt the emptiness her mother caused when she died. Lacy had tried her best to harden her heart. Anger sometimes eased the pain, but only momentarily.

Moving out across the grassy lawn, past the vegetable garden and the hot springs pool, Lacy followed the road to the cemetery. The warmth of the July sun bore down on her, but Lacy gave it little thought. The tall pines that sheltered the graves would offer her shade and keep her cool. She often thought this was the most perfect place for sorting out her thoughts. It comforted her, even though it reminded her of death and sorrow.

"I suppose I'm strange that way," she said, walking to her father's gravestone. She had placed flowers there earlier when gathering blossoms for Beth's bouquet. Somehow it just seemed appropriate.

"Pa, I'm still trying to get you justice. I'm hoping God has told you as much."

She glanced up through the trees to the cloudless blue sky. "I just want you to know that I'll never give up. Even if everyone else forgets—I won't."

Across the valley, the mountains stood in majestic splendor. The snow was gone now, but only for a short time. Lacy knew that soon enough it would return, and the chill of winter would be upon them. Frankly, she liked the cold. When the winter storms came, there was less traffic—fewer people. She liked that. She could imagine herself leaving Gallatin House to head up into the mountains. Sometimes Lacy even entertained herself with thoughts of just writing her sisters a letter and taking off. Maybe now that Beth was married, she'd do just that.

She'd heard Hank talk about whether they would remain in the area or move north to accommodate the railroad. There had even been discussion as to whether or not Gallatin House was even needed. The store was doing a great deal of business and would no doubt continue to do so whether they moved it or not. If they did move, Gwen and Hank could tend the store, while Beth and Nick would have the blacksmith shop. There really wouldn't be a place for Lacy in either of their families.

How sad it would be when everyone went their own way. Lacy couldn't imagine life without her sisters being there to advise her. Not that she'd always listened.

She smiled. "I suppose I really don't listen much at all."

She heard someone coming up the road behind her and turned. Dave Shepard tipped his hat as he came closer. "I hope you don't mind the intrusion. I saw you head over here."

Lacy felt her heart skip a beat. Her feelings for Dave confused her. She found him annoying and demanding, yet at the same time, there was something about him that caused her to catch her breath.

"I don't mind," she said, moving to a stand of aspen trees. The green leaves fluttered almost musically in the breeze. "I just came here to think."

Dave eyed her as if to challenge her statement, then looked off toward the mountains. "You think too much."

Lacy shook her head. "I don't think that's possible. A great many folks don't bother to think at all."

"Well, I've been thinking plenty. I want you to stop trying

to find your father's killer. I know you made a promise to Gwen regarding it."

"I also told her I couldn't keep that promise," Lacy replied.

"There's too much at stake here, Lacy. You've got to realize you'll only end up getting hurt."

She frowned. "There is a lot at stake, and that's exactly why I can't stay out of it. I should have known better than to tell you about Cubby and what he'd heard. I should have known that if I wanted anything done, I'd have to do it myself."

Turning to leave, Lacy was shocked when Dave grabbed her and pushed her up against the trunk of an aspen. "You listen to me, Lacy Gallatin. This isn't serving coffee with laudanum to keep cowboys from drinking themselves into a reckless state of mind."

"I never thought it was," she said, feeling rather light-headed. There was something about Dave Shepard's touch that left her unable to think clearly. "I only . . . I just don't like . . . well, that you aren't doing anything about it."

"I've been doing more than you realize. I already had suspicions about Rafe and Wyman and what they might know. I don't need you getting in the middle of it. In fact, if you're not careful, you'll ruin all the hard work I've already done."

"What hard work?"

He shook his head but continued to hold her fast. "Lacy, I'm good at my job. That's why the sheriff hired me. I'm good at figuring out people. When you add that to my tracking abilities and the fact that I'm a crack shot, I make a pretty decent deputy, if I do say so myself. I think there is far more going on than meets the eye, where Rafe is concerned. I think he might very well be tied in with the highwaymen, as well as hold the key to unlocking the truth about your father's death."

"Then why haven't you arrested him?" Lacy asked in an accusing tone.

"Lacy, you've got to understand that I don't have enough evidence to hold him. And until I do, I don't want to scare him off or cause him to do something foolish to cover his tracks. I want him relaxed. I want him to think that he's played all of his cards just right and that no one has any reason to suspect him."

"I don't see how that makes sense." She suddenly felt very self-conscious. Dave had been holding her in place for several minutes now, and it felt as if his fingers were burning holes right through the material of her dress and into her shoulders. She tried to move, but he held her fast.

"The idea is to give him enough rope with which to hang himself," Dave explained. He seemed oblivious to Lacy's attempts to break his hold. "Rafe and Wyman are evil, there's no doubt about it. But I have to handle this in a way that will result in a legally successful conclusion. If I act too fast or arouse their suspicions too soon, we might very well never know the truth."

She searched his face. "Why have you never told me this before?"

"Because the less you know, the better. I don't want any-one trying to see what I know by getting to you. I won't put you in danger that way, and you need to not put yourself in danger, either."

"But I could help," Lacy offered. "I'm a good tracker and rider. You know I can handle a gun."

"No."

"But why?" Her voice held a pleading tone. "Why won't you let me help you?"

Dave pulled her tight against his chest and bent her backward ever so slightly. Lacy didn't even have time to close her eyes before his mouth captured hers in a long, passionate kiss.

When he pulled away, Lacy felt as if every thought she'd had in her head had fled. She looked at him in stunned silence while he watched her, assessing her response.

Finally Dave chuckled. "I wish I'd known earlier it was that easy to shut you up."

Cubby saw Dave Shepard kissing Lacy and pounded his fist against his side. *No wonder she won't consider courting me. She already has someone.* He frowned.

"That ought to be me kissing her," he muttered.

He thought of marching over to the cemetery and challenging Dave to a gunfight. Cubby played the scene out in his head. He would stand at one end of the road, and Dave would be at the other. They'd walk toward each other and when they got close enough, he would draw his gun and shoot Dave dead.

"Then she'd love me," Cubby said softly. "If there were no Dave Shepard, Lacy would have to love me."

# CHAPTER TWENTY-FOUR

"Bishop has sent that no-good Lassiter and his nephew to Bozeman to get the legal papers for the land," Rafe told Wyman. "I've agreed to give Ellie over to Hank as soon as I have the signed deed in hand." He gave a maniacal laugh. "I didn't say, however, what kind of shape she'd be in."

Wyman offered Rafe a look that suggested he didn't exactly get his boss's meaning. "What kind of shape should she be in?"

"The last thing I need is for this mess to give any of the other girls an idea as to how they can earn their freedom. I've never been one to tolerate sass or defiance, and them that's been with me for a while know it full well. Giving in to

Bishop's demands might suggest that I'm getting soft. I don't need that kind of reputation."

"Well, I don't know what you can do about it now." Wyman rubbed at his jaw. "You've already agreed to the deal, and while it wasn't accomplished as fast as Bishop wanted it, it's too late to go back on it now."

Rafe shook his head and poured himself a beer. "I don't intend to go back on it. I merely intend to put across my point to the other girls."

"And how will you do that?"

"That's where you come in." Rafe tossed back the beer, then slammed the mug to the bar. "I want you to teach Ellie a lesson, and I want the other girls to know exactly what's going on."

Wyman smiled, and understanding flooded his expression. "I think I'm going to enjoy this."

"Just don't enjoy it too much. I don't want her dead."

Wyman shrugged. "I don't have to kill her to prove a point."

⌘

"So I presume Nick and Beth got off on their trip," Patience said as she served Gwen hot tea and cakes.

"Yes. They'll only be gone a few days, but I think it will be good for them to be alone."

Patience nodded. "I completely agree. Are you taking care of Justin?"

Gwen leaned back in the soft, cushioned chairs and shook her head. "No. He's with Simon, and frankly, I'm glad. I've been so tired just trying to keep up with the chores that I would never have the ability to keep up with a young boy."

"They can be trying. I remember when Dave was little. Goodness, but it was often like he was three or four children instead of just one."

Gwen nodded and picked at the cake. "Lacy was that way, too. She could run rings around Beth and me. So maybe it's not just a boy thing."

"Has Lacy been able to take on some of the extra chores in Beth's absence?"

"She has, but she's got enough of her own work to handle. And," Gwen said, picking up her cup of tea, "Lacy isn't nearly as thorough as Beth. If Lacy sees a stain on the tablecloth, she'll give it a good scrubbing, but if it doesn't come out, she lets it go and moves on to something else. Beth would work with it until that stain was gone. I've seen times when she was battling a mark for hours in the evening, long after the rest of us had concluded our work."

"Sometimes those things become personal challenges," Patience said. "Oh, did I tell you that young Ben Mills came to work for us? Jerry hired him off the Koeber ranch."

"I hadn't heard."

"Jerry wants to expand. He figures with the railroad finally coming in—even if it's not through Gallatin Crossing—it would be profitable to increase the herd size and offer to sell beef to the workers."

"That does sound smart," Gwen said, suppressing a yawn. She put down her tea and closed her eyes for a moment while Patience continued talking about their plans. The last thing she remembered was Patience saying something about Jerry also purchasing some piglets to fatten.

When Gwen woke up a little later, she found Patience had covered her with a blanket. She noted from the clock on the mantel that she hadn't been asleep much more than an hour, but she was embarrassed to have nodded off like that.

"Patience?" Gwen called out, pulling the blanket away.

"I see you're awake. Did you have a good rest?" Patience asked as she came into the room. She smiled lovingly. "I couldn't bear to wake you. I hope you'll forgive me."

"I was thinking much the same—hoping you would forgive me for falling asleep." Gwen stood and began to fold the blanket. "I feel so ashamed. I don't know what's gotten into me. Sometimes I don't sleep very well at night, and with all the worry about Ellie and Simon and Beth's wedding plans . . . well, I've met myself coming and going."

"Might there be something else?" Patience asked, coming to take the blanket from Gwen.

Gwen threw her a confused look. "What do you mean?"

"Might you be with child?"

The question hit Gwen like a bolt of lightning. "Pregnant?" She hadn't considered the possibility at all. As much as she longed for a child of her own, Gwen hadn't even been able to stop and think about such things for a long time.

But with Patience looking at her with a knowing smile, Gwen began to do a mental calculation. She touched her hand to her stomach. It was possible. She looked at Patience. "I'm pregnant?"

Patience laughed. "Well, only time will tell for certain, but that would be my guess. Some women have horrible morning sickness, while others have fainting spells and dizziness. For me, I was always tired and always hungry."

Gwen nodded. "I have had a bit of an appetite lately." She sank into the chair and shook her head. "But I never once thought about it being a baby causing all the fuss."

Patience put the blanket aside and came to sit beside Gwen. "How far along do you suppose you are?"

"It's been at least two months since . . . well . . . since my last . . ." She let the words trail off, feeling suddenly embarrassed by the intimacy of discussing such things as monthly cycles. "It might have been three months. I can't recall clearly."

"In another month or two, you should be able to feel some movement. It's like the tiniest flutter of wings at first. My mama used to say it was the angels keeping the baby company."

Gwen smiled at the thought. "Hank will be so excited. We've wanted this very much. I was so jealous of Millie that I could hardly stand myself. And then Beth married and instantly became a mother, as well."

"And now you will join them. How exciting. Oh, I will start sewing things for the little one immediately. What fun this will be!"

Gwen could only nod at the thought. She was going to have a baby. The very idea left her feeling both overwhelmed and happy at the same time.

∞

Lacy heard the first scream and stopped what she was doing to investigate. A second cry came very nearly on the heels of the first. Someone was clearly in trouble, and immediately Lacy thought of the bear. She grabbed up the revolver and headed out the back door with Major at her side.

"No! Stop!" The cry came from one of the prostitute rooms.

Lacy couldn't be sure, but she thought it sounded like Ellie. "Come on, boy. Let's see what's going on."

She stepped cautiously toward the saloon. The sound of commotion—fighting—could be heard. This was accompanied by a man yelling obscenities and accusations. Lacy listened for a moment but couldn't clearly make out what was being said.

The woman screamed again and then came the sound of splintering wood. Lacy pressed on, though apprehension and fear coursed up her spine. She had no way of knowing exactly what was happening, but it was violent and wrong.

Major growled when they came to the door of one of the rooms. Lacy felt her stomach sicken. It was Ellie's room. She thought to knock but knew she'd never be heard. The man was continuing his tirade and now Lacy could tell it was Wyman.

She pushed open the door just as Wyman threw Ellie into the wall. The woman slid down to the floor. Her eyes fought to remain open, and Lacy wondered if she could even focus on the man standing in front of her.

"What do you think you're doing?" Lacy called out. "Get away from her. Stop it!"

"Mind your own business," Wyman demanded. He picked Ellie up and slammed her against the wall again. She moaned softly, but this time there was nothing else. He threw a punch into the nearly unconscious woman's face.

Lacy grew sick at the thought that she might witness Ellie's murder if something didn't stop Wyman. It was then she remembered her revolver. She brought the gun up and pointed it at the enraged man.

"I said stop."

Wyman glanced at her only momentarily, but it was enough for him to spy the piece. "And I said to mind your own business. You're trespassing. Now get off this land."

"Not without her. Rafe has already made a deal with Hank to set her free. I'm taking Ellie home with me."

Wyman laughed and let Ellie fall to the floor. He took a step in Lacy's direction but stopped when she cocked the gun. "Are you planning to shoot me over a prostitute?"

"If need be, I will."

There must have been something in her expression that betrayed the truth of the matter to Wyman. He folded his arms against his chest and narrowed his eyes. His gaze was unnerving, but Lacy held her ground.

"You have no right to beat her. You've very nearly killed her—just look at her face," Lacy said, her anger building.

"She got mouthy with me. That was reason enough."

"There's never a good reason for hitting another person, especially a woman."

Wyman guffawed at this. He threw his head back and laughed so loud that Lacy wasn't entirely sure he hadn't lost what little sanity he possessed. The gun grew heavy in her hand. Her arm began to burn from the stress, but she remained fast.

"What's going on here?"

Lacy turned to see Dave standing in the open doorway. "Thank goodness you're here. Wyman was trying to kill Ellie."

Dave gave Lacy a hard look. "Put the gun away.

"Wyman, what's this all about?"

Lacy felt a sense of confusion at Dave's angry tone. He'd looked at her as if she'd started this entire thing. She uncocked the revolver and put it in her apron pocket. The long barrel made it awkward at best, but it seemed the least threatening thing she could do.

"It was personal business," Wyman replied. "An employee situation that Rafe asked me to deal with."

Lacy rushed to Ellie's side and gently lifted the unconscious woman's face. She was nearly unrecognizable, her face bloody and broken. "Take him to jail, Dave. He would have killed her if I hadn't come in when I did."

"I wouldn't have killed her," Wyman protested. "I had no thought to kill her—just punish her."

"Well, it seems you've punished her enough."

"Arrest him, Dave."

Dave turned to Lacy. "Let's put our attention to getting Ellie the help she needs. I can deal with this varmint later."

Lacy realized the sense in that. She nodded. "Help me lift her. We'll take her to Gallatin House."

"She's not going anywhere until Rafe gets his signed papers."

Dave was already lifting Ellie in his arms. Lacy stepped up to Wyman and narrowed her eyes. "I still have a loaded revolver, Wyman, and frankly, I would just as soon use it as not."

"Not a very Christian thing to say," Wyman mused. He looked at Lacy as if she were a silly little girl, speaking of things she didn't understand.

"I'm not feeling particularly Christian at this point." Lacy could feel the weight of the revolver in her pocket. Her breath was coming in a pant, and her heart raced at the very thought of what she might have to do.

"You'd best leave it alone, Wyman. She's mad enough to do it," Dave said as he moved with Ellie to the door. "If you enjoy life, you'll leave us alone and go report to Rafe that you've done your job."

Lacy waited only a moment longer before turning to follow Dave out of the room. She'd never been so angry in all of her life. The hatred she felt at this moment startled her. No, it terrified her. Where was such rage borne?

"Where should we take her?"

"The top room, where we worked on the stage man. We can go up the back way. It'll be quicker." Lacy hurried to get ahead of Dave. She held the door for him and grabbed towels and water as he carried Ellie up the stairs.

Lacy squeezed by him in the hall upstairs and hurried to open the bedroom door. She put the towels and water aside. "Put her on the bed."

She pulled back the blanket and sheet as Dave lowered Ellie to the mattress. Lacy gasped again to see the brutality Ellie had endured. She put her hand to her mouth. How could anyone do something so heinous to another human being?

"It's pretty bad," Dave admitted. "I'd best go for the doctor. Where are Hank and Gwen?"

"They're . . . ah . . ." Lacy couldn't think. Fear and shock blended with her anger, leaving her weak and helpless. She thought she might even pass out. *You have to be strong,* she told herself. But it did little good.

Dave came to her and took hold of her shoulders. "Lacy? Are you all right?"

"I . . . um. . . ." She shook her head. "I tried my best."

"You have to help Ellie. Don't think about what you've seen today or even what she looks like now. You are her only help."

Lacy met his sympathetic gaze and nodded very slowly. "I . . . want to help her."

He touched Lacy's cheek. "I know you do. But you can't help her if you fall to pieces on me."

She swallowed hard and drew a deep breath. "But what if she dies?" Lacy's shoulders began to shake as tears came to her eyes. "What if she dies because I wasn't fast enough to help her? What if I fail her, too?"

Dave pulled Lacy into his arms and gently stroked her hair. "You haven't failed anyone. I know this is way too much for any one person to handle, but you have to be strong. I need to get help, and you have to tend to her now. Can you do that, Lacy?"

She sniffed back the tears and nodded against Dave's chest. "I'll do it."

He pulled her back and smiled. "Now tell me where Gwen and Hank have gone."

She nodded again and the shock seemed to clear a bit from her mind. "Hank's at the store. Gwen went to see your mother."

"And Simon?"

Lacy hadn't thought of how enraged Simon was going to be when he came home to find Ellie like this. "He's in Bozeman with Justin. They're getting the signed deed that will give Rafe the land behind the saloon."

Dave blew out a heavy breath. "All right. I'll go tell Hank what's happened and get him over here. You do what you can, and I'll find the doctor."

Ellie began to moan, and this helped Lacy to put aside her last bits of doubt. She broke away from Dave and hurried to the woman's side. Taking up a towel and dipping it in the water, Lacy spoke softly.

"It's all right, Ellie. I'm here. I'll help you."

# CHAPTER TWENTY-FIVE

It seemed like Dave had been gone forever, and Hank still hadn't come to help Lacy. She tried to focus on cleaning up the cuts on Ellie's face. The swelling was far more prominent than the actual wounds. Wyman had bloodied Ellie's nose and cut her lip badly. There was also a cut above her eye, but it was the swelling and discoloration already setting in that distorted the young woman's face so much.

Not knowing what else to do, Lacy decided to undress Ellie and get her into a nightgown. Blood on the mattress startled Lacy at first. It didn't register for several minutes; then Lacy remembered Beth telling her about the pregnancy. Now it appeared Ellie would lose the baby.

She was immediately taken back in time to when their mother had been trying to deliver.

"She's bleeding," nine-year-old Gwen had announced. "We need a doctor."

"We need Papa," Beth said. "Lacy, you've got to go get him."

Gwen nodded. "Yes. Go get him. He'll know what to do."

Lacy frowned and pushed the memory aside when she heard someone just outside the door. She rushed to see who it was and felt a great amount of relief when Gwen hurried inside.

"I just got back. Hank was on his way over here and said there was an emergency."

"There is." Lacy hugged Gwen close for a moment. "I'm so scared. Ellie's bleeding, and I don't know what to do. I think she's lost the baby."

Gwen paled. "Oh no." She left Lacy and went to Ellie's bedside. It took only a moment of considering the situation. "Lacy, get plenty of towels and more hot water. We've got to try and stop the bleeding until the doctor can get here. Otherwise, she might very well die."

∽∾

By nine that night, the doctor felt he'd done all that he could. Ellie had lost the baby, as well as a great deal of blood. She looked as pale as the bedsheets and didn't so much as moan in her unconscious state.

Lacy felt as though she were staring death in the face as she looked down at Ellie. The doctor closed his bag and gave Lacy and then Gwen a sympathetic shake of his head.

"It's in God's hands now. We'll have to just watch her through the night."

"We have a room for you," Gwen said. "Come, and I'll have my husband show you to it."

They stepped from the room, leaving Lacy with Ellie. It wasn't long before Gwen returned. "Why don't you go get something to eat? I'll stay with her for a while. You can relieve me later."

Lacy made her way downstairs and headed into the kitchen. She couldn't remember the last time she'd had something to eat, and now her stomach rumbled just at the thought of food. She sliced a piece of bread and covered it with butter. Lacy had just started to eat when Dave Shepard appeared.

"How is she?"

"It's hard to tell. Doc said we'd have to wait and see."

Dave frowned and poured himself a cup of coffee. Lacy could see he was deep in thought. She swallowed another bite of bread to keep from berating him with questions, but her mind wouldn't let her rest.

"If she dies, will you charge Wyman with murder?" Lacy asked.

"Yes." He said it without pause.

Lacy could hear the anger in his voice even with that single word. She knew how he felt. "I'm glad you came when you did," she finally said.

He looked at her and shook his head. "It wasn't soon enough."

"I made it over there shortly after her first scream, and it wasn't fast enough to stop Wyman from doing what he did. We did what we could."

Hank returned just then. "The doctor is settled in. He said to wake him if Ellie's condition worsens."

"You won't let Rafe get her back, will you, Hank?" Lacy looked at her brother-in-law and then to Dave. "She can't go back."

"No. We won't let that happen," Hank replied. His face took on a dark expression. "I suppose one of us should go next door and tell Rafe what's going on."

Dave put down his mug. "I can do it. I am the law, after all."

"I could come with you, if you think he might cause trouble," Hank said.

"We both could," Lacy said.

Dave shook his head. "I don't want anyone involved. The less we do to irritate this situation, the better it will be—for Ellie."

Lacy knew he was speaking the truth. If they caused too much fuss, Rafe would only find a way to take it out on Ellie later. Especially if Hank and Dave couldn't keep her from having to return. For once, she didn't question Dave's decision. And she couldn't be sure, but she thought she saw relief in his eyes.

Dave looked up to find Lacy watching him. He felt compelled to offer her some kind of assurance. "I'll make certain Rafe knows she's not coming back."

Lacy nodded as if satisfied that he was telling the truth, then got to her feet. "I'm going to go relieve Gwen. I'm sure she's tired."

"Let us know if we can do anything," Hank called after her.

Dave watched her go. His mind was jumbled with images and thoughts of all that had happened. He knew Lacy had been tested to the breaking point today, and all he could think of was how she felt she had failed. Failed again, she had said. She seemed to carry the weight of the world on her slim shoulders.

"I can't figure out what's keeping Simon and Justin," Hank told Dave. He put down the book he'd been holding for the last hour. "Simon isn't going to handle this well. His instinct will be to kill Wyman."

Dave nodded. "I figure it, too. It might be in Wyman's best interest if I did arrest him."

"I can't figure anyone hurting a woman like that." Hank scowled. "That's got to be one evil kind of man."

"It's the way he and Rafe have always settled things," Dave said. "Men like that don't know any other way. If other people get caught in the middle, it really doesn't matter to them. When I tried to talk to Wyman about what happened, he wouldn't tell me any more than he already had. He said it was something Rafe had asked him to take care of."

"Maybe that would be enough to see Rafe arrested, too," Hank suggested.

For just a moment, Dave felt a sense of anger surge. Did everyone think him a complete idiot when it came to doing his job? Now Hank was trying to offer advice. Before he could reply, however, Hank was checking his watch.

"I've just got a bad feeling about this, Dave. I think maybe I ought to go looking for Simon and Justin. Simon assured me he'd be back before nightfall, and there's no reason he shouldn't have been."

Dave got to his feet. "I'll go. I can talk to Rafe afterward. The ladies might need you." He grabbed his hat and headed for the door. He hated the uneasiness that coursed through his body. Simon was a sensible man, and he wouldn't endanger his nephew by waiting so late to return home. It was possible his horse had grown lame or that someone had needed his help. But Dave had a feeling something much more sinister kept Simon from returning.

Retrieving his horse from the Lassiters', Dave also borrowed a lantern and headed out. In the distance he heard the unmistakable sound of thunder. He caught sight of the lightning flashes to the south and again heard the rumbles that followed. They could use the rain, but at this time of year the storms were far too often dry and only served to set the forested areas on fire.

The horse was nervous about the approaching storm and whinnied softly as Dave urged him forward. Neither mount nor rider wanted to be out on this night.

About a mile down the road toward Bozeman, Dave heard something ahead and stopped to listen. The slow, plodding steps of horses, along with another sound that Dave couldn't quite identify, drifted on the night air. As the noise grew louder, Dave could finally make out sobbing. He put his heels to the side of the gelding and closed the distance.

Justin Lassiter sat atop the smaller of two horses. He was crying uncontrollably, but he still managed to hold on to the reins of his horse, as well as those of the horse behind him.

He startled and pulled back hard on the reins as Dave approached. "Don't . . . don't hurt us," he cried out.

"I'm not here to hurt you, son. It's me. Deputy Shepard."

"We were robbed," the boy said, fighting to control his voice.

Dave came up even. "Where's Simon?"

"He's on that horse. They killed him and tied him to it." Justin began to cry. "He didn't . . . didn't do nothin' wrong. They were just . . . just bad men."

Dave felt sickened. Bile rose in the back of his throat. He jumped from the horse and hurried to light the lantern. He held it up to see Simon.

Someone had tied the man's hands to his feet, looping the rope under the belly of the horse. They'd also cinched Simon around the waist and tied his rope off on the saddle horn. Dave gently lifted Simon's face. It was unrecognizable. Someone had pistol-whipped him. Blood caked his face and shirt.

Dave felt the man's ragged breath against his hand and nearly dropped the lantern. "He's not dead. He will be, though, if we don't get him help right away." Dave put out the lantern and jumped back on his horse. "Come on, Justin. We have to hurry."

❧

"I'm sorry you had to come home to such chaos," Hank told Gwen.

She turned from the wardrobe where she'd been studying her clothes. She felt confident about her condition, but having just seen Ellie lose her child, Gwen also knew a great fearfulness.

"I can't believe anyone would want to hurt another person that way." She shook her head. "Sometimes I wonder if it wouldn't be better to live in a big city."

"There are problems there, as well," Hank said. "No place is ever perfect."

She nodded. "I suppose there's always good with the bad."

He came to her and opened his arms to her. "I agree. You are my dearest blessing."

Gwen stepped into his embrace and rested her head against his chest. "And you are mine. I feel so safe knowing you're here." She thought again of the child she carried. "I can't help but think back a year ago. Things were so different, and a year from now they'll be even more different."

"Time has a way of doing that to a person."

"Especially when additional people come into your life," she said and pulled back.

Hank ran his hand down the side of her face. "I'm glad you came into my life. I can't begin to imagine living without you. I want to be the husband you need me to be—the godly man you desire I be. I keep praying that I won't disappoint you."

"I could never be disappointed in you, Hank. You're everything I could have ever wanted in a husband. You're the man I want as father for my children." She smiled despite her fears. "And in a few months, you can demonstrate just how good you are at that, as well."

Gwen waited for the meaning of her statement to dawn on him. Hank's eyes widened, and he took a step back to look at her. "Are you sure?"

"Sure enough. I haven't talked to the doctor about it yet, but Patience and I discussed it today. I'm pretty confident that I am going to have a baby."

Hank looked completely stunned, and for a minute, Gwen worried that he wasn't happy about the news. She frowned. "Are you upset with me?"

He looked at her as if she'd gone crazy. "No. Not at all." He came to her and took hold of her again. "I'm just surprised—that's all." He hugged her close. "Pleasantly surprised. I know how much—"

"Hank!"

Dave's voice bellowed from downstairs. Gwen jumped and

Hank dropped his hold. They both rushed for the bedroom door.

"Get the doctor, Hank. It's Simon," Dave said as he struggled to carry the larger man.

Gwen saw Simon's bloodied shirt and face. She put her hand to her mouth and gasped. Hank hurried to help Dave with the body.

"We need to get him to bed. Gwen, go wake the doctor, and I'll help Dave."

Gwen nodded. She waited only a moment as Dave and Hank started up the stairs, then turned to see Justin watching them, as well. His face was dirty and tear-streaked. She could see the terror in his eyes and knew that he must have witnessed whatever had happened. Instinctively, she went to him and took him in her arms.

"Come on. We'll get the doctor. Then I'll help you get cleaned up."

✐

The days passed in the heat of summer with both Ellie and Simon recovering very slowly. The doctor came and went, and Lacy found it encouraging to hear him say that both would survive their attacks.

Ellie's swollen face was nearly back to normal, but the bruising was still very evident. She cried upon learning about the baby. Lacy had held her close as Ellie sobbed out her sorrow. The poor baby had been innocent of the ugliness Ellie had been exposed to, and she thought perhaps losing the child had been a merciful thing. But still, it cut a deep wound into Ellie's heart.

On the fifth day, Gwen and Lacy told the recovering Ellie about Simon. She immediately insisted on seeing him.

"The doctor doesn't want you out of bed for another week," Lacy protested. "You could grow too weak and lose more blood. You have to take it easy."

"I want to be with him. I want to know that he's going to be all right."

Gwen looked to Lacy and then nodded. "We can surely set it up so that they can be near each other. We'll tack up a rope across the wall and hang a sheet to give them privacy when needed, but otherwise they can be in the same room."

Ellie settled back against her pillows. "Thank you, Gwen. I promise I won't be a bother."

By nightfall, Ellie was settled into the bed next to Simon's. Hank had carried her over and maneuvered the bed close enough that Ellie could see Simon and hold his hand. She was surprisingly strong and didn't shed a single tear. Lacy admired her for that. Ellie didn't want to upset Simon, so she made light of the situation.

"They told me you were being a difficult patient," she told him.

He gave her a weak smile. "Looks like you were the difficult one." The look on his swollen and battered face spoke more than his words.

Lacy knew that Hank had already explained everything to Simon. She marveled that Ellie and Simon could say so much to each other without speaking another word. Ellie simply took Simon's hand in hers and let the healing begin.

Exiting the room, Lacy marveled that love could be so intense, so vast. The circumstances that had created this situation had been unfair—so completely unreasonable.

Neither Ellie nor Simon had done anything that deserved this outcome.

"Is Uncle Simon going to be all right?" Justin asked her. He sat perched at the top of the stairs.

"He's doing very well, thanks to you."

"What do you mean?"

Lacy sat down on the step beside him. "I mean, if you hadn't gotten him home, he might not be all right."

"I didn't know how to get home, but the man who told the other men to tie Uncle Simon up said the horses would know and to just follow the trail. I was so scared."

Lacy nodded. "I can imagine. It took real bravery to put aside that fear. Your father and mother will be so proud of you."

Justin had said very little about the incident, and even Dave had struggled to get the boy to remember anything about the attack or the men who were behind it. Now it seemed in this casual moment, he was beginning to remember what had taken place.

"So there were three men?" Lacy asked, making it sound as if it weren't important at all.

Justin nodded. "Yeah. Three. They all had guns, but the one who talked all the time, he had a rifle."

Lacy kept her voice soft. "What did he talk about?"

Justin seemed to think about this for a moment. "He said Uncle Simon had to pay for his sins. Uncle Simon told him we didn't have much money, but that they could have whatever he had so long as he didn't hurt me." The words tumbled out from the boy's mouth. "The man said his problem wasn't with me."

Lacy stiffened. That meant the attack had been planned against Simon. It was personal and not just the random act of highwaymen. "Did the man say what kind of problem he had with Simon?"

Justin shook his head. "He just said Uncle Simon had to pay for his sins." Justin frowned. "Then one of the other men told Uncle Simon to get off his horse. He did and the two men beat him up. One of them hit him with their revolver." He looked up at her and the fear was in his eyes again. "I thought they killed him."

Lacy put her arm around Justin. "But they didn't. God was looking out for you."

"But doesn't God punish people for their sins?"

"If you're thinking God had this happen to make Simon pay for his sins, then you're wrong. Simon loves Jesus, and Jesus already died for your uncle's sins. Those men were bad, evil people. They were upset with Simon for some other reason, and that was just their way of taking revenge on him. It had nothing to do with God."

Justin leaned against her and allowed Lacy to hold him close. He said nothing more, and Lacy couldn't help but wonder if he believed her. She thought again of how the men knew Simon personally. This had been a planned attack. Someone had known Simon was going to be on that road.

She thought of the reason Simon had gone to Bozeman in the first place. He was bringing back the deed papers for Hank and Rafe. But surely Rafe wouldn't have wanted Simon harmed. He was glad to be getting the land. Would he have arranged something like this and risk losing the land? Lacy shook her head. It didn't make sense, but maybe Dave would have some clearer thought on the matter. At the least, she fervently hoped he might be able to use this new information to catch the men at large.

# CHAPTER TWENTY-SIX

"So where's my deed?" Rafe demanded as he sauntered into the store.

Hank looked up. "I have it," he said, watching Rafe the whole time. "It's blood-stained but still in one piece."

Rafe looked at him oddly and shrugged. "So long as it's legal."

Hank crossed his arms. "You wouldn't know anything about the attack that nearly killed Simon, would you?"

"Why should I?" His expression looked taunting.

"Someone has to know something, Rafe. I just figured you might have heard something at the saloon."

Rafe leaned against a flour barrel and shook his head. "No one's said a word to me about it. I didn't even know Ellie was that bad off until Dave came over to talk to me. You can imagine my surprise when he said she might die."

"Yes, I can well imagine." Hank did nothing to hide his sarcasm. He'd dealt with enough liars to know the man was being deceptive, at least where Ellie was concerned.

"I didn't figure Wyman did that much harm to her. She's taken a worse beating from me."

"Maybe she wasn't expecting a child at the time."

Rafe narrowed his eyes. "She's pregnant?"

Hank nodded slowly. "She was. She lost the baby and nearly bled to death, thanks to Wyman."

"Stupid girl. She knew better than to let herself get that way. It was probably Lassiter's, and she thought they'd just go off and have a happy little family."

"They might have, if not for you and Wyman," Hank said angrily. He reached under the counter and produced the smudged deed. "Here. Take this and be done with it. Send Ellie's things over to the house before nightfall. I'll never let her step foot on your property again."

"She doesn't own anything. She came to me with nothing, and that's the way she'll leave," Rafe said, taking the paper. He looked it over for a moment. "This better be completely legal." He pulled Ellie's contract out and handed it over to Hank. "I'm not going to be happy if you've found a way to cheat me."

"You're the only one who seems to favor that kind of business dealing," Hank said, shaking his head. He began tearing up Ellie's contract. "Just so you know, neither you nor Wyman are welcome in my store again. You want supplies, you can go elsewhere for them."

Rafe looked at him in disbelief. "You can't do that."

"I can and have. I have the right to refuse you service, just as you have the right to refuse me service at the saloon."

"But town's too far away. That's not fair. You don't drink, so I'm not denying you anything. I need the things you offer here."

"That's too bad, Rafe. You should have thought about that a long time ago. You aren't a good neighbor. I'd just as soon see you move on. I'd still be happy to buy you out."

"Ha! That'll never happen," Rafe declared. He stomped off toward the door. "Mark my words, Bishop. I plan to create an entire empire here, and this will see to it." He held up the deed. "You were a fool to trade the land for that worthless piece of trash, but it's to my benefit."

Hank continued to stare out the door long after Rafe had gone. He wondered if Rafe might be right. Maybe it had been foolish to give the land away so easily. On the other hand, Hank knew the day was coming—and probably sooner than his wife or her sisters would want to hear—that they would need to make a decision about leaving the area.

It was almost lunchtime, so Hank closed the store and headed to Gallatin House. He was nearly to the front steps when he caught sight of two people walking toward him from the direction of the Lassiters'. It was Beth and Nick. Dread washed over him at the thought of having to explain to the couple what all had transpired in their absence.

"Hello, Hank." Beth crossed the distance and gave him a hug. "As you can see, we're back."

She possessed a glow that suggested their days camping in the mountains had agreed with Beth. Nick came forward and shook Hank's hand. "I hope Justin didn't cause anyone too much trouble."

Hank frowned. "Look, some things happened while you were gone. It'd be best if you sat with me on the porch and let me explain."

"What's wrong?" Beth asked. "Is it Justin? My sisters?"

Hank put his arm around her and led her to the porch bench. "Everyone is fine . . . now. But there has been some trouble."

"What kind of trouble?" Nick asked.

Hank explained in as few details as possible. Beth hurried inside as Hank concluded, desperate to see for herself that everyone was all right. Nick lingered, however.

"Do you have any idea who tried to kill Simon?" Anger flickered in his eyes.

"No. Justin said there were three men. They sounded to be the same highwaymen who've been attacking others on the road. Dave Shepard told me he thinks it's more than just a few men. He believes there may be as many as eight who are working together. However, this particular trio seemed to single Simon out for some kind of revenge. I'm not sure exactly why. They told him, though, that he had to pay for his sins."

"What sins?"

Hank shrugged. "I don't know. Neither did Simon."

Nick frowned. "We have to put a stop to this. They could have killed him—Justin too."

"I know. And next time it could be one of the women."

"How's Ellie doing?"

"Well, it was hard for her to realize she'd lost the baby. She's doing much better. In fact, she's been eager to get up and tend to Simon's needs. The doctor wants her in bed for a full two weeks, but I doubt we'll keep her there."

Nick smiled. "She sure loves him. I'm blessed by that."

"And Simon loves her. When he finally became conscious, he asked about her and Justin right off."

"How's Justin handling all of this?"

"About as well as can be expected. He was traumatized by the robbery. There's no doubt about that. Then those miserable no-accounts left him to find his way back here, thinking that Simon was dead. He has terrible dreams at night. He's taken to sharing Lacy's room for comfort, but he still wakes up screaming."

"I should have been here," Nick said glumly.

"Don't beat yourself up over it. You had no way of knowing anything like this was going to happen. If I'd thought there was danger, I would never have let Simon head out, much less take Justin. We hadn't had any trouble around here for some time, and we figured things might be getting back to normal."

"You fellas going to come inside?" Lacy asked. "We've got lunch on the table." She smiled at Nick. "Good to have you and Beth home."

Nick got to his feet. "I'm glad to be back—though sorry to return to so many problems. If you don't mind, I'll grab a bite later. I want to see Simon and talk to him."

"I kind of figured you would," Hank replied. "He's upstairs."

◦◦◦

Nick hadn't known what to expect, but seeing Simon's face still so bruised and swollen made his stomach knot. "Well, brother of mine, you sure seem to know how to have a good time."

Simon smiled, revealing a hole where his tooth should have been. "I see . . . you finally decided to come home." His upper lip had several stitches, making it difficult to talk.

"Looks like I got here a little late." Nick pulled up a chair and took a seat. He noted the empty bed on the other side of Simon. "Where's Ellie? I heard she wouldn't leave your side."

"The doc . . . took her off to the other room. Wanted to have . . . a private place . . . to examine her. She'll be back . . . soon enough. She hasn't left my side . . . for much . . . of any other reason."

"So that gives us a minute to talk privately," Nick said. "What do you know about this attack?"

"Not much. There were three men." He paused for a moment. "They started beating on me . . . after that . . . I don't remember anything." Simon drew a deep breath and grimaced. "I have two . . . broken ribs . . . maybe a fracture in my left arm. Doc splinted it. He . . . taped the ribs. My head took most of the damage . . . got stitches all over."

"Well, that's the hardest part of you," Nick said with a laugh. "At least that's what Ma used to say."

Simon smiled and nodded. "Usually after I'd fallen . . . out of a tree or . . . from the barn loft."

"Since I was bringing lunch up for Simon," Hank said from the doorway, "I thought I'd bring you something, as well, Nick." He came into the room with a large tray. Dave Shepard followed behind with two mugs of coffee.

"With Ellie busy elsewhere, I thought we might talk about your attack," Dave said. He handed Nick his coffee and put Simon's on the bedside table. "Let's get you sitting up."

Nick quickly set his coffee on the dresser and went to his brother's left side, while Dave handled the right. They tried to be as gentle as possible, but it was clear their actions caused pain. Simon grunted thanks, then settled back against the pillows.

"I went out to the area where you were waylaid," Dave said. "I looked it over for any evidence that might prove who robbed you. I didn't find anything. I've talked to Justin, too, but he's told me about as much as he can. There were three of them, they had their faces covered and wore black. They had guns and were larger than life."

Simon nodded. "That's how I remember them, too." He smiled, but it was a weak attempt.

Hank put the tray across Simon's lap, then turned to hand Nick a separate plate. "I've asked anyone who's come into the store if they've heard or seen anything that might help. Since the men who attacked you took your knife and rifle, I thought maybe someone had tried to sell them or was even seen using them. But so far nothing."

"What about them saying that you had to pay for your sins?" Nick asked. "That seemed odd to me. Did we have someone with a dispute over business matters?"

Simon considered this a minute. "No. I've tried to think about that. Other than having troubles . . . with Rafe and Wyman . . . can't think of anyone who'd hold me a grudge."

"And Rafe and Wyman were both at the saloon," Dave said. "I know because I saw them there myself. Of course, that doesn't mean they couldn't have gotten someone to do the job. Maybe even tried to make it look like highwaymen to lead us in the wrong direction."

"That could be," Nick said, nodding. "It sounds like the kind of underhanded thing Rafe would do." He stared at his brother as he tried to handle eating and balancing the tray. Nick felt grieved to see Simon in such pain. With every bite of food his brother took, there was evidence of misery in his expression. This only served to further Nick's anger. Someone needed to pay for this.

"What about having Ellie talk to the other girls?" Hank suggested. "Maybe we could encourage Regina to come visit. I know they were friends. Maybe she would have heard something said about the attack."

"It's worth a try," Dave said.

"So long . . . as she doesn't have . . . to go there," Simon said. "I don't want her . . . in any danger. Regina's a good gal." He paused and drew another ragged breath. "She's a genuine friend to Ellie. . . . None of the others care about her."

Hank and Dave nodded. "We wouldn't let her get anywhere near that place, so you don't have to worry about that," Dave told him.

Nick picked at the fried trout on his plate. "Hank told me he gave Rafe the deed to the land and tore up Ellie's contract. I guess that leaves you two free to do as you please. I hope you know I'll be keeping an eye out for both of you, at least until you're on your feet again."

Simon met his brother's gaze and nodded slightly. "I know. I can count . . . on all of you to be there for us. Ellie and I . . . well . . . we wouldn't be alive right now . . . if not for that."

❧

It seemed strange to Beth that she should call the Lassiter place home. "But I am a Lassiter now," she reminded herself.

She moved around the small kitchen, smiling at the neat order Millie had made of the place. Millie had come over earlier in the evening to tell Beth where things were and to encourage Beth to rearrange things to suit her own needs.

*"It's your home now,"* Millie had said. The truth of it had given Beth such a peace of mind.

"My home," she said, looking around the room.

The small kitchen still held a decidedly masculine appearance, as did the rest of the house. Beth would change that soon enough. She had plans to put her own touches on things. Millie had made some nice curtains for the upstairs bedrooms, but downstairs the window coverings were simple dark wool. They had been chosen more for keeping the cold out during winter than for any other purpose.

Beth fingered the brown material and considered what she might prefer. Maybe she could create something light and airy for the summer months and revert to the heavier curtains when the cold returned.

"I'm glad you're home," Justin said, making his way down the log steps.

Beth smiled. "I'm glad, too. I'm sorry you had such a bad time while we were away."

He shrugged and moved around to the small dining table to sit down. He leaned his face against his left hand. "I thought Uncle Simon was dead."

She joined him, hearing the fear that remained in his voice. "That must have been horribly frightening."

Justin looked at her and nodded. "I didn't know how in the world I was going to tell Pa, and I guess I was worried, too, that maybe Uncle Simon would turn into a ghost."

Beth did her best not to smile at the suggestion. Justin's little-boy fears were valid, even if they were rather skewed. "You know, your uncle loves Jesus. If he had died, he would have just gone on to paradise. Just like Jesus told the thief on the cross. Do you remember that?"

Justin shook his head. Beth folded her hands together. "Well, when they put Jesus on the cross, there were two thieves who were also being killed. There was one on each side. One was a miserable man who hated everyone. He mocked Jesus and wasn't at all nice. But the other man . . . well . . . he seemed to realize that Jesus was the Son of God. And he seemed to understand that Jesus could save him, even though the world was putting them both to death."

"How did he know?" Justin asked.

"I think God's Spirit whispered it to his heart," Beth answered. "I think when that man looked into Jesus' eyes, he knew that he was in the presence of God himself."

"What happened then?"

"The thief asked Jesus to remember him when Jesus entered into His kingdom. Jesus told the man, 'Today shalt thou be with me in paradise.' Jesus promised the man that he could go where Jesus was going—that he didn't have to be afraid anymore."

"I wish . . . I wish I wasn't afraid." Justin looked at the table. "Those men scared me real bad."

Beth reached out and covered his hand with her own. "You don't have to be afraid anymore. Your father and I will take care of you, and God will watch over all of us."

"But sometimes at night, I have really bad dreams." Justin looked up at her wide-eyed, as if seeing those ghosts from his nightmares. "I don't mean to."

"Of course you don't mean to. But I want you to listen to me. You don't have to be afraid anymore, and you certainly do not have to bear this alone. Your father and I love you very much, and our room is just a few steps away from yours. If you have a bad dream, you can come to us."

"And you'll let me stay with you?" he asked hopefully.

"Yes, or we'll come and stay with you until you feel better," Beth said in a soothing manner. "My mama used to do that for me, and now I want to do that for you."

Justin got up and went to Beth. Wrapping his arms around her, he sighed. "I'm so glad you're home, Mama."

"Me too." Beth kissed the top of the boy's head and held him close. "There is no place I'd rather be."

# CHAPTER TWENTY-SEVEN

"I wish you wouldn't go," Beth told Simon and Ellie.

With August had come the couple's very small wedding and the decision to leave for Tacoma, Washington.

"It's best for both of us," Simon said after a quick glance at Ellie. "If we stayed here, I'd be too tempted to kill Wyman."

Beth's sharp intake of breath must have caught Simon's attention, because he smiled and quickly added, "Besides, the money's too good to pass up. The Northern Pacific needs ironworkers for the shop there. I figure it'll be a good place for a new start."

"I suppose so," Beth said, "but I'll miss you both."

"I'll miss you, too, Beth," Ellie said, smiling rather shyly. "You've been a real friend to me. I won't forget that."

"Besides, now we're sisters," Beth added.

"I've never had a sister before." Ellie looked at Simon and then back to Ellie. "In fact, it seems forever since I had any family."

"Well, you have them now, and being a sister is something I know very well."

"That's the last of it," Nick said. He climbed on top of the wagon that he and Forrest had been helping to load. He handed a rope to his uncle, then secured the canvas while Forrest tied it down tight. "You shouldn't have too bad of a time going over the passes," Nick added. "There really isn't a whole lot here."

"I figure we can buy what we need soon enough," Simon answered.

Nick jumped down and came to where Beth stood. He looked at his brother and Ellie and nodded. "I suppose you know what you're doing. I'm not suggesting you don't, but . . . well . . ." He left the thought unspoken.

Simon grabbed Nick's shoulder. "I know. But this is the right thing to do. I prayed about it and so did Ellie. It's best we start our new life elsewhere. Dave's never been able to learn anything about my attack, and I worry that somehow I'll bring on more trouble if I stay here in the area. Not to mention that Ellie would have to see Rafe and the others all the time. That just isn't fair."

Nick embraced his brother in a big bear hug. "I know. Just don't forget where I'm at."

"You will come visit us, won't you?" Ellie asked Beth. The hope in her expression was too much to deny.

"We'll certainly do what we can." She gave Ellie a hug. "Now, you write me lots of letters, and I promise to answer them."

Ellie nodded and when she pulled away, there were tears

in her eyes. "I'll never forget you or your family. When Lacy told me she might do some traveling, I told her she'd always have a place to stay with us."

Since when did Lacy plan to travel? Beth bit back her concerns and just smiled. Nick put his arm around her while Simon helped Ellie up into the wagon.

"Thanks again, little brother," Simon said once he was seated. He took the reins in hand and released the brake.

The brothers exchanged a look, and Beth imagined all of the unspoken things they might be telling each other. She knew how she'd feel if this were one of her sisters leaving for parts unknown.

Finally, Simon slapped the reins gently across the backside of the matched black Percherons. Ellie turned and waved until they had moved so far down the road that the gentle curve took them from sight.

"It's going to be different without them here," Nick said. "I suppose it was for the best, though. A man has to do what's right for his family."

Beth felt a twinge of concern, but it passed quickly. She smiled. "Before you know it, we'll be hearing from them, and it won't seem so bad. Besides, with Justin in the house, you can hardly get bored."

Nick laughed. "I wasn't worried about getting bored. I have you, after all." He gave her a wicked grin and a wink. "I was more concerned about keeping up with all the work."

∽

Although he'd acted rather secretive about the entire affair, Hank called a community meeting for the night of

Wednesday, August twenty-fifth. He had told Beth and Gwen that he would have preferred having it on a Saturday, but Rafe had protested that Saturdays were his busiest day, so Hank had taken pity on him.

Once everyone was convened in Gallatin House, Hank came to the front of the room and called the meeting to order. Beth couldn't imagine what was important enough to hold such a gathering. Gwen was completely clueless as to what her husband had planned. Lacy had even tried to get information out of Dave, but it was to no avail. Beth settled in and put her arm around Justin as Hank began.

"I know you're all wondering what could possibly have been important enough to call you away from your regular duties. I'm afraid the news isn't all that good, but it requires our consideration."

"What news is that?" Rafe asked. He crossed his arms, clearly annoyed by being summoned into the piety of Gallatin House. Gwen had told him quite plainly that he couldn't chew tobacco or smoke while at the meeting, and Lacy made him clean off his muddy boots before entering the house. Beth could see he was more than a little anxious to be on his way.

"I'm going to let someone else explain exactly what news I'm talking about. Mr. Murphy, will you come up?"

Beth tensed. Adrian Murphy maneuvered from the back of the room to stand beside Hank. He looked out and caught her gaze. He smiled broadly, causing Beth to quickly look away.

"It's good to see you folks again, but . . ." He paused and let his smile fade. "I'm afraid the news isn't what you'd hoped to hear. We can now confirm that the Northern Pacific will lay tracks well to the north of this location."

"That's hogwash," Rafe declared. "I've got it on good authority that it's gonna come right through here." This caused a rush of murmurings.

Adrian held his hands up for silence. "I don't know who's been telling you such a thing, Mr. Reynolds, but it's not true. I just came from headquarters. The tracks will go in north, passing through Bozeman and out to Butte. There will be land for sale along the tracks, and it would be in your best interest to consider getting in early on the opportunity to buy. You could easily move your town and relocate to accommodate the railroad and benefit your community."

"That's crazy talk," Rafe said, shaking his head. "We got too much going for us here. The stage runs right through, and I'm planning to build a new hotel. Should get started on it before winter sets in."

Beth cringed at the idea of a full-fledged brothel going up next door. It was bad enough that Rafe had the small rooms attached to the back of the saloon. Once he built a bigger establishment, there would be nothing but chaos.

"That alone would cause me to relocate," Forrest said in reply.

Several people laughed, but many others nodded in agreement.

"It's not so bad for you ranchers," Adrian continued. "I can tell you without a doubt that several towns will spring up along the route. I don't think anyone will end up more than four or five miles at most from a town along the railroad."

Beth listened as the talk continued. People asked Adrian questions, and others argued about the sensibility of trying to start over. A part of her wanted to cry. When the discussion got more heated, Beth excused herself, telling Nick she and Justin were going to go to the kitchen to prepare some refreshments. Nick was so completely caught up in the discussion, he didn't really give her a second glance.

"I want to stay with Pa," Justin said, surprising her.

Beth couldn't understand why a boy his age would prefer sitting in a meeting to eating cookies, but she only nodded. She made her way to the kitchen and tied on an apron. The thought of moving—again—played out in her mind. The packing and unpacking, the building and cleaning. It all promised more work and aggravation than she wanted to face. Even silly things like establishing the flower and vegetable gardens seemed daunting, not to mention trying to make new friends. But perhaps most everyone would relocate to the same area.

She checked the large pot of coffee on the stove, then went to work arranging cookies on a platter. Why should it matter where the railroad went in? she wondered. Towns had existed for years without a railroad.

"Why doesn't someone point that out?" she muttered to herself.

Beth put the cookies out on one of the dining room tables and drew a deep breath. She knew her feelings about the situation didn't account for much at all. The Northern Pacific had certainly never once asked for her opinion. If they had, they would have gotten an earful.

Hank's booming voice sounded, and Beth could hear that the formal part of the meeting was breaking up. Soon everyone would adjourn for refreshments and more heated arguments that they would call discussions. She hurried into the kitchen to retrieve coffee mugs and nearly jumped at the sight of Adrian Murphy.

"Is there something you want, Mr. Murphy?" she asked.

"I wanted to see you. Is it true you married Nick Lassiter?"

Beth met his gaze. "Yes. Yes, I'm happy to say I did."

He frowned. "I guess we were never meant to be."

She looked at him and shook her head. "No."

He moved closer and took some of the cups from her. He let his warm fingers slide over her hand. "I think that's a real shame. I know I could have made you happy, Beth."

Again, she shook her head. "I don't think so. I like staying in one place, and you're threatening even the security I have living here."

"I didn't mean to. I only came to give you all a fair chance to make a move before someone else snaps up all the good land. The railroad has an easement, you know—property they're given and even extra for the purpose of encouraging towns to be built. Once word gets out, it'll go fast, and what's left will be sold at prices so high no one will want to pay them."

Beth turned away and carried the cups to the dining room. Murphy followed as she knew he would. She went about arranging the cups, then hurried back to the kitchen for more.

Adrian paced after her faithfully. He didn't try to talk, at least, and for that, Beth was grateful. When she retrieved all the cups, Beth took a hot pad and reached for the coffeepot.

"Why don't you let me carry that?" Adrian said, coming to her side. He leaned down and whispered in her ear, "If I can't marry you, at least I can help you."

Beth put the pot down with a *thunk* and turned to Adrian. "Do what you like. I need to go check on something else."

He put his hand on her arm and smiled. "I didn't mean to offend you."

Squaring her shoulders, Beth met his gaze, then looked at his hand until he dropped his hold. When he let her go, she smiled. "Good evening, Mr. Murphy."

Nick looked at Beth as she kissed Justin good-night and sent him off to bed. The house was strangely quiet, or maybe it was the silence that seemed to blanket Nick's heart that made it seem so. He kept reliving the picture of Beth and Adrian Murphy together. Murphy had a possessive hold on her and was smiling as if she'd just agreed to run away with him. Nick had quickly turned Justin away before he could spy the same scene and ask questions, but now Nick had questions of his own.

"Did you know Murphy was back in town?"

Beth was already busy folding clean dish towels. She looked up and shook her head. "No, I have to say I was quite surprised to see him."

Nick nodded and then began pacing the floor. He went first to the window and then checked on the fireplace. He toyed with the poker a few minutes and even added a log, but he couldn't seem to calm his racing thoughts.

"I saw you two alone in the kitchen," Nick finally blurted out. He straightened and marched to where Beth sat. "You want to tell me what that was all about?"

Beth looked stunned. "It wasn't about anything. He followed me into the kitchen and asked if it was true that I'd married you."

"And what did you tell him?"

She looked at him as though he'd lost his mind. "What do you suppose I told him?"

"Seems odd that he wouldn't just leave you alone once you told him you were a married woman."

"Nicholas Lassiter, are you accusing me of wrongdoing?" She put the towel aside and got to her feet.

He could see the fire in her eyes but pressed another question. "I'm not accusing, I'm just asking what was going on. I saw him whisper in your ear and put his hand on your arm. I turned Justin away so he wouldn't see."

"See what? Me about to drop the pot of coffee?" She put her hands on her hips. "Jealousy does not become you, Mr. Lassiter. I seem to recall a couple of other times when such things reared up between us. I won't have it. I'm in love with you. I pledged my life to you." She waved her hands upward. "I pledged it before God and witnesses. Do you really suppose I would throw out a promise so lightly?"

Nick began to see how silly he sounded—how awful it was to be thinking such accusations. Beth had never done anything to give him doubts about her love. He sighed.

"I'm sorry, Beth. I didn't mean to accuse you. It's just . . . I know Murphy wanted you for himself. He seemed too familiar."

She shrugged. "Wanting something doesn't make it so. If that were the case, I'd never have to worry about leaving this area or having anyone ever get sick again. In fact, I have a whole list of wants that I'm pretty sure will go unfulfilled, but I want them just the same."

He smiled and stepped forward. "Forgive me, Beth. Please. I was stupid. I see that now. I guess I just saw red."

Her expression softened. "Nick, you don't ever have to worry about me being unfaithful. I love you with all of my heart, and even if that weren't enough—and it is—I wouldn't sin against God in such a manner. The harm it would do us would never be worth the price. The harm it would bring to Justin would be even worse to overcome. I want no part of any such thing."

He drew her into his arms and just held her for several minutes. It almost frightened him to realize how much he needed her.

"I love you, Beth. I'm not sure I could live without you."

# CHAPTER TWENTY-EIGHT

"Ellie says they are both well and that the trip went fine," Beth said as she scanned the letter they had received from the couple. "She says it's a lot more damp there, more rain and such. Simon started his new job, but she doesn't say much about how he likes it. She said the railroad provided them with a small furnished house to live in." Beth looked up to find Nick taking it all in.

"It sounds like she's happy," Nick commented.

"Yes," Beth agreed. "I suppose we'll hear more about Simon's work in the next letter."

"I miss Uncle Simon. Do you think we could go visit him someday?" Justin asked. He had just finished his supper and was delaying his chores by asking the question.

"I think we probably will . . . one day," Nick said before Beth could comment. "Would you like that?"

Justin nodded enthusiastically. "Maybe we could take the train. Grandpa and me took the train for a long ways when we came here. I like riding on the train."

Nick laughed. "Do you know I've never ridden on a train?"

"Truly?" Justin asked. "I rode on another train a long time ago when we went to see Uncle David in St. Louis. Did you ever ride a train, Mama?"

Beth shook her head and got up from the table. This kind of talk was making her nervous. Folding the letter, she put it aside and began to gather the dishes. "We were much too poor to travel by train."

"Well, we ain't poor now, are we, Pa?"

"We *aren't* poor," Nick corrected and answered at the same time. "But we do have responsibilities. A fellow can't just be running around all over the countryside when he has a job to do. And you have schooling to do. Your mother's been working hard to help you keep up with your studies."

"I know, but we could always take my books with me." Justin looked at Beth as if for confirmation.

"No matter what, we have horses that need to be fed and wood that needs cutting tonight," Beth countered. "We need to get our chores done." She took a stack of dishes to the kitchen and drew a deep breath.

*I cannot let these things bother me. It's only reasonable that Nick would want to visit Simon someday. It's not the same as pulling up and moving.*

But even as she told herself these things, Beth wasn't convinced.

Another letter followed a few days later. This one came from Simon, and Nick eagerly shared the news with Beth.

"He says the work is good. He likes working in the machine shops. He makes parts to repair the locomotives. He also says that the railroad is working to lay track in our direction. Apparently they're coming at it from both sides."

"I'm glad he's happy," Beth said. "Justin is still working on his studies. Maybe you could wait and share the rest with us at supper. He might get too excited if he hears about the letter now."

Nick folded the paper and put it in his pocket. "Simon says there's plenty of work to be had, and if I want a job, he can get me one." He kissed her on the cheek. "I'll be out at the forge if you need me."

Beth wasn't sure why he'd shared the information about Simon getting him a job. She tried to focus on the piecrust she was making, but Nick's comment began to eat at her peace. Was Simon encouraging Nick to leave Gallatin Crossing?

This thought was on her mind long after Nick shared the full letter. Beth found sleep impossible that night as Simon's information and Nick's comments continued to dance in her thoughts.

"It gives us something else to consider," Nick had said at supper. "If the town falls apart, we could think about joining Simon and Ellie instead of moving north."

"I don't want to move at all," Beth had told him, but he hadn't listened. He had gone on about how it would be hard to remain here and earn a living, and how Rafe's plans to enlarge his business would only serve to bring in less-desirable clientele.

Beth clenched and unclenched her fists. The tightness in

her chest increased with every worried thought. It just wasn't fair. Here she finally had the husband she'd dreamed of and a home of her own—not to mention a son. She was happy, and yet now it seemed to be threatened by one little letter from Simon.

She got up from the bed, leaving Nick sleeping soundly. Obviously, he had no worries about the future. Beth pulled on her robe and made her way downstairs. She didn't bother to light the lamp but instead went to her rocking chair and sat in the dark.

"I want to be at peace about this," she said softly, "but I don't know how." She thought of all the things that had been said regarding their little community. If they couldn't make a living, there was no hope of keeping the town alive. They would have no choice but to relocate.

She leaned her head back and rocked. There had to be a way to save Gallatin Crossing—to keep from moving once again. Beth thought of her mother packing their belongings for yet another move. Her mother was always a cheerful woman, and even when forced to leave the comfort of her home for yet another place, she had always managed to keep a smile on her face.

Beth honestly didn't know how her mother had endured. For ten years, she had picked up and left the home she'd made for herself and family without so much as a second glance back. She had always treated each new location as an adventure, encouraging the girls to set up their rooms to suit them and make it feel like home.

"But I'm not her," Beth whispered. "I can't pretend to be all right with leaving. That would be a lie."

A hint of smoke in the air caused Beth to open her eyes.

She sniffed again and was surprised at how strong it smelled. Getting to her feet, she went to check the fireplace in case the damper had somehow closed. It was fine, and the embers had died out long ago, leaving the room chilled and dark.

Beth went to the kitchen and checked the woodstove. It was still plenty warm but not emitting smoke. Where was it coming from?

Walking toward the front door, Beth realized the smell was stronger here. She opened the door and looked outside to find a strange glow lighting up the night. Panic seized her as she stepped outside. It took only a moment to realize the blacksmith shop and stables were on fire.

"Nick!" she called, rushing back into the house. "Nick!"

She raced up the stairs and opened the door to Justin's room. "Justin, wake up!"

The boy barely roused. Realizing she needed more help, Beth went to get her husband. "Nick, there's a fire!" she shouted, hurrying to his bedside.

"What?" he asked groggily. "What are you talking about?"

"The shop is on fire," she said, shaking him. "Wake up!"

Nick bolted out of bed at this. "What happened?" He began yanking on his clothes.

Beth realized her own state, but rather than dress, she just grabbed her clothes and moved to the door. "I was trying to wake up Justin."

"I'll get him. You get out of the house—it could all catch and go up any minute."

"I'll get his clothes first," she said, following Nick to the boy's room.

"What's wrong, Papa?" Justin asked as Nick whisked him out of the bed.

"There's a fire, son. We have to get out of the house."

Beth hurried to collect what she could in the dark. The smoke was growing thicker by the minute, and she couldn't suppress a cough as she followed Nick and Justin downstairs.

"Take him to Gallatin House," Nick ordered as he put the boy on his feet.

"Justin, get your boots," Beth told him.

They went out into the chilled night air and crossed the yard. Looking back, Beth could see Nick attempting to enter the shop. "Don't go in there!" she called.

"I have to try to fight it," Nick hollered back.

"It's too late," she told him, hoping he would stop. "We can't do anything about it, Nick. It's too far gone."

Nick stopped and seemed to assess the situation. "I have to get the horses away from the stable."

Beth glanced to the corral and saw the next day's stage team pacing nervously from side to side. "I'll help you."

Nick turned. "No. Go to your sisters. Get Hank and Dave."

She knew she could never hope to hold Nick back from risking his life, but maybe another man could. Getting her brother-in-law and the deputy seemed the wisest thing she could do.

"Come on, Justin," she said, nudging him forward. "We need to hurry."

They ran the short distance to Gallatin House and hurried to wake the others. Beth was nearly hysterical by the time she reached the top of the stairs. She pounded on Gwen and Hank's door, while Justin went to wake Lacy.

"Beth?" Hank questioned at the sight of her.

"The shop and stables are on fire," she said. "Nick's there alone. He sent me here for you and Dave."

Hank said nothing more. He went back into the room, leaving the door open. Gwen was now climbing out of bed. "What's wrong?"

"Lassiters' is on fire," Hank explained.

Gwen immediately began to dress. "What can we do to help?"

"You can't do anything," he told her. "I won't have you risking yourself or the baby."

This comment caused Beth to momentarily put aside her panic. "Baby?" she murmured.

"I'll get Dave," Hank said, pulling on his boots. He raced past Beth just as Lacy and Justin joined her.

Beth looked at Lacy. "Did you know that Gwen was going to have a baby?"

"I didn't tell anyone but Hank," Gwen explained. "I learned the day Ellie lost her baby. I didn't think it would be right to celebrate." She sighed and lit a lamp. "Now's not the appropriate time for a celebration, either."

"But it is wonderful news," Beth said. "I'm so sorry that you didn't feel like you could tell us."

"Don't be. I knew the right time would come. It just seems troubles have come first."

"What caused the fire?" Lacy asked, hugging Justin close.

Beth shook her head. "I don't know. I just know it's bad. I don't think they can save the shop, and with everything connected the way it is, I'm afraid we may lose the house, as well."

"Oh no," Gwen said. "Beth, I am so sorry."

"Why don't we get dressed and see what we can do," Lacy suggested.

Beth nodded. "I have some things here for Justin. He has his boots."

Lacy picked through the things Beth held. "Come on, Justin. Let's go back to my room."

The boy looked at Beth for a moment. She could see the fear in his eyes. "It's all right. Go with your Aunt Lacy. I need to get dressed, too."

Gwen helped Beth with the buttons on her gown, and Beth did likewise for her sister.

"I don't know what we'll do. I'm so afraid," Beth said, tears sliding down her cheeks.

"Nonsense. You can come here and stay and we'll figure it all out. It's not like we don't have room. You and Nick can take your old room, and Justin can stay in one of the others or with Lacy."

"It's not that," Beth said, sobbing. "If Nick's lost the shop, he won't have work. Simon's already sent a letter saying he can get him a job in Tacoma. Oh, Gwen, I don't want to leave."

∞

"We saw the fire," Evan said, jogging to where Nick stood, pumping water into a bucket. Uncle Forrest wasn't far behind.

"I don't know what happened. I suppose a spark from the forge could have ignited something."

Evan moved toward the shop. "Maybe we can get some of the tools out."

Nick brought the bucket and started toward the entrance. "That's what I've been trying to do." He coughed hard and water sloshed around the bucket's rim. "I'm not making much progress." He pointed to a small pile of things.

Forrest joined them just as a beam crashed down inside the building. "It's not worth risking your lives over, boys. It's only material things. Where are Justin and Beth?"

"Gallatin House," Nick said, turning to look at his uncle. He tried to fathom the meaning of what Forrest had just said. Surely he didn't want Nick to just give up.

Another beam broke lose and fell to the floor of the already-blazing shop. Forrest pulled both men back with him. "We can't go in there. It's too dangerous."

"But all of my tools and yours are in there," Nick declared. "Not to mention the wagon Evan has been working on and—"

"And nothing." Forrest turned Nick to look him in the eyes. "You can't give up your life for something that can be replaced."

"What happened, Nick?" Hank asked. He and Dave joined the trio with a look of disbelief.

"I don't know. Beth woke up and realized it was on fire. I don't know what happened." Nick put the bucket down and shook his head. "I just don't know."

"Let's get things out of the house," Hank suggested. "It doesn't look like it's spread that far yet."

"It won't be long, though," Dave cautioned. "The wind's picking up."

"There you go, Nick. We can't save the shop, but we can get as much out of the house as possible," Forrest offered.

The men worked quickly to do what they could. Furniture, clothing, and bedding were thrown haphazardly onto the road away from the house. Nick lost track of how many trips they made, but when the fire finally broke through the wall of the house, the place was empty except for the beds upstairs and the stove in the kitchen. *Of course, we didn't have all that much,* Nick thought as the home he'd known went up in flames.

Rafe and his bunch stood watching from the porch of the saloon. They hadn't offered to help, which broke all codes of frontier life. Nick didn't care. As far as he was concerned, Rafe had never been much good to anyone but himself.

Night turned to dawn and then full daylight, revealing the sorry charred and smoking remains. Thankfully, the wind had died down, and the fire had been contained to the Lassiters' property.

Beth came out to stand beside Nick. She didn't say anything, but Nick could see the anguish in her eyes. He wanted to comfort her, but he had no words. What possible encouragement could he offer, when he had so many questions and doubts of his own?

"What are we gonna do now?" Justin asked.

Nick looked down and met his son's gaze. "I don't know."

"Well, for one thing, you're going to stay with us," Gwen declared.

Hank nodded. "We'll get your things stored in the shed so they're out of the elements."

"Lacy's got breakfast ready, so why don't you come on over to the house? We have a stage in at noon, and we need to make a plan. Are the horses all right?" Gwen asked.

Nick nodded. "I put them in the far pasture with the others."

"Good. That will work out well," Hank said. "I think Gwen's right. Let's eat and then figure out what to do next."

"We're going to head home, Nick," Forrest said. "Evan and I need to let Millie know what's going on. She's been feeling poorly, and we think the baby may come any day now."

Nick nodded and watched as the people around him went their separate ways. Only Beth remained at his side. She reached for his hand, but he barely felt her touch.

He stared at the smoldering remains of his home and business. "Why would God let this happen?"

Beth shook her head. "I've been asking the same question."

"It just doesn't make sense."

"I know," Beth said softly. "Few bad things do."

# CHAPTER TWENTY-NINE

Beth looked at the food on her plate but had no stomach for it. She pushed around the eggs but ate nothing.

"Once things cool off," Hank began, "we can see if anything in the shop is salvageable."

Nick seemed fixed on his coffee cup. He said nothing, and Beth worried where his thoughts had taken him. Why did this have to happen now—on the heels of Simon's letter? The timing couldn't have been worse.

A fire, of course, would never be welcome, no matter the timing. Still, it wasn't the fire and destruction that preoccupied Beth's thoughts as much as the way her husband might decide to resolve the situation.

"You know, you and your family are welcome here as long

as you like," Hank said, looking to Gwen. She nodded and waited for Hank to continue. "We can even help you rebuild a corral and shelter for the horses while you stay with us. That way you can at least keep up with the stage."

"That's so kind of you," Beth said in a barely audible voice. She was afraid to say too much, for fear it might cause Nick to reject the idea. She didn't know him well enough, even now, to be able to anticipate his reaction to this situation.

"You're family," Hank stated. "Look, I know this is devastating, but I'll lend you whatever you need to get through. It might not be wise to rebuild everything, what with the town's existence being so questionable, but we can do enough to allow you to continue to earn a living. I can also get additional blacksmith supplies."

Nick finally put his coffee cup down. "I don't have any way to pay for such things. We were barely able to meet all our needs on the stage salary as it was. The side jobs from the various ranchers helped keep things running smoothly, but it won't be enough to rebuild—not with winter coming on."

"But surely if we stay here," Beth put in, "I can work at Gallatin House and earn some money. That would help us rebuild."

Nick frowned. "I won't have this family be dependent on you working a job. I'm the man of the house, and I will see to my family's needs."

"But sometimes," Hank countered, "we have to turn to others for help."

"That's right," Gwen added. "The Bible says we're to bear one another's burdens. That's what being a family is all about."

Beth looked at Nick. "Everyone knows you've always

worked hard and can provide for your family. Don't let your pride get the best of you. Things will come back around. We can rebuild in time." She tried to sound as encouraging as she could, hoping against all hope that he wouldn't consider any other possibility.

"If the town is going to be relocated anyway," Nick said after a few moments of silence, "then there's no reason to rebuild."

"That is a valid point." Hank put down his fork. "In fact, maybe it helps to make the decision that much easier. I've asked Adrian Murphy to wire his superiors and get us an exact location and availability of land that the Northern Pacific has for sale. Once he gets back to us, we'll know better. You could relocate the shop and secure the stage contract by building near the rail line."

Nick shook his head. "I'm not talking about relocating to the railroad or rebuilding, for that matter. Simon wrote and told me he could easily get me a job with the railroad in Tacoma. I see now that letter must have come for a reason—especially since the fire destroyed everything that would keep me here."

Beth found she couldn't take any more of the conversation. "If you'll excuse me," she said, getting up quickly. She hurried from the room and fled the house.

Without thought as to how it might look, she hiked her blue skirt and ran down the road in the direction of the cemetery. If someone had seen her, they might have thought she were being pursued by a bear or a highwayman, but Beth ran from something entirely different. Unfortunately, her heartbreak seemed to keep perfect pace with her, meeting her face-to-face when she finally came to halt at her father's grave.

"Why does this have to happen?" she asked, staring at the small headstone that bore her father's name. "Why now? Why in this way? Why . . . when I finally had all the things I'd dreamed of?" She buried her face in her hands and began to cry.

Falling to her knees, Beth longed for the comfort of her husband. If only Nick would come to her and tell her it was all a mistake—that he would never want her to be unhappy and therefore would never force her to leave all that she loved.

But instead of Nick's embrace, Beth found herself wrapped in her sister's arms. She recognized Gwen's perfume without even looking up. For several minutes, Gwen said nothing. She just held Beth close and let her cry. Beth remembered times when she'd been much younger that Gwen had done much the same.

"I can't do this," Beth finally managed to say.

"I kept thinking of what you had confessed to us—your relief when Pa died, because you didn't want him to move us again. Now Nick speaks of leaving, and I know it must pierce your heart with many sorrows."

Beth looked up and nodded. "I don't want to go. I don't want things to change."

"But they *have* changed, Beth. You married. You left Gallatin House for a home of your own. Now that home has been destroyed, but your family is still very much in place. Your husband and son need you."

"But I have needs, too," she said, sniffing back tears.

Gwen relaxed her hold on Beth and eased off her knees

to sit on the ground. "Sometimes needs are based on illusions and false understandings."

"What are you saying?" Beth asked. "That I don't know what I want? That I'm not really sick and tired of moving from place to place—that it's an illusion and not a real problem?"

Gwen lowered her gaze and shook her head. "I know it's real to you. But, Beth, your marriage is more important than the place you live. You made a commitment to Nick—a commitment to be obedient and to trust him for the future. You promised to love him until death separated you. Are you willing to just cast that promise aside?"

Beth considered Gwen's words. Was she willing to walk away from Nick and the marriage—from Justin and her motherhood—just because they might find it necessary to relocate?

For a long moment, Beth wasn't sure what to say. The fact was, she could see herself doing it, and that frightened her. She loved Nick—didn't she? Would she really not keep her vows to him and God if he decided to move them to Tacoma?

Gwen reached over and took hold of Beth's hands. "I know this hurts you. I know you cannot begin to imagine how this could work out for the good of anything, but I'm telling you that God can take such tragedy and turn it into something wonderful."

Beth's anger got the best of her, and she jerked her hands away. "How can you say that? How can you possibly know that?"

Her sister looked at her oddly. "How? Because I've lived it. We lost Mama and then Pa, we moved from place to place, we had to work our fingers raw to keep us fed and clothed. I lost a husband. I loved Harvey dearly. He died, and I couldn't see anything good in that. My entire life has been filled with challenges, but God has shown himself faithful. If we hadn't come here, I wouldn't have met Harvey and married—and I certainly would never have met Hank. If Harvey hadn't died, I couldn't have married Hank, and I wouldn't now carry his child. I have to see the good with the bad."

Beth felt stupid for having challenged her sister. They had all endured suffering and sadness. Beth's situation certainly didn't rank above the misery of others. "I'm sorry," she said softly. She looked toward the eastern mountains. They had already been kissed with their first snow. It wouldn't be all that long before the days would grow short and cold.

"I know you didn't mean anything by it," Gwen continued. "I just want you to see that your place is with your husband, and your faith has to be in God. They both love you, Beth. Nick, as a man, has his limitations, but God's love surpasses all of them. God knows your pain, but I promise you He has a plan, even in this."

"I wish I could know what it was," Beth replied. "I certainly can't see anything good in this."

"Then ask Him to show you," Gwen suggested.

Beth looked at her sister, knowing the wisdom of her advice. "I'm afraid. What if He shows me, and I cannot bear what the truth of it is?"

Gwen nodded. "Then we must pray that God will also give you strength to face whatever it might be. He won't leave you orphaned in this. He can ease this sorrow and strengthen your heart so that you can not only endure what you must, but you can come through victorious and strong—even happy."

"I want to believe that," Beth said. "I truly do."

The noon stage brought very few passengers. Nick brought up the horses and began changing out the team while the people filed into Gallatin House for their lunch.

"What happened, Nick?" the driver asked.

"Not sure, Fred. Woke up to it last night. Whole place burned before we could do much, but we did get everyone to safety."

"So your missus and little boy are all right, then?"

Nick worked to unhitch the team. "Yeah, they're fine. We're staying here temporarily. I managed to get the horses to the far pasture, and so I can continue to work the stage stop. I'm gonna have to get some additional feed, though. All the hay was lost."

Fred nodded and pulled off his neckerchief to wipe his face. "So you can still handle us coming through?"

"For now," Nick replied. He didn't know what else to tell the man. "You'd best get your lunch, Fred. I have this under control."

The older man studied Nick for a moment, then pocketed his neckerchief. "Guess I am a bit famished. You holler if you need anything."

"What I need, you can't provide."

Nick didn't wait for his response but moved the exhausted team out away from the stage and tied them off at one of the hitching posts at the store. He then began the task of positioning and securing the fresh team of four. Once they were hitched, he collected the now-cooled-down horses and led them to the pasture, where they would find water and grass. After the stage left, Nick planned to ride out to the Shepards' place and see about getting some hay on credit. He hated the idea, but he had to at least honor his contract. It wouldn't be long before the stage line would send someone to renegotiate it anyway. Nick would see his duties through until that happened.

"So did you figure out what caused the fire?" Rafe asked as Nick walked back from the pasture to Gallatin House.

He looked up to find Rafe casually leaning against the door as if he didn't have a care in the world.

"No. Dave Shepard plans to investigate it, but otherwise, I don't have any idea," Nick said, not even bothering to stop.

"I'm wondering if you'd like to sell your land to me," Rafe said.

This did cause Nick to stop in midstep. "What?"

Rafe shrugged. "I'm just wondering if you plan to sell out."

"I hadn't really thought about it." Nick hadn't figured anyone would be interested in making him an offer on the land alone—especially not Rafe, who'd just managed to wheedle the property behind his place out of Hank.

"Well, I can make you a good offer. Not as much as it might have been worth with the house and stable, but a fair deal, nevertheless."

"I'll think about it, Rafe."

The man smiled. "Good. Glad you aren't against considering it."

Nick nodded and turned to head to where the stage was already reloading. He caught sight of Beth on the path just ahead. She'd obviously overheard his discussion with Rafe and looked quite upset. The destruction of their home had left her very shaken and emotional. She'd run off at breakfast, and when he'd started to go after her, Gwen had waved him back, asking him to let her talk to Beth.

The stage pulled out, kicking up dust and leaving the road

strangely deserted. Nick decided perhaps he should try to speak to Beth about the situation. He hardly felt capable of comforting her, but he didn't want her to think he didn't care.

"Walk with me?" he asked, meeting her questioning gaze.

She nodded and took his offered hand. Nick drew a deep breath. "Where's Justin?"

"Working with Lacy. He was rather disappointed that we managed to save his schoolbooks," Beth answered.

Nick could hear that she was trying her best to sound unconcerned with what she'd witnessed between him and Rafe. He wondered how to best broach the subject, but Beth put an end to that when she questioned him.

"So Rafe wants to buy you out?"

"Yes. I was surprised, but he asked."

"And what did you say?"

Nick blew out a heavy breath. "I told him I'd consider it. I figured you probably overheard."

Beth nodded. "I just wasn't sure I'd heard right."

They followed the road in the direction the stage had gone. Nick couldn't bear the idea of walking the other direction and being faced with the reminder of all that he'd lost.

"It's already September, Beth. We really need to think quickly on this."

"On what, exactly?"

"On our decision about where to move."

"But I don't want to move." She stopped and looked at Nick with a pleading look that went straight through him.

"I know, but there isn't anything here for us. At least, not for long. The stage contract is nearly up—for Gallatin House, too, as I understand it."

"But that doesn't mean anything," Beth said, clearly upset. "The railroad won't come in for another year or two, and until then, this is the best place for the stage to stop. It's established and a perfect location. We shouldn't have to worry about leaving for at least that long."

"But it seems senseless to rebuild, only to leave in two years."

"Not if you figure it will give us extra time."

He looked at her and shook his head. "Extra time for what?"

"Well," Beth began, "we can save money. We can stay at Gallatin House and earn our keep. Maybe you could take Hank up on his offer and build a corral and keep working with the stage company. We could use the extra time to figure out what we need to do."

"But what if I already think I know what I need to do?"

She looked at him with a frown. "Don't I have any say in this?"

"Don't you trust me as your husband to look out for your best interest?"

Beth turned away from him as if to walk back to Gallatin House. She stopped all of a sudden, however, and marched back. "You don't care how I feel about this. When you read that letter from Simon, you only thought of him. I like it here. No, I *love* it here. I don't want to go anywhere else."

"Are you telling me that you wouldn't go, even if I decided it was best for our family?"

"There you go again. *You* will decide. You don't care about what I want."

"That's not true, Beth." His frustration grew. "I'm your husband, however, and I have to do what I can to take care of you and Justin. I have responsibilities that go beyond mere sentiment."

She looked at him as if he'd somehow betrayed her. With tears welling in her eyes, Beth turned away. He could see her slim shoulders shaking as she cried. He hated himself for causing her tears. He wanted to assure her that they could stay, but in truth, he didn't think that was possible.

"Please know that I love you, Beth. I don't want to hurt you."

"Then don't make me leave," she whispered.

He shook his head. She wasn't going to make this any easier. Either he would break her heart or leave a huge uncertainty in his own. There was no easy answer here—no sure choice that would promise prosperity and peace. He started to walk away but glanced back over his shoulder.

"Even if you can't trust me, Beth, I would think you'd trust God. You're the one who told me He could always be counted on to guide a person to truth."

He walked down the road, leaving her there to think about his words. Nick looked skyward and wondered why God remained silent. Hadn't folks assured him that no matter what, all you had to do was pray and God would answer? So where was He in all of this?

*I want to trust you in this. I truly want to believe that you will see me through—that you will guide me to truth, just like folks say. All of my life, though, one thing or another has happened to steal away the things I love. First with Annie, then Justin, and now Beth. What am I missing, Lord? What have I failed to do?*

# CHAPTER THIRTY

"Mama?" Justin called at the door to Beth's room.

Beth looked up and forced a smile. "Come on in."

Justin crossed the room to sit beside her on the corner of her bed. Beth knew he was upset. He'd seen her crying when she'd returned to Gallatin House. She hadn't been able to hide it from anyone. She'd come upstairs, hoping that no one would follow.

"Are you sad about the fire?"

Beth nodded. "That and so much else."

"Like leaving?"

She looked at him, surprised that he should vocalize her fear. "Why do you say that?"

"Because when Pa was talking about that at breakfast, you ran off."

Beth had forgotten Justin's presence at the table that morning. "I was rude to do that, but I was . . . well . . . I was afraid."

"But why?" He looked at her with such innocence in his expression.

Beth knew he didn't understand, and she searched for the right words. "I love it here. My sisters are here. I don't want to leave."

Justin nodded. "I didn't want to leave my home, either. Even when Grandpa and Grandma were real strict. I liked it there."

Beth considered his statement. "Then you know how I feel."

"Grandpa said that sometimes we had to let go of a thing in order to get something better."

"But I can't imagine anything being better than what I have right here." She gazed around the room and smiled at the familiarity. "I've lived here longer than any other place in my life. It comforts me."

"But what about Pa and me?"

"What do you mean?" Beth looked back at the boy and could see his lip tremble.

"If Pa decides to move to where Uncle Simon is . . . are you gonna stop being my mama?"

The question overwhelmed Beth momentarily. How could she allow her own selfishness to cause this child more uncertainty and pain? Even if she had to move again—to leave all that she had known comfort in—she couldn't lose Nick and Justin.

She reached out to pull Justin into her arms. "No. I'll never stop being your mama. It would make me very sad to leave, but I would go with you and your father. I made a promise to love you both, and that's a promise that will last forever, because my love will last forever."

Justin wrapped his small arms around her and hugged her tight. Beth held him close, feeling his anxiety fade away in her embrace. It wouldn't be easy to go to Tacoma, but if that's what Nick concluded was best, she would find the strength. Like Gwen said, her place was with Nick and Justin. She couldn't allow this child's life to be turned upside down even one more time. Not only that, but she couldn't betray her love for her husband in such a manner.

It wasn't that her heart had changed in regard to wanting to stay, but Beth knew the people in her life were far more important than where she lived. Somehow, she would endure whatever came her way in order for them to be secure and happy.

Had that been the secret to her mother's ability to be cheerful, no matter how many times their father had moved them? Maybe she had comforted herself in knowing that her home wasn't in a building or on a piece of land, but rather it was with the family she loved. Things seemed a little clearer in light of that thought, and Beth felt a bit of peace enter her heart.

Somehow, some way, God would see her through this.

He would make it right.

"Can you and your sisters come quick?" Forrest asked Gwen. "Millie's havin' the baby, and she's askin' for you."

Gwen looked up, rather startled by this declaration. The only time she'd ever tried to deliver a baby was at her mother's bedside. "I'm hardly a midwife," she told him.

"She wants you. That's all I know. She asked for all of you girls."

"We can come," Beth said, coming down the stairs. She looked to where Nick sat reading a week-old newspaper. "If that's all right with you, Nick. Justin's already in bed."

He didn't even look up. "Of course it's all right for you to help." His voice was stilted.

Lacy got up from her chair reluctantly. Gwen saw her younger sister's doubtful expression and thought it mirrored her own heart. Nevertheless, she couldn't leave Millie without comfort. "We'll come. Hopefully you'll get the doctor there before we have to worry about anything. First babies often take quite a while to be born."

"I'll go ahead for the doctor, then," Forrest said, sounding greatly relieved.

"I'll walk the ladies over to your house," Hank told him. "We'll see to everything."

Forrest nodded. "Thanks. I feel a sight better just knowing Millie will have other women to help her." He hurried back outside.

"Do you suppose Millie has everything she needs at the house?" Lacy asked. "Should we take anything with us?"

"It's not that far," Hank said. "You can send me back for things if you find you need something else."

Gwen smiled and took the shawl he handed her. "Grab

356

our aprons, Lacy. Otherwise, I'm sure Millie has probably set everything in order. You know how she is about that."

They headed down the road with Hank holding a lantern to light the way. Evan and Millie's place wasn't that far, and the ladies could have easily gone ahead without him, but Gwen was glad for her husband's company. She knew he would understand as she spoke.

"I can't lie. This is rather unnerving for me."

"Me too," Beth said, nodding. "I was just thinking of Mama."

"Yes," Lacy whispered. "If it weren't for Millie counting on us, I wouldn't have agreed to come."

"I can understand your discomfort," Hank said, putting his arm around Gwen's waist. "This must surely stir up memories. Just know that I'll be praying for you. I'll sit with Evan, and we'll both pray while we wait for the doctor."

Gwen was touched by his comment. "With you praying, I know we'll be just fine." She smiled because she truly believed the words.

Millie was sitting up in bed when they arrived. Evan was at her side and looked rather pale and confused by the entire process.

"Why don't you go sit with Hank?" Gwen suggested. "We'll make sure Millie is comfortable and that you know what's happening."

"Yes, come with me, Evan. We can occupy ourselves with a good game of chess."

"I . . . ah . . ." He looked at Millie, who nodded. "I guess so."

He made his way out of the room, and Lacy closed the door behind him. Millie seemed to let out a sigh of relief.

"He's been a nervous ninny ever since the pains started coming regularly."

"How long ago was that?" Gwen asked, rolling up her sleeves.

"About two hours ago. Forrest and Evan were working out back, and I didn't want to bother them, but the pains were so strong after about an hour, I had to face the truth. This baby is on its way." She smiled but quickly grabbed her abdomen. "Oh, it's starting again." She bent forward as far as her protruding stomach would allow and moaned.

Beth quickly donned her apron, and Gwen did likewise. For a moment, Lacy just stood at the door, looking rather dumbfounded.

"Put your apron on, Lacy, then come help me. We need to check and see how far along she is." Gwen moved to the far side of the bed.

They waited for Millie's contraction to pass, then helped her to lie flat. "This isn't at all comfortable," she confessed. "I feel like this baby is knocking the very air out of my lungs."

Gwen smiled and pulled back the covers. "Babies have a way of doing that, or so I'm told. Did I tell you that I'm going to have a little one?"

Millie shook her head. "That's wonderful news! When?"

"The end of January." Gwen knelt on the floor to check the baby's progress. "I don't see the baby's head yet, so that's good. We've got a fair amount of time, hopefully." She felt Millie's abdomen, trying to remember what she'd heard about such matters. How in the world could she tell if the baby was head down or not? She felt so unprepared to help. Just as she had with her mother.

Gwen frowned, remembering the curse that death would

be her constant companion. She had fought to put aside such memories, knowing that God had delivered her from that nonsense, but it still haunted her on occasion.

She covered Millie back up and helped her roll to her side. "If you want to sit back up, that's fine. We'll help you to be as comfortable as possible."

"I'm fine here for now. I have to say I'm already exhausted. I was almost hoping you'd tell me the baby would be here right away."

Lacy laughed nervously. "Beth and I are relieved she didn't."

Beth nodded. "Sorry, Millie, but I'm in complete agreement with Lacy. Let's have the doctor deliver this one."

Millie chuckled. "I don't suppose any of us have a choice. Little ones tend to come in their own time, as I hear it."

∞

It was just after midnight when the baby's cry filled the Cromwell house. Beth marveled at the wrinkled, squalling infant. The baby boy squinted his eyes against the light and seemed all the more unhappy when the doctor began cleaning out his mouth.

"It's a fine little boy," the doctor told Millie.

She laughed. "I could have figured as much. Evan told me our first would be a son."

Gwen took the baby from the doctor, and Beth and Lacy moved with her across the room to help with cleaning and dressing the infant.

"He's so tiny," Lacy said. "Is he big enough?"

"For what?" Beth asked with a grin. "He isn't going to be playing ball with Justin anytime soon."

Gwen laughed. "They're always small like this when they're born."

"He didn't feel small," Millie called out.

"He's a perfect size," the doctor said as he continued to work on Millie. "Felt like he might be about seven pounds."

"Not even as big as Calvin J. Whiskers," Gwen said, gently smoothing the baby's blond hair in place. "That cat must weight at least ten pounds."

Beth continued to stare in awe. He was surely the most marvelous of all God's miracles, she thought. What a perfect wonder. Her heart flooded with longing to have her own child. Justin meant so much to her, but she wanted to give him brothers and sisters. She wanted to give Nick a baby, as well.

She almost laughed out loud. It was so like God to change her perspective with something so little—yet so intricately special. Leaving this community of hers no longer mattered in light of the idea of bearing Nick another son or even a daughter.

"I'm sure glad it's all over," Lacy said, easing onto a chair. "I just kept thinking of Mama and all that we went through."

Gwen nodded. "I know. I thought of her, too. She went through so much."

"Most women do," the doctor said, throwing a smile over his shoulder, "but they endure it because of the joy to come."

"But in the case of our mother," Lacy said, "there was no joy. She died."

"She knew the risk," the doctor said, turning his attention

back to Millie. "Most women do and face it willingly—even knowing it could take their life."

"He's right," Millie said. "I would have gone through far worse for my baby—for Evan."

Beth knew the truth in what was said. Their mother loved them very much and her desire for a large family was well-known to each of them. She hadn't died unaware of the risk; she died knowing the possible cost.

"She understood," Beth said.

"What?" Gwen asked.

"She knew having babies was a danger because she already had the three of us," Beth explained. "But that didn't stop her from having more, and I suppose it really didn't have much to do with Pa moving us around from place to place."

"And it didn't have to do with curses," Gwen said softly.

"But if I'd been able to find Pa . . ." Lacy's sad words caused Beth to go to her sister.

"No. It didn't even have anything to do with that. It's just the way life and death can be."

"I wish I could believe that," Lacy said.

"Well, we've turned rather maudlin on this happy occasion," Gwen said, straightening. "I suggest we put aside our sorrows and focus on the joy of this new life."

Beth crossed the room. "I'll go let the men know."

She went to the bedroom door and opened it to find her husband, as well as Evan, Forrest, and Hank. Beth laughed. "You all look fit to be tied."

"Is it . . . is she . . ." Evan couldn't finish the question.

"Millie is fine. So is your son. Congratulations."

"A boy!" he gasped. "It's a boy! I knew it. A boy!" Evan slapped at his father's arm. "Didn't I tell you?"

Forrest laughed. "Indeed, you did. Guess we'll be hearing about this for some time to come." The other men laughed and went to congratulate Evan.

Beth caught her husband's gaze and smiled. She hadn't been able to talk to him all evening, and now that was all she longed for. She hoped the smile would convey her heart until they could be alone. Nick watched her for a moment and gave her a hint of a smile. There was no real joy in his expression, but Beth didn't expect it. She'd hurt him, and she knew that she needed to make things right.

"So what are you going to call this boy of yours?" Hank asked.

Evan sat down hard on the nearest chair. "I . . . ah . . . can't . . ." His eyes rolled back and he slumped over. Had Forrest not been there, his son would have passed out cold on the floor.

"I guess we'll have to wait for that information," Forrest said, laughing. "The proud papa has just fainted dead away."

❧

"Nick, I've been a fool," Beth confessed once they were alone in their bedroom. She hoped he'd be patient enough to hear her out.

He propped up his pillow and looked at her from the bed. "Go on," he said, putting his hands behind his head.

"Well, to begin with, I want to apologize for the things I said and how I acted. I know you were hurt, and that was never my intention." She toyed with the robe of her dressing gown and began to pace.

"I realized today when I was talking to Justin—and then later tonight when Millie had the baby—that all I really need or want, I have. I have you and Justin and more love than I could ever have hoped for. The place I live shouldn't matter, so long as you two are there."

Nick said nothing, and Beth was afraid to look at him. She drew a deep breath and continued to move from one end of the room to the other. "I guess it took me a long while to realize that, but now that I have . . . well . . . I'm hoping you will forgive me. I'll go wherever you want me to. It would be hard to leave and never see my sisters again, but if that's what you want, I'll stand beside your decision."

"What makes you think I would ever want that?" he asked softly.

Beth looked at him. "What do you mean?"

"Why do you think I'm heartless enough to ever take you so far away that you would never see your sisters again?"

She bit at her lower lip for a moment and shook her head. "I don't have an answer for that. I suppose because our father brought us out here so far away from everyone we knew, it just seemed possible that my husband might do the same."

"Come here, Beth."

She walked slowly to the bed and stopped. "I've loved you for a long time, even before you were willing to admit your love for me," he said. Reaching for her hand, Nick pulled her down to sit beside him.

Beth nearly melted into a puddle when he put his hand on her cheek and caressed her face. "I will never hurt you on purpose. I know I'll fail you somewhere along the way, but it won't be for lack of trying. I love you. You're my heart—my life. We'll stay here if we can. If the stage company is willing to renew my contract for another year, I'll do so and work things out with Hank."

"You will?" She could hardly believe his words, yet they were exactly what she had longed to hear.

He grinned and pulled her against him. Nick kissed her gently and pulled back. "Only if you'll be here with me," he breathed against her lips.

"Wild horses couldn't drag me away," she said with a giggle.

"I think you should know," Dave Shepard told Nick a week later, "the sheriff doesn't think your fire was an accident."

Nick looked at Dave and shook his head. "What are you saying?"

"The sheriff had a friend of his take a look at the remains. His friend used to be a fire chief in a big city back East and has been trained to recognize arson. When I told Sheriff Cummings that it seemed suspicious to me, he asked his friend to ride out and take a look. He did, and the fact of the matter is, the fire didn't start anywhere near the forge."

Nick looked at the remains of his shop and home and felt sick. "You mean someone *meant* to do this?"

"It looks that way. I immediately thought of the fellows who tried to kill Simon. You don't suppose they came here thinking to pay him back for whatever grudge they held against him?"

"I don't know. Most folks in the area know that Simon

and Ellie moved off. I can't imagine anyone thinking that burning down the place would punish Simon."

Dave looked at him quite seriously. "Do you have any enemies, Nick? Anyone you've offended of late?"

Nick shook his head. "No one that's told me to my face." He tried to think of anyone who might want to cause harm to him or his family.

"Well, I have my suspicions," Dave said, "but for now I'll keep them to myself." He kicked at the dirt with the toe of his boot. "I wouldn't want to start something without more proof."

"If you know who it is, then tell me. That fire could have killed my family," Nick said angrily. "I deserve to know."

"It's just speculation at this point," Dave replied. "I don't want to get you thinking in one place, just in case something comes to mind later that might lead us in another direction to finding the real culprit. I'll let you know if I get something more solid to go on."

"I suppose I understand," Nick said, not exactly happy to let the matter drop.

"I hope you'll stick around for a while," Dave told him. They turned and walked back toward Gallatin House. "Here, I mean. I think it would benefit everyone."

"I'm here for the time being. I told Beth we'd wait and talk to the stage company. If they renew my contract for another year, then we'll be around at least that long."

"Good. That ought to give us time to decide what to do with the town, as well."

"That was kind of my thought on the matter. Your father has offered to give me hay for the horses."

"It's been a good summer with plenty of moisture. Pa's got quite a bit of hay put up; I don't think he's gonna miss it."

With screeching laughter, Beth and Justin came bounding from around the side of the house, both their faces covered in white powder. They ran as fast as they could and were laughing so hard, they could hardly stand by the time they spotted Nick and Dave. Beth came to an immediate stop and pulled back on Justin's collar to keep him from running into his father.

"What's going on with you two?" Nick asked, looking at the ghostly features of his wife and son.

"Mama's teaching me to play a joke."

Nick raised a brow and looked to Beth for explanation. She only shrugged and acted innocent of the matter. "Our son has a . . . vivid . . . imagination." She nudged Justin. "You'd best go wash your face." He frowned, but when she bent and whispered in his ear, he giggled and was quickly off and running for the house. Beth pulled up her apron and wiped at the mess.

Dave grinned and tipped his hat. "I believe I'll go see what's for lunch."

Beth looked up, powder still dusting her hair, and nodded. "Oh, I think that's a splendid idea." She started to follow after Dave, but Nick pulled her back.

"Oh, no you don't, Mrs. Lassiter. I want to know what kind of corruption you're teaching my son and why."

Beth sighed in his arms and kissed him on the neck. "Someone has to carry on the tradition."

"What tradition is that?"

She kissed him again, and Nick very nearly forgot what it was they were talking about. "Wouldn't you rather talk about something else?" She rose on her tiptoes and kissed his lips. "Or maybe not talk at all?"

Nick tightened his grip on her. "I suppose it can wait until later." He grinned down at the woman he'd loved for so very long. "And then again, maybe it's best I don't even know."

She nodded solemnly. "I think you're right. It's better you be surprised."

Nick chuckled. "With you, Bethany Lassiter, I'm always surprised."

"Good," Beth replied. "Lady Effingham would be pleased to know that I've carried on her legacy of keeping the menfolk in her life guessing." She closed her eyes for a kiss, but when it didn't come, she looked up in confusion. "Aren't you going to kiss me?"

"Maybe. But first tell me: Who in the world is Lady Effingham?"